*W*hat the critics are saying...

&

5 *coffee cups* "Ms. O'Clare has written a sizzling tale of mystery, thievery, and love. Her characters are mesmerizing and have an appeal that keeps you riveted to your seat." ~ *Coffee Time Romance*

4 1/2 *Stars* "Lorie O'Clare has penned another excellent book with memorable characters, and a plot that keeps you on the edge of your seat." ~ *Romance Junkies*

4 1/2 *Stars* "If you're in the mood for a fantastic romantic suspense book, then you won't want to miss getting "Caught" by Lorie O'Clare." ~ *eCataRomance*

4 *cupids* "The battle of wills, hot sex scenes and the chase for the thief keep you spellbound from start to finish." ~ *Cupid's Library Reviews*

4 1/2 *roses* "Whether you're a new fan to Ms. O'Clare or you've read her before, you won't be disappointed in Caught!" ~ *A Romance Review*

Lorie O'Clare

CAUGHT !

ELLORA'S CAVE
ROMANTICA PUBLISHING

An Ellora's Cave Romantica Publication

www.ellorascave.com

Caught!

ISBN # 1419953567
ALL RIGHTS RESERVED.
Caught! Copyright © 2005 Lorie O'Clare
Edited by Sue-Ellen Gower
Cover art by Syneca

Electronic book Publication March 2005
Trade paperback Publication April 2006

Warning:

The following material contains graphic sexual content meant for mature readers. This story has been rated E–rotic by a minimum of three independent reviewers.

Ellora's Cave Publishing offers three levels of Romantica™ reading entertainment: S (S-ensuous), E (E-rotic), and X (X-treme).

S-*ensuous* love scenes are explicit and leave nothing to the imagination.

E-*rotic* love scenes are explicit, leave nothing to the imagination, and are high in volume per the overall word count. In addition, some E-rated titles might contain fantasy material that some readers find objectionable, such as bondage, submission, same sex encounters, forced seductions, and so forth. E-rated titles are the most graphic titles we carry; it is common, for instance, for an author to use words such as "fucking", "cock", "pussy", and such within their work of literature.

X-*treme* titles differ from E-rated titles only in plot premise and storyline execution. Unlike E-rated titles, stories designated with the letter X tend to contain controversial subject matter not for the faint of heart.

Also by Lorie O'Clare

ε⌒)

And look for her Nuworld Series from Cerridwen Press at
www.cerridwenpress.com

About the Author

෨

All my life, I've wondered at how people fall into the routines of life. The paths we travel seemed to be well-trodden by society. We go to school, fall in love, find a line of work (and hope and pray it is one we like), have children and do our best to mold them into good people who will travel the same path. This is the path so commonly referred to as the "real world".

The characters in my books are destined to stray down a different path other than the one society suggests. Each story leads the reader into a world altered slightly from the one they know. For me, this is what good fiction is about, an opportunity to escape from the daily grind and wander down someone else's path.

Lorie welcomes mail from readers. You can write to her c/o Ellora's Cave Publishing at 1056 Home Avenue, Akron, OH 44310-3502.

Caught!

છ

Trademarks Acknowledgement

~

Chapter One

§

Roxanne Isley lifted the stack of files from the floor, and grunted. This had better be all her boss needed, because she would not haul one more load up those stairs. Her lower back ached, and her fingertips felt numb after flipping through the packed cabinets to find the ones he needed.

"Roxanne." Her boss's voice boomed off the stairwell.

She jumped from the unexpected sound, and adjusted the stack in her arms so they wouldn't scatter across the basement floor. The dark and musty space around her housed files from their accounts, which were over a year old. Leaving the small room, she managed to lock the door and work her way down the hallway, past other small rooms where other offices in the building kept their archives. The stairway ahead of her cast light down the stairs, flooding a small amount of space in front of her.

She didn't have to look to the top of the stairs to see Jordan Hall standing there. His aura made his presence known without the man needing to say a word. Over the two years she had worked for him, Roxanne had accepted the fact that all Jordan Hall had to do was enter the room, and the pressure would build between her legs.

She'd kept him out of her thoughts while she dated Jeffrey Mills. But now that he was gone and she was free, Jordan had become a presence hard to ignore.

As he stood at the top of the stairs, Roxanne felt the swelling grow and the ache begin, that she could only blame on the amount of time that had passed since her last sexual encounter. Ever since parting with Jeffrey when he'd accepted the job in Italy, she hadn't had time to do much dating. Her boss seemed to keep her too busy to even think about going out after work.

Besides, she told herself, Jordan Hall was so damned hot he could probably make a virgin swoon. Well, Roxanne was no virgin, but the man definitely could be a distraction. Of course, she had grown accustomed to how Jordan made her body react with his mere presence. She worked for him though, and a professional business relationship was all that would ever be between the two of them.

Those thoughts had been easy enough to abide by when Jeffrey had been in her life. She'd been so happy with him. But his career was his life. When Jeffrey had told her of the position in Italy, all she could do was encourage him. And it had been tempting to suggest she go with him. But there was nothing for her there, and being completely dependent on a man, no matter how secure he was, had never appealed to her.

Roxanne's sandals tapped across the basement floor. She nudged the service elevator button with her elbow and then rode silently to the next floor where her boss waited for her. She passed him without a word, but her nerve endings came to life when she walked within inches of him, heat crawling through her. Her nipples hardened while an ache carved through her with a dagger's strength, piercing the swelling that throbbed in her cunt. It was all she could do not to alter her course by inches so their bodies would touch.

"There you are. I've been waiting those files." Jordan took the stack from her and led the way to the elevator that would take them to their offices on the seventh floor.

Of course you have, she felt like saying. *That's why I'm hauling them up these blasted stairs*.

But Roxanne knew better than to get smart with her boss. Even if Jordan Hall wasn't the owner of Hall Enterprises, the most successful investment firm in town, and even if he didn't sign her paycheck every two weeks, something about the way he carried himself made a person want to stand at attention in his presence. That fact alone encouraged something inside Roxanne to do just the opposite. She didn't deny that looking at him made her ache to have him pounding deep within her, but that wasn't something he needed to know.

"I pulled every one you asked to see," she said, with the pleasant tone she'd mastered since working with Jordan. "I also grabbed the older files on a few of them. It might make preparing the summary easier to do, and more thorough."

Those midnight-colored eyes of his took their time strolling over her, and her body tingled from his gaze.

"Telling me how to do my job now, are you?" Jordan followed her into the elevator, taking his time to admire her backside.

Roxanne was more than a spitfire. His assistant had intelligence too, a mix in a woman that was hard to find. And word around the office was that she was now available. He doubted seriously that she would stay that way long. Roxanne would be one hell of a catch for any man.

The doors dinged open onto the quiet floor of Hall Enterprises, a company he'd built up from scratch and was damned proud of. Roxanne opened the glass doors leading into the secretarial pool, and stood to the side so that he could enter. She looked up at him with dark brown eyes. Her lashes fluttered over them, giving him a look he hoped was flirtatious.

"Call for you on line one, Mr. Hall," Dorothy said as they entered.

"I'll take those." Roxanne reached for the files in his hands.

Jordan didn't mean to touch her when they exchanged files, but his fingertips brushed against her arms. Memories of school, and getting a hard-on when a pretty girl walked by, or gave him a knowing look, rushed through him. Roxanne had managed that and all he'd done was brush his fingertips against her skin.

He cleared his throat, adjusting his tie that suddenly felt too tight, and ordered his cock to sleep. There was work to do, and now wasn't the time or the place for such thoughts.

Taking the call in the outer lobby, he watched Roxanne walk down the hallway to his office.

"I hope you're ready to work late again," he told her, entering his office.

He was unable to keep his gaze from her perfectly rounded ass when she bent over her desk.

"Why should tonight be any different?" she countered, not looking at him, which was a damn good thing since he was afraid she would have caught him drooling.

He moved to the other side of his desk and put several pieces of paper from different stacks into one pile. He organized what he would need for their work that afternoon. Roxanne kept him on his toes, and he didn't want to appear inefficient in her presence.

She had set the files on the long mahogany table, and then opened the cabinet in the wall where he kept coffee, as well as a small stash of office supplies. She grabbed the can of regular coffee—no decaf for this man—and a fresh legal pad, then turned to face Jordan.

"We'll start with the newer accounts, and work our way back," he decided out loud, finding it hard not to notice the round curve of her rear end as she moved around her desk.

Bringing her into his own office had been purely selfish. But she did such damn good work, and knew as much about his business as he did. He'd never thought working as a team was his forte. Working alone had made him successful. Opening Hall Enterprises and hiring other accountants allowed him to grow, but when it came to seeking out new business, he was a one-man team. It was damn nice having her so close to him though.

"However you want to do it," she mumbled, sitting down at her desk.

Roxanne had grown accustomed to his meticulous nature—everything about the man was perfect. She knew her opinion of him didn't stem from a crush, or infatuation. Her heart didn't have the ability to create such longings. Roxanne knew her body needed sex, and had been deprived for too long. Jeffrey had been gone for almost six months now. Her reaction to Jordan blossomed from need, and she could control that.

After Jeffrey, any man who had entered her life was just that—a man. Roxanne couldn't risk any more pain right now. So acknowledging Jordan's qualities only meant she understood the type of employee her boss expected her to be. Jordan Hall wasn't an easy man to work for—the high turnover of office clerks proved that point. Roxanne saw in Jordan what others failed to see however. He couldn't help his appearance—how incredibly sexy he was. Roxanne did as he instructed, but she never cowered, she didn't waver under his commands, and she never hesitated in telling him her opinion. As a result, the two of them worked well together.

"I brought up the extra files because I'm sick of running up and down those stairs," she said, and then dropped the writing pad on her desk. She turned to dump coffee into the filter, and then poured water from the small sink next to the cabinet into the glass coffeepot. "Everything should be here that you need. And you're going to need them."

Roxanne couldn't tell if Jordan laughed or grunted at her assumption, but she didn't care. She left the coffeepot as the black drips began to bubble, its sound comforting somehow, and then sat at the smaller desk, which was opposite her boss' desk and over to the side of the room.

There had been talk on the floor when Jordan moved her into his office less than a year ago, putting her desk in the same room as his.

Although she still had a cubicle in the junior accountant's area where her filing cabinet and shelves filled with reference books and computer discs remained, she spent most of her days in Jordan's office. She knew more than half the women and some of the men thought the two of them were having some kind of affair on the side, but Roxanne never stooped to office gossip, and so ignored their inquiring looks and suggestive whispers when she supposedly was out of earshot.

Any woman who spent time with this man would be target for gossip. Jordan Hall had a reputation as a man who took what he wanted. Hair the color of a raven's, and eyes that were almost black added mystery to his height and muscular physique. In another time he would have been a perfect knight, or rogue tearing across the countryside, a ruler controlling all around him. There was something carnal, yet alluring about him. The entire package made him appear intimidating, seductive, a man on a mission.

But fantasizing about him like that didn't necessarily mean he would be like that in real life. She'd imagined an aggressive side with Jeffrey, but that hadn't been his nature. And she was so strong-willed that her fantasy wouldn't be right if she asked the man to control her. Her imagination conjured up someone who was stronger than she was, would take charge without being told to, would see what she wanted and give it to her before she could ask. Thoughts of being controlled, yet cherished as an equal were pure fantasy. No man existed who could fill the image she'd created.

"Ready when you are, boss," she said, and looked down when he raised an eyebrow at her informal way of addressing him.

"Let's start with Uphouse." He moved the file in front of him, glancing up while Roxanne focused on her computer screen. "He'll be coming to town tomorrow and we need to make sure we have a good portfolio lined up for him as well."

Once Jordan focused on work, it wasn't hard for Roxanne to do the same. She pulled data, balanced accounts, and prepared summaries. Her legal pad had scribbled notes covering several pages when she moved to the printer to pull the account she had just printed.

Hours passed before she realized it. She loved working with numbers, watching how they were able to make people's money work for them. And the way Jordan got into what he did best, watching him as he discussed his clients' accounts, made suggestions that would be presented to the individual, made him even more impressive.

"Just leave the report on your desk." Jordan cupped his hands behind his head and stretched. "You can type it in the morning."

"A few of these older files have some discrepancies in them," Roxanne added, trying not to stare at him while he stretched. "I'll go over those tomorrow, too."

Steady raindrops tapped the windows behind him, and Roxanne focused on the darkness streaked by the drops of water on the panes for a moment, before nodding. They had worked late every night that week, and exhaustion slowly consumed her. A hot bath and her fluffy slippers sounded in order. Now all she had to do was make it across town before she fell asleep.

Roxanne stood, grabbing her purse from the floor underneath her desk. "I'll have the report on your desk by the time you're here in the morning."

They walked across the tiled lobby floor in an easy silence. Rain pelted the double glass doors in front of them and beyond that, darkness spread, interrupted by wavering floodlights from the parking area.

"Give me your keys." Jordan held his hand, palm up, in front of her, and offered no further explanation when Roxanne looked at him in surprise.

The last thing she wanted was to wade across the many puddles in her heeled sandals to her car parked on the opposite side of the parking lot. Maybe Jordan guessed her thoughts. She fumbled through her purse and produced her key ring.

"Wait here," he instructed, and then disappeared into the rainy darkness outside.

Jordan took long strides through the parking lot as rain pelted his suit. The downfall remained steady, but lack of wind kept the temperature tolerable. His mind wasn't on the weather, though. The company's largest client would be in town the next day.

Over the next several days, Jordan needed to show the man that his money created more profit with Hall Enterprises than any other company the man worked with.

And thanks to Roxanne, Jordan knew his company was one of several his client did business with. Without her he wouldn't be as organized, on top of things. Clients loved to feel they were the sole focus of your attention. With Roxanne by his side, he always had his client's information up to date, and at his fingertips.

If Jordan had his way, by the end of the week his client would put all of his business with their company.

But there were the discrepancies, and he kicked himself for not noticing them sooner. Again, he had Roxanne to thank for her thorough perusal of the files.

Only one discrepancy existed on the client's file. He knew he didn't have to tell Roxanne that finding a way to fix that slight error in the books would be imperative if tomorrow's meeting was to be a success.

Many companies had gone under due to faulty bookkeeping, and Jordan wasn't about to let that happen to Hall Enterprises. He'd worked too hard, burned too much midnight oil, and given up too much of his life to let the inadequacy of some office help take him down.

Jordan pushed the button on his key chain and the car beeped in the damp blackness of the night. His thoughts remained on work as he started the engine and turned on headlights. He stared for a moment through the rain-soaked windshield before starting the wipers. In less than a few months he would be forty. Very few men experienced the success he'd obtained by his age. And he knew hard work and attention to every detail were the keys to his success. Jordan never missed an opportunity when he saw one, and many envied him his accomplishments. The discrepancies bothered him, though. Roxanne would handle it, he told himself, and slipped the car into gear. She was a gem to have by his side.

Jordan praised his keen sense of observation that he'd had the insight to hire the young woman who had been fresh out of college with no real experience. Roxanne had more drive in her than many seasoned businessmen. But she had more than that. Roxanne not only possessed the intelligence and keen attentiveness to run his office, but the woman was sexy as hell. Almost an impossible combination to find in a lady as far as Jordan was concerned.

The one thing the woman lacked was knowledge of how incredibly perfect she was. That quality appealed to Jordan the most, and over the past two years he had taken her and molded her into being his perfect assistant.

She was more than just another accountant in his office. He had worked with Roxanne so that she responded to him, no matter his request. Of course, he had kept his requests work-related, but she answered to him and him only.

But working side by side with an incredibly beautiful woman had its drawbacks. Not many men would sympathize with him, but Jordan knew that more than once Roxanne had prevented him from being as efficient as he could have been had the woman not distracted his thoughts.

Just thinking about her made him harder than any other woman ever had. And he'd fantasized more than once about her submitting to sexual requests just as she did work-related ones. The thought of her on her knees in front of him, while he stood over her, stroking her hair, and feeling that hot mouth close over his cock, just about made him explode like a teenage boy.

Roxanne wasn't the tallest of women, but she liked wearing heels, which not only added height, but helped display legs that were made to wrap around a man. They were long and thin, curving perfectly at the calf. Her ass had a shape to it that Jordan liked, firm and not too round. And her waist was narrow enough that he was sure he could wrap his hands around it.

But he had to admit that he was a breast man, and Roxanne had a pair on her that could stop traffic. She liked wearing those one-piece dresses that clung to her in such a way that more than once he had a perfect outline of those shapely breasts. He bet she had large nipples too.

Jordan pulled his phone from his pocket when he felt it vibrate. He gave his head a quick shake to get tits off the brain and glanced at the small, black cellular phone.

"You can wait," he said, as he stared at the glowing box displaying the home number of one of his executives.

Jordan had heard that the man planned to invite him to dinner — suck up, he thought with a scowl.

"Tonight's dinner will be my treat." Jordan smiled, possibly for the first time that day.

Yes, the time had come to put the matters of business for the day to rest. He didn't allow himself much social time, but after working this hard with Roxanne to prepare for their client, he had one thing on his mind. That hot little secretary of his needed a break too, and he knew just how to help her relax.

He drove his car through the dark parking lot toward the building where she waited for him.

Roxanne stood inside the doors, alone in the lobby, and probably the only one left in the twelve-story office building. Sane people left work a lot earlier than this.

She let her gaze fall out of focus as she stared through the blurred glass into the darkness and watched Jordan disappear. A flash of lightning, followed by a quick clap of thunder, brought her to attention, and she grew aware of every sound around her.

Roxanne turned quickly when a tapping noise sounded, only to scan the empty lobby cast with long shadows. She surveyed the large open area, her surroundings familiar. Well waxed tiles on the floor glistened with every flash of lightning, and the high ceiling made the thunder echo. With a sigh, she turned to face the doors and wait. Once again tapping sounded behind her, and she turned again, almost tripping over her own toes.

"Would you quit it," she scowled to herself. "It's nothing but pipes."

The sound of her own voice calmed her a bit, but her senses remained heightened, and every minute sound alerted her. She felt on edge, and blamed it on lack of sleep. The tapping sounded again, but she refused to turn this time, although prickles down her spine made her anxious to leave. Maybe she should just wait for Jordan outside.

Roxanne pushed the handle to open the glass door. Damp air surrounded her, and at the same time she felt the toes of her pantyhose saturate with water. Rain hit her arms and soaked through the material of her dress. She hadn't taken more than a step when headlights approached her. Roxanne frowned when she recognized Jordan's tan Porsche, instead of her own Probe. Why the hell had he taken her keys if it wasn't to bring her car to her?

"Why are you standing in the rain?" Jordan exited his car and walked around, then took her arm. He slid his card through the security box, pressed the necessary buttons and escorted her back into the building. "Look at you. You're soaked."

"I thought you were bringing my car to me." Roxanne wiped rain from her face with her free hand, since she was unable to release her other arm from Jordan's grasp. Her chin-length bangs that she had been trying to grow out forever, it seemed, stuck to her cheek, and she brushed them aside. Her mood turned sour as she realized she must look a wreck now in front of Jordan, who, although a bit damp, still looked sexy as hell.

"I'm going to take you to dinner." Jordan released her and stood appraising her. "But now we need to clean you up. What possessed you to stand outside?"

Roxanne felt foolish and frustrated at the same time. It was just like Jordan to assume she would want to go to dinner with him. She had planned on taking herself home to a hot bath. Her emotions laced with aggravation at his pompous attitude, and a sense of excitement that he had thought to reward her hard work by taking her to dinner.

"I heard something," she mumbled, doing her best to dry herself with her hand.

Jordan didn't respond, and the silence grew between the two of them. Roxanne decided her actions didn't require justifying, and straightened.

"Why did you ask for the keys to my car, and then not bring it to me?"

After all, her workday had ended, and now Jordan Hall was just a man, not her boss. She felt a tremble when she met his gaze, and narrowed her lips into a thin line, feeling herself grow wet, knowing she would submit to him if she didn't stand her ground. "And why would you assume I would go to dinner with you?"

"I would never leave you anywhere if you weren't safe." Jordan spoke quietly, almost a whisper, sounding so calm she blinked, momentarily forgetting her guard. "We need to get you dry before we go eat."

She licked her lips and wondered what it would be like to kiss this virile man. At the same time she realized he hadn't answered her question. She didn't need him thinking for her.

Jordan turned, putting his hand on the back of her head, and guided them back to the elevator. His hand slid from her head to between her shoulder blades, and remained there until the doors opened on the seventh floor. Roxanne felt certain her dress dried on her backside just from the heat of his touch.

"I can dry myself in the bathroom." Roxanne slowed when they reached the bathrooms, but Jordan's fingers pressed into her skin on her back, angling her beyond the restroom doors.

They walked silently to their office, and then Jordan took her arms and backed her up against his desk, so that her rear end rested on the edge.

"I want to dry you off." Jordan placed his index finger under her chin, lifting her head so that he could meet her gaze. "You need to trust me."

Overwhelming domination swirled in those black eyes, captivating her.

She laughed, trying to make light of the situation that had her pussy throbbing. "I've never had a reason not to trust you. But I'm quite capable of drying myself off."

You're all alone in this building with him, and I bet if you asked him to fuck you right here, he would. Roxanne struggled to ignore the voice taunting her thoughts.

Jordan turned as if he hadn't heard her, slipping his overcoat onto the chair, and then opening the cabinets next to the sink.

Roxanne remained glued to the edge of his desk, allowing herself an eyeful of the man while his back was turned. She should walk out of the office. The bathroom was the safest place for her to put herself back in order. But damn, did he make it hard for her to just walk out on him.

His white shirt spread over a broad, muscular back, and then narrowed into his work slacks, which covered what she was sure had to be the perfect male ass. Jordan turned at that moment, and with her eyes set at the level of his ass, she found she now saw a bulge through his pants. She wondered, while quickly averting her gaze, if the fullness she had noticed was due to the pleats in the slacks, or if he was simply very well-endowed.

"Hold out your arms." Jordan returned to stand in front of her with several white towels in his hands. He leaned into her slightly, placing two towels on the desk next to her, then unfolded the one he still held.

She raised her arms, her heart pounding. Jordan never offered explanations with his instructions. But his instructions had never been on such a personal level before.

"Like this." Jordan took one of her wrists and stretched her arm so that it straightened parallel to her shoulder. She did the same with her other arm, her heartbeat pulsing in her pussy lips, distracting her while it swelled and moistened.

Jordan began towel-drying her arms, caressing them gently with the towel. "The rain soaked you, didn't it?"

The roughness of the small towel sent chills rushing through her. And she didn't answer right away.

Jordan met her gaze, stroking her skin with small movements. Those black eyes captured her, captivated her, and she didn't look away. Barely able to breathe, pressure built, making her ache for him.

If he were to spread her legs apart, and place his mouth on that growing ache, she knew he could relieve her of so many months of pent-up sexual desire. She imagined him running his tongue over her smoothly shaved skin, and breaking the dam of desire that her battery-operated toys had failed to do.

"If you'd stayed inside, done as you were told..." he continued, his voice a mere whisper, his face less than a foot from hers while he stroked her with the towel.

He moved the towel, encircling her neck, drying the skin there while her body tingled like an overexposed nerve ending.

The way he watched her, his expression relaxed, his presence overwhelming her by how close he stood, she wondered if she would ever be dry again. The more he rubbed her with that towel, the more wet she became.

Jordan moved the towel over the top of her dress, his hand grazing over her breast.

Roxanne jumped, squealing in surprise.

"I think that's enough. I feel better now, thank you," she rushed to say, while almost tripping when she moved away from him, crossing her arms across her chest.

"You aren't dry." Jordan straightened, offering her that intent look she so often noticed when he was focused on one of their accounts.

"And I never will be at that rate," she mumbled, but then heat rushed over her cheeks. "Umm, it's late, and I'm tired. I think I'll just head home now. I'll see you tomorrow."

Roxanne darted for the door, feeling foolish and unable to focus her thoughts while her cunt pulsated violently with need. She hadn't had sex for a long time. Hell, she hadn't experienced that much foreplay in a long time. And her body screamed in protest when she forced one foot in front of the other, and marched out of his office.

Halfway to the secretarial pool, she stopped in her tracks.

Her keys!

Jordan Hall had her keys, the bastard. Roxanne took a deep breath, did an about-face, and marched back into her boss's office. He leaned against his desk in the exact spot she had been moments before, arms crossed, as if waiting for her to return. Which, of course, was exactly what he was doing. He knew he had her keys.

She held her hand out, palm up. "My keys," she demanded.

He nodded to his coat, tossed over her office chair. "In my pocket," he said.

She studied him for a second longer. He appeared the predator, waiting for his prey to play right into his preset trap. If only she knew his game, but those dark eyes revealed nothing, just watched her without blinking. Roxanne grabbed his coat and held it by the collar as she stuffed her hand into one pocket, and then the other.

"Jordan, where are my keys?" She sighed.

"They're in the inside pocket." He still hadn't moved.

Roxanne took a deep breath, and reached inside his coat, searching for the pocket. Jordan pushed himself from his desk and took a step toward her. She stepped around her chair, blocking him, and at the same time holding his coat higher, feeling silly when she used it to shield herself. He stopped and crossed his arms.

"Do you think I'm going to attack you?" He sounded amused.

Damn the man to hell for making her want him so desperately.

"I know you're not."

She pulled her keys free and draped his coat over her chair. Could Jordan tell how sexually aroused she was? Her nipples were hardened peaks, and her pantyhose were soaked next to her pussy. She was as wet there as her toes were from the rain.

Although her heart pounded from nerves while she watched her boss warily, Roxanne knew one thing beyond a shadow of doubt. She did trust him. After two years of working with the man, she knew he was fair, and that he could be kind. Jordan had plotted an agenda, and she could guess his attempts to dry her had aroused him as much as it had her. But Roxanne knew that Jordan wouldn't do anything to her without her wanting it. And, oh baby, did her body want it. Damn.

"Good night, Jordan." Roxanne slipped her keys into her purse and turned again to leave his office.

"You won't get scared again walking through the building alone?" His tone offered a quiet challenge, making her breath catch in her throat.

She almost stumbled in the doorway, but managed to maintain her composure and headed again toward the elevator.

"I'll be fine," she called out, and kept walking.

She hadn't made it to the secretarial pool when the lights on the floor went out. Roxanne stopped in her tracks while her eyes adjusted.

"Jordan?" she called, although she knew he had simply turned them out since they were both leaving the floor.

But Jordan didn't respond.

Roxanne steadied herself by reaching for Dorothy, the receptionist's, desk. Her eyes adjusted and she glanced at the row of cubicles, then back toward the hallway where the executive offices were. She didn't see Jordan approach, and she continued to stand, not moving, once again listening to every sound in the building. This time the pipes remained silent. She was surrounded by a quiet darkness charged with sexual energy. Where was Jordan?

Roxanne stepped toward the elevator, looking over her shoulder, wondering where in the hell he was, while her cum-soaked pantyhose dampened her inner thighs.

She reached for the elevator button, which glowed in the surrounding darkness, and shrieked as long fingers encircled her wrist.

"I want to take you to dinner," Jordan whispered in her ear.

Every inch of Roxanne's backside turned to gooseflesh as nerve endings exploded. Jordan's body pushed up against her, and the hardness of him pressed against the upper part of her ass. She sucked in air, trying to think of a response, but she couldn't think of anything coy to say.

The only thing that popped into her head was that she wanted *him* for dinner, but she sure as hell wasn't going to say that. She struggled for balance in her heels, while her mind focused on the thick, long, hard-as-a-rock shaft pressed against her, fogging her senses with lust.

Jordan loosened his grip on her wrist then slid his hand up her arm until he cupped her neck. Taking her chin, he turned her head and she moved her body of her own accord, until he had her facing him.

Still holding her by her chin, his black eyes studied her, and then his gaze lowered to her lips. When his mouth lowered over hers, she felt his heat before tasting it. But when the tips of their tongues touched, white sparks exploded behind her closed eyes, and the explosion trickled down through her body, making her knees tremble.

"Jordan," she gasped into his mouth.

He pushed her up against the wall next to the elevator.

"Do you realize how beautiful you are?" he whispered, dropping to his knees in front of her.

Roxanne opened her mouth to talk, but couldn't manage to utter a word. His hands gripped her outer thighs, his touch strong and so damned hot. She placed her palms on the wall behind her, needing to hold on to something solid before she melted into a puddle of lust at his feet. The cool wallpaper behind her back did nothing to calm her fiery nerves.

Jordan slid his fingers under her dress, gliding his touch up either side of her. He raised her dress slowly, entranced with the view that appeared before him. The scent of her desire made him mad with need, his cock suddenly throbbing like a caged animal, demanding its freedom.

Gripping the top of her pantyhose, he eased them down her thighs, her dress falling once again to conceal from him a perfect view of her exposed pussy.

His brain was on fire. Her skin was so damned smooth under her hose, her legs perfectly shaped, trim and firm. If he continued to torture himself like this he would lose all sense of reality. She wasn't going to fight him, and he wouldn't take her by force. But if he didn't focus, he would get too rough. Roxanne was willing, but skittish. Moving too fast would ruin it for both of them.

Taking each of her feet delicately in his hands, he removed her sandals, and then her hose. Red polish on her toenails flattered her feet nicely. He cupped her ankles, and then slowly glided his hands back up her legs.

Standing took more effort than he'd guessed. Blood pumped through his veins, surging toward his dick. Thinking became an annoying task. But he had to focus, keep his attention on pleasing Roxanne. Too many nights he'd lay thinking about her, and now was the time to make his intentions clear.

He straightened, seeing how her desire flushed her cheeks, made her dark orbs burn with passion. There was no way he could look away, but at the same time, his cock needed freedom.

Roxanne slid her fingers over the feverish throb between her legs, trying to rub the ache into some form of mild submission while watching Jordan free his cock from his pants. She couldn't stop her mouth from opening when the thick, swollen member appeared in the dim light that barely flooded in through the glass doors leading to the hallway.

"Oh dear Lord," she gasped, and then felt heat burn her cheeks while embarrassment rushed through her.

Jordan was fucking huge! His long fingers held the swollen cock, her mouth going dry, and then wet again, as she watched him stroke the velvet skin covering the rock-hardness. The head of his cock was smooth, round and engorged, a beast waiting to conquer. And more than anything, at that moment, she wanted that cock slammed into her with all the force the man could muster.

"Is there a problem?" Jordan's breath tortured her skin while he placed moist kisses down her on-fire cheeks.

She lowered her head, worked for words to say, but she couldn't think of a thing to say that wouldn't embarrass her more.

"Roxanne," Jordan whispered, torturing her further with the simple mention of her name.

She looked up, but forgot to think when she stared into his handsome face. Even attempting a smile took work.

"It's okay, sweetheart." He brushed his lips against hers.

They were so moist, so hot, and she was feeling worse than an awkward teenager. Opening to him, tasting coffee mixed with the heat of his mouth, sent her over the edge.

She let out a murmur, or maybe it was simply a plea for more. Jordan growled into her mouth, deepening the kiss, while his body leaned into hers.

"I need you now," he grumbled, breaking the kiss and leaving her working to catch her breath.

Jordan pressed her hard against the wall, lifted one of her legs, then the other, pinning her so that she couldn't move. The head of his shaft rubbed against her swollen lips while she tried to move her ass to ease his entrance.

"Be still, woman," he growled in her ear, and Roxanne froze.

Then he thrust. Roxanne hit her head against the wall and saw stars when he pounded into the depths of her womb.

He drove deep inside her, hitting that spot she'd never been able to reach with her toys. Wave after wave of pent-up desire rushed through her, so that when Roxanne opened her eyes, all she could see was a spectrum of colors.

"Oh. God." She didn't remember sex being this good.

Jordan Hall reached depths within her that she knew had never been reached before. And the man had stamina like she never imagined. With every thrust her inner muscles clamped around him, soaking both of them with her juices.

She dug her fingers into the flesh on his shoulders. Her juices streamed and tickled her ass, while he impaled her repeatedly.

"Don't stop," she wailed. *Please never stop.*

Hair fell in her face, while her head tapped the wall behind her, but she didn't care about either. All of her attention focused on that wonderful cock nailing every aching pressure point deep within her.

Roxanne could tell by how Jordan's entire body seemed to contort that he was about ready to explode. At the same time, her inner muscles swelled, peaking, building to a pressure point as she readied herself for possibly the largest orgasm she had ever experienced. She worked to clear her thoughts, wanting nothing to interfere with the climax she wanted desperately to experience. When Jordan lunged for the final time, her lower back scraped the wall, but her inner body exploded in a shower of light and molten heat that left her limp and numb. Never before had she experienced sex like this, and with the one man she had sworn she would never touch.

Chapter Two

ක

After getting her car for her, Jordan waited for Roxanne to leave the parking lot in her Probe, before taking off. The urge to follow her back to her house overwhelmed him, and he stopped before reaching the exit of the lot and pinched the bridge of his nose.

Best thing to do right now would be to bury himself in work.

The ride home didn't last long enough for Jordan to turn his thoughts toward work. He pushed the button on the white box clipped to his sun visor, and his garage door silently slid open as he pulled his Porsche onto his blacktop drive. Jordan heard the familiar beep of his security system as he entered his kitchen, and reached for the mail that Millie, his housekeeper, had left on the counter. He barely looked at it before tossing the unopened envelopes back where they had been.

Roxanne had distracted his thoughts before, but after tonight, Jordan started to think the rest of his night would be ruined for getting any work done. What a hot fucking ride she had been. And to think she had worked next to him for the past two years and he had waited this long to find out how good she was.

Damn. He must be getting old. Jordan walked through his house toward the back patio, and then stepped outside to turn on the hot tub. If he had done that woman before tonight however, he realized he might not have made all the profits he had over the past year. She would have kept him way too busy.

Jordan had a feeling that Roxanne was the kind of lady who would want more and soon. He grinned at the thought, and tested the temperature of the water. He almost laughed out loud when he felt the vibration of his cell phone.

"Jordan here," he said, still smiling.

"Jordan." The voice of one of his senior accountants, Ralph Layette, made the smile on Jordan's face disappear. "I think we might have a problem."

* * * * *

Roxanne toweled dry in a rush as the phone rang for the second time. Her pale blue robe hung on the hook of her bathroom door, and she threw one arm into it, and then the other as she left damp footprints on her carpet.

"Hello," she said, after grabbing the cordless from its cradle.

"Are you up already?" Her best friend, Joanie, sounded way too cheerful for the early hour. But that was Joanie.

"Just hopped out of the shower." Roxanne crooked the phone between her shoulder and cheek and ran her towel over her legs as she headed toward her bedroom.

"I just wanted to see if you could meet for lunch. I got the invitations in the mail yesterday and you've just got to see them." Joanie sounded so excited that Roxanne couldn't help but smile.

"These are the ones you and I picked out? The ones with the roses on them?"

Roxanne remembered the day she and Joanie had chosen wedding invitations, napkins, and so many other little necessities for her friend's upcoming wedding. The day had left Roxanne feeling a little down, since she doubted she would ever be able to plan such an event for herself. After Jeffrey had left town, it just seemed like too much work to try and establish a relationship with a man. It always led to heartache. But Joanie had reveled in every moment, and Roxanne wanted to be there for her best friend.

"Yes. Meet at my house around twelve-thirty?"

"Sounds good." Roxanne told her friend goodbye and then pushed the "off" button on her phone before tossing it on her bed.

Matisse, her well-fed, long-haired white cat, stood up and stretched, and sniffed at the phone, which lay next to her.

Roxanne ran her hand over the cat's silky white fur. "Sorry, sweetie. Did I wake you?"

The cat offered a scratchy meow, and Roxanne turned to begin applying her makeup. She towel-dried her hair, and flinched as she ran fingers over a couple of tender areas on the back of her head.

Heat raced through her as she thought about the night before. What a fool she had been. Granted, Jordan Hall had given her the best sex she had experienced in her entire life, but what did that say about her?

The man had taken her like a common whore. They hadn't even completely undressed, and of all things, up against the wall in the secretarial pool.

Heat flushed from her cheeks to her tummy as humiliation rushed through her. This was her boss. She worked side by side with the man every single day. Not only would she have to face him today, but she would spend her entire day with him. Roxanne blew out a frustrated breath of air.

"Well, girl, you fucked up big this time," she said to herself in the mirror, and reached for her blow-dryer. "You don't want to lose your job so you're just going to have to make the best of it."

The drive across town wasn't as bad, Roxanne realized as she shifted lanes easily, since she had left her house forty minutes earlier than normal. The report would be complete and on Jordan's desk before he arrived that morning. There were a few other accounts in her in-tray she wanted to have done before lunch, and Jordan's meeting with their biggest client was today.

Hopefully the two of them wouldn't experience too much time alone.

Roxanne's tummy did nasty flip-flops wondering how he would react to her today. She scolded herself to focus on her tasks, and not on her well-endowed boss.

A couple of the other executives were in their offices when Roxanne arrived, and she greeted each of them as she always did, while making her way to Jordan's office at the end of the hall. Although he never arrived much before ten, Roxanne still breathed a sigh of relief when she flipped on the light and surveyed the empty office. Her computer hummed as it booted up, and she turned Jordan's on as well, as she always did, then started coffee. Within thirty minutes she had the report complete and on her boss's desk. His desk...where it all had started. Roxanne ran her fingers over the edge of it, remembering how the man had successfully managed to dominate her and turn her into complete putty in his hands. A tingling between her legs reminded her that he had done a damn good job of it too.

She reached for a pad of yellow sticky notes, and scratched out a comment to attach to the report. One of the accounts hadn't balanced accurately. It appeared the bank showed a smaller balance than their records did. She had contacted the bank and verified the amount, and then adjusted their records.

"Please ask Mr. Uphouse if he made a personal withdrawal without notifying us," she mumbled as she wrote the message.

"Roxanne?" She jumped at the sound of Dorothy's voice, and turned to press the button on her phone.

"Yeah, Dorothy?" She looked at the small speaker attached to her phone.

Glancing at the half-open office door, she leaned back in her chair, stretching her legs under her desk, and massaged a sore muscle in her shoulder.

"Mr. Hall is on line one for you."

Roxanne sat up straight. Everything inside her turned to stone. Her gut clenched, her throat constricted, and for a moment she couldn't respond or move her finger from the speaker button.

This power Jordan had managed over her was infuriating, and she gritted her teeth to fight it off. Thinking about how he had taken her, made her want him all over again and had her nerves on edge, which really pissed her off.

"Thanks, Dorothy," she managed, clearing her throat and forcing herself to relax.

Get a grip on yourself, she scolded, as she pressed her hands together prayer fashion, and held them to her lips. Last night was a one-night fling. The two of them worked very closely together, and both were consenting adults. She knew he had enjoyed himself too. The smile he had offered her while they dressed, or more like adjusted their clothing afterward, had been proof of that. They hadn't said much, but she knew a good fuck meant both of them had gotten off.

However, today was a new day. The man was her boss, and she could keep their relationship professional, just as it had been for the past two years.

"Yes, boss," she said as she picked up the phone, trying to sound as nonchalant as she always did.

"I need you to print the accounts payable file on Roger Uphouse. Pull the file on his overseas account, and be at the Garrison Lounge at one-thirty. Roger will be there and you will join us to explain the transactions if he has questions."

"Not a problem." She was proud of her confident tone, her relaxed-sounding voice. If only her insides would calm down. "I'll be there."

Roxanne glanced at Jordan's desk, where the Uphouse file rested with the note she had just stuck to it. He must have the rest of his files, since they weren't in the office, but this one held the bank transactions. She wondered if he knew about the discrepancy.

And although she didn't like it, Jordan offered no explanation as to why he wanted that particular file. Nor did he bother to let her know why her presence was needed. That was so like him, always in control and never bothering to fill her in on details. Man, did he need some serious training!

Well, it was a good thing she had found the discrepancy, and didn't need to ask Jordan any questions. As always, Roxanne would be prepared.

Training? Wait a minute, what was she thinking? Jordan was her boss, and that was it. Some other woman could train him. This was his company, and all she needed to focus on was doing her job to the best of her ability.

She gave herself a mental shake, reminding herself once again that last night had simply been a much-needed good fuck. There was no way she could spare her heart again for possible heartbreak.

Slowly she gathered what she would need for the luncheon, once again going over the file so she would be prepared for any questions.

The Garrison Lounge was one of the most exquisite restaurants in town, and during the day, a common retreat for executives to wine and dine favorite clients. Roxanne had met Jordan there once before, and knew the place reeked of class and elegance.

She glanced down at the conservative dress she had chosen for the day. Granted, she was simply an accountant for Hall Enterprises, but it wouldn't hurt to put on something a bit more chic for the luncheon meeting.

Going over wedding plans with Joanie would have to be put on hold until another day.

* * * * *

The two men sat at a corner table, and Roxanne greeted both with a smile as the host pulled her seat for her. "Good afternoon, gentleman."

"I don't believe we have had the pleasure of meeting." Roger Uphouse extended a hand across the table. The man had a rugged Texan look about him, and Roxanne guessed him to be in his mid-forties. Light brown hair had slight streaks of gray running through it, but his clean-shaven face showed no wrinkles or worry lines. Overall he was a fairly attractive man. Roger grinned as Roxanne accepted his hand.

"Well now, Jordan, this attractive lady could soothe any concerned client you might have," he added. "Jordan told me you'd bring the transaction reports I asked to see."

Roxanne released her hand but couldn't reach for the files she'd pulled from her briefcase before Jordan took them.

He handed them to Uphouse. "Yes. We have printouts right here. And if you approve of what I've done, we can make arrangements to move your other accounts in a similar fashion."

The last thing he wanted was Uphouse focusing all of his attention on Roxanne. There had been no time to get to the office before this meeting. He knew he could have had Roxanne fax the file to him, but damn it, he'd wanted to see her.

Roger Uphouse took the printout that Roxanne had brought with her, and compared the two. He wrinkled his brow, taking time to compare the figures. After several minutes of silence, he looked across the table, smiling. "Good move, Hall," Uphouse said. "I like your keen eye for the market. Normally I like to approve all transactions of my monies, but this stock moved so quickly, that you made a good call in switching money as you did."

Roxanne wanted to know what transaction Uphouse referred to, but she held her tongue. She could only guess that somehow Jordan had been the one to take the money from the account that showed an off balance, and use it to purchase some stock. But why wouldn't he have made a note in the file if he had done so? Jordan would ream any employee for pulling a stunt like that, and it wasn't like the man to do anything different than what he would expect of his employees. All she could do was wait for later to get her answers.

The waiter arrived to take their orders, and Roxanne found her knowledge wasn't needed when Jordan answered most of the questions Roger asked. The millionaire smiled at her occasionally, but Jordan never looked her way. He focused on business and, for the most part, Roxanne focused on her salad.

The business suit she had selected when she stopped home before her meeting with the two men was comfortable. Her tan suit jacket, white silk blouse, and knee-length skirt fit the atmosphere perfectly. She crossed her legs, and then looked up in time to see Roger glance her way and their eyes met briefly. But Jordan never swayed from the topic at hand.

The three of them continued the discussion of Roger's overseas accounts as they headed for the exit, but once outside the building, Roger stopped Roxanne with a hand to her elbow.

"We've spent this entire luncheon discussing nothing but business." Roger had a friendly smile, and Roxanne felt comfortable with him.

"I thought that was what business luncheons were for," she teased, and found Roger had a warm laugh.

"I would be honored if you would join me later today for a drink. Jordan told me earlier that you have a knack for the market. I would love to pick your brain a bit."

"Roxanne has a busy afternoon on her calendar." Jordan spoke before Roxanne could respond.

More than anything he wanted to touch her, give Uphouse the clue that Roxanne wasn't available. But he didn't have that right, and for some reason, that irked him more than Uphouse's way too chivalrous attitude.

When Uphouse looked like he would comment, Jordan decided he needed to be more clear. "It might be best for you to call the office later today. I'm not sure yet what meetings she will need to attend," he added, knowing Roxanne knew he had no idea what was on her schedule.

She set her own schedule, hell, she arranged his days for him. And maybe he had been out of line, but damn it, he hadn't had a chance to talk to her since last night. There was no way what they had done would be just a one-night stand. He wouldn't have it.

"Sounds good," Roger nodded, and then said his farewells.

Roxanne let her polite smile fade when Roger turned toward his car. Without a word to Jordan, she turned and marched toward her own car.

What kind of nerve did that man think he had? There were no afternoon meetings. Not only did Roxanne arrange her own schedule, she set Jordan's schedule as well. More times than not, he didn't have a clue what was on his agenda until he consulted with her.

Roxanne pulled her car door open with more force than needed, and tossed her briefcase to the passenger side.

Jordan had parked several cars down, and when she glanced up his gaze met hers. She made no attempt at hiding her anger as she pursed her lips and glared at him. As usual, however, his expression remained calm. The sun caught his black hair, making it shine, but his eyes were as dark as a night sky as they held her gaze captive. Without opening his car door, he walked over to her. Roxanne forced herself to get into her car, but couldn't shut her door before Jordan opened it again.

"What are you doing?" Roxanne felt surprise dampen her anger when Jordan took her arm and pulled her out of the car. She glanced around the parking lot nervously, but being midafternoon, the place was fairly quiet.

"Do you really think Uphouse gives a rat's ass how well you can play the market?" His tone brought her pause, and she simply stared at him. "The man is loaded. If he wants to fuck he can pay for a whore."

Roxanne's mouth opened when she realized Jordan's implication. She shut it quickly and swallowed, then straightened to take on the intimidating man who had her pinned between her car and her car door.

"If someone asks me to do something after work, I am more than capable of telling them whether or not I will be available." She put her hands on her hips and dared to face those black eyes. "We do not have a heavy work load this afternoon, and if I wish to see the man after work that is my prerogative."

"And if I decide that I want every file audited this afternoon that is my prerogative." Jordan took Roxanne by the shoulders, wanting more than anything to shake some sense into her. Instead he brushed his thumbs over the curve of her shoulders, forcing his tone to soften. "Get yourself back to work. I'll be there shortly."

"You can't suddenly load me down with work just to make sure I don't go out tonight." Roxanne turned as if to get out of the car again, but doing so would have made her run into Jordan, who had a hand on her car door, and another on the roof of her car.

"Those files haven't been audited in a while." He knew he couldn't keep her at work late every night, but he would do everything in his power to keep her from seeing Uphouse.

The man didn't live here, Jordan did, and he needed to see Roxanne again. There was no way she could have much of a social life with the hours she kept. It wasn't hard to hear the office gossip, to know she no longer had a boyfriend.

"Get back to work." Now wasn't the time, but he would arrange to talk to her further in a more intimate setting.

Roxanne slammed her fists against the steering wheel after Jordan closed her car door for her. He fought a grin, loving her fiery temper. She would be worth every minute of taming.

* * * * *

As it turned out, Jordan didn't return to the office until almost five. Roxanne had been kept fairly busy with phone calls, but if Roger Uphouse had tried to reach her, Dorothy hadn't put the call through. At five before five, Roxanne shut her computer down, and headed toward the elevator.

"Have a good evening, Dorothy," she smiled, and then noticed Jordan standing by one of the filing cabinets, surveying an open file he had spread over the top of the cabinet.

He glanced at the wall clock, and then at Roxanne. She ignored him, and turned to leave. It crossed her mind that she should go over a few phone messages with him, and any other day she would have. But at the moment, she felt too outraged and baffled by his behavior earlier that day. He had acted like he owned her.

She let the glass doors to Hall Enterprises close silently behind her and hurried to the elevator before its doors closed. Jordan returned his attention to the file on top of the cabinet and she studied him while the elevator doors closed.

His image—that perfect body, his strong powerful features, the way he looked so in control, even when he simply looked over a file—distracted her thoughts during her drive home.

Roxanne had just stepped out of her hot bubble bath, the one she didn't get the night before, when the phone rang. She wrapped her towel around her, dabbing at herself until she picked up the phone.

"Roxanne?" The man's voice didn't sound familiar.

"Who is this?"

"Roger Uphouse. I hope I'm not reaching you at a bad time."

Roxanne padded across her now damp carpet to her room, and tossed her towel over the back of her chair next to her computer desk. She plopped on her bed, and stroked Matisse, who stretched to make the job easier.

"No, it's not a bad time." She stared at her painted toenails, and Matisse rubbed against her foot. "But how did you get this number?"

"When I called your office and your receptionist told me you were on the other line, she was kind enough to give me your last name. Directory assistance did the rest." There was a smile in Roger's tone, and Roxanne couldn't help but grin at his boyish tone, but she wondered why she hadn't received a message that Roger had called. "I had some work to finish, but find myself now here alone at my suite. I thought I'd check to see if you're free this evening."

Matisse hopped to the floor and trotted out of the room. Roxanne leaned against her pillow and ran her hand down her naked body. It had been more than apparent that Jordan didn't want her to see this man.

If he wants to fuck, he can pay for a whore. The words he'd thrown in her face still got her ire up. She circled her nipple with her fingernail, and watched it pucker as she considered Roger's offer.

"What did you have in mind?" She didn't see anything wrong with knowing the man's intention firsthand. Jordan could be completely off-base about what Roger wanted.

"There's a nice lounge downstairs. I'm at the Marriott South. I'd like your company, Roxanne. You seem intelligent, and you are very beautiful. Let me send my car for you, and we will see how the night goes."

Roxanne knew the Marriott to be one of the nicer hotels in downtown Kansas City. She rolled off her bed and walked through her house, which had grown dark as evening had set in, toward her kitchen. She slid a wineglass free from the wooden rack that hung above her sink, and poured wine as she considered Roger's proposal.

"Well, Roger, I just got out of a hot bath, and hadn't planned on going anywhere this evening. How long will you be in town?"

"Probably for a week, or so. Just have a drink with me this evening. Tomorrow night I can take you dancing." Roger's pleasant tone tempted her. He didn't make demands like some men did.

"Why don't we have that drink tomorrow evening?" Roxanne turned to stare at her dark kitchen, and leaned her bare back against her counter. "I don't think I have a heavy schedule tomorrow, so maybe we can make a night of it."

"Roxanne, that sounds wonderful." Roger chuckled into the phone. "Now don't you let Hall work you to death. He doesn't realize the treasure he has at his fingertips."

Roxanne pondered the man's final words as she bade him good night. She wasn't too sure Roger Uphouse knew Jordan as well as he thought he did.

"So you're going to go out with the man anyway?" The voice through the darkness made Roxanne jump, and chilled wine spilled down the front of her naked body.

She turned to see the tall, forbidding shadow leaning against her back door at the other end of the kitchen. How long had Jordan Hall been standing there?

Chapter Three

🔖

Roxanne had thrown him a curveball. Not only had he inaccurately concluded how she would react toward him after he'd fucked her silly, he had discovered that she apparently had no intention of seeking him out for round two. Jordan didn't like reading a person wrong, and he seldom did. When she responded to Uphouse's flirting earlier that day, he had decided the best thing to do would be to help Roxanne see how she needed to keep her priorities straight. She answered to him first.

He had no problem with scooping up her afternoon messages when he'd arrived at the office. He brought them to her often enough that Dorothy didn't think anything of it. And he knew he would find a message from Uphouse among them. Roger had left a message saying he would try to reach her at her house that evening. Jordan decided a social call might be in order, but when he approached her front door, he realized the silly woman hadn't closed her blinds yet. Through the dim light in her house, he had watched her walk to her kitchen without a stitch of clothing on. The front door had been locked, but he found the back door opened without a squeak.

"What the hell are you doing in my house?" Roxanne glared at her him through the unlit room, temporarily forgetting her nudity in front of him.

"I told you not to go out with him." Jordan pushed away from the wall, and took her glass from her, setting it on the counter before she could react.

He pulled the towel, which hung around the refrigerator handle, and then rubbed it down her front.

Roxanne slapped at him, and jumped backward at the same time. "Would you quit always trying to dry me?"

"I will when you quit getting wet every time we're alone together."

His double meaning wasn't missed. Roxanne stared at him without a response for one moment, and then growled her frustration. She stormed out of the kitchen, knowing clothes were imperative at that moment. She didn't make it halfway to her room before Jordan grabbed her arm and spun her around.

"All he wants to do is fuck you," he hissed, as he held her wrist pinned in the air.

Although the only light filtered from the bedroom, Jordan's black eyes glowed with strong emotion.

"And you, what do you want?" she snarled, ready to slap some sense—and manners—into this man.

Jordan pinned her wrist to the wall behind her. The impact made the picture frame, hanging inches from her hand, rattle. She reached to push his chest backward, but he grabbed that wrist and pinned it against the wall as well. Roxanne glared at him, as she stood bare-ass naked against the wall, with her hands pinned on either side of her head.

"What I don't want is a one-night stand." Jordan didn't press against her, but stood a good foot away, not lowering his gaze once, but focused on her brown eyes that at the moment swarmed with anger. "And you're not going to start sleeping around."

"Not that it's any of your business, but I haven't had sex with anyone in a long time before last night," she hissed through clenched teeth and then struggled against his grip. "Now let me go."

Jordan released her wrists, but instead of pulling his hands free from her, he ran them down the undersides of her arms. When he bent his head to brush his lips over hers, Roxanne found it hard to breathe. Jordan Hall had entered her space, made her being part of his being, and she wasn't sure how or when he had done it.

"Letting you go isn't an option," he whispered into her mouth, and then deepened the kiss.

He would calm her anger. If it took all evening, she would know he meant what he said. It had been a long time since someone had gotten under his skin the way Roxanne had. There was no way he would let her slip through his fingers. She was too hot, too damned sexy to allow her to stray from him.

Roxanne felt drugged from the spell she felt certain the man had planted on her. Her mind fogged with need, her rational thought slipping while the ache inside her began throbbing without shame.

Jordan released her mouth, tracing a fiery path across her cheek to her ear. She sucked in air, trying her damnedest to maintain control of the situation before she begged him to fuck her again.

"Would you have me take you up against a wall again?" Jordan's voice scraped over her naked body, like wicked fingernails, giving her exotic chills.

Roxanne blinked, fighting the fog that enveloped her senses. Why did he have to ask her how or where she wanted it? Jordan knew how to make decisions, and she was all for him deciding the position right now. All she knew was that she wanted—no—she *needed* him to satisfy her again as he had last night. She raised her hands to his chest, pushing without success.

Jordan grabbed her shoulders and turned her toward the only lit room in her home. His hands slid down her arms while he moved her toward the light, grabbing her wrists and pinning them behind her back. She walked as his captive into her bedroom. Jordan pushed her forward, causing her to fall on to her bed. She rolled over quickly, her legs bent and spread enough that the scent of her juices teased her nostrils.

"You're trying to control me," she managed, words suddenly hard to form.

Jordan stood over, definitely the sexiest man she'd ever laid eyes on.

He took his time undressing, allowing her time to watch those long fingers while he unbuttoned his shirt, to those penetrating black orbs, glazed thick with desire. Roxanne sucked in a breath when he shrugged his shirt from his shoulders. Thick black curls spread across well-developed muscles.

"Maybe you need to be controlled." Jordan laid his work shirt over her chair and then freed his belt from his slacks.

She watched him sit, and noted how hard his stomach was, not one ripple of fat appearing as he rested on her chair and took off his shoes, and then socks.

"I need respect." Her tits ached from desire causing them to swell.

And she needed so much more, too. She grabbed one of her nipples and twisted it hard, feeling the shriek of need race down her abdomen to her pussy, which she quickly rubbed with her other hand.

"You are one horny little bitch, aren't you?" Jordan growled, and she bit her lip, liking the guttural sound of his voice. "Do you need it again that bad?"

"I'm not the only one who needs it," she accused, enjoying watching the striptease occurring in front of her.

Rubbing her clit as he unzipped his pants, and then removed them along with his underwear, the small nub of flesh swelled against her finger, her cream soaking her fingers.

The large cock that danced in front of her, surrounded by thick black curls, made her mouth water. She sat up without thought, and reached for it.

"Oh yes, baby. This is all you need." Jordan grabbed the back of her head, although she didn't resist, and held her as she sucked his cock into her mouth, lapping at it eagerly. "Damn, babe. That's it. Show my cock how badly you want it."

But she wasn't the only one with needs, she'd been right. Jordan closed his eyes when she ran her moist lips along his dick. She licked and sucked at him, taking him in until her throat filled with him, then pulled back so that she could lap at him with her tongue. Jordan groaned, unable to tell her with words what she was doing to him.

Jordan pulled his cock free, and pushed her back on the bed.

He knelt on the edge of the bed, in between her legs. She ran her fingertips over his chest and the slight touch made him want to roll his eyes back in his head. He wouldn't look away from her though, wouldn't miss a moment of enjoying the sultry body lying in front of him.

"You have perfect tits, sweetheart," Jordan whispered as he grabbed them with his hands, giving them a rough squeeze.

He sucked in one nipple, and then moved to the other one, nibbling first, and then soothing as his warm lips surrounded her areola. Roxanne let her eyes roll back as she closed them, and rolled her hips upward underneath him, fucking the air between them.

"And this is the most beautiful pussy I have ever seen," he said, after leaving a moist trail with his tongue down her stomach until he breathed on her soaked, glistening lips. His fingers parted her and he lapped at the cum that awaited him there.

Roxanne groaned when he sucked her swollen clit, and then whipped it with his tongue. She exploded with her first orgasm, and his entire mouth covered the heat between her legs as his tongue did a wicked number, tracing a path again and again from her pussy to her clit.

Jordan's mouth was glazed with her pussy juices when he surfaced and crawled over her, until he stared with powerful lust down at her. "Are you ready for me?"

"Yes, please," she whispered, barely able to speak.

"I'm going to beat that pussy with my cock."

Roxanne reached for his cock, unable to wait any longer, and aimed it at her pussy, then let go in a hurry when he plunged deep. She screamed and threw her head back, as he rose up to rest on his knees, and then took her legs and rested her ankles on his shoulders. He grabbed her tits and squeezed, as his balls slapped her ass and his cock pressed deeper and deeper with each lunge.

Jordan leaned forward, pressing her legs up between the two of them, as he continued to turn her world sideways with the depth he reached with his thick cock. He kissed her open mouth and his tongue raced deep into her throat. She groaned and grabbed his shoulders, returning the kiss with as much eagerness.

His final pound brought tears to her eyes as he grunted and growled and exploded inside her, then slowed but remained in her scalding pussy. She allowed one leg to slide from his shoulder, and Jordan adjusted himself and placed her other leg on her bed. She felt more sated than she could ever remember, knowing movement wasn't an option at the moment, and having no desire to go anywhere.

"Do you feel better now?" she murmured, and Jordan chuckled.

He slid down the bed, and then sat on the edge, and Roxanne decided to attempt a sitting position, then ran fingers through her tousled hair, knowing she had to look like a just-fucked mess at the moment.

"So tell me why you want to see Roger Uphouse?" Jordan turned to watch her and she met his gaze, his black eyes clear once again, yet appearing dangerously predatory.

The way he looked at her made her insides flip-flop. The man had moved something inside Roxanne, and that didn't sit well with her. Jordan had come to some conclusion that since she worked for him, he had sole rights to her. He was egotistical, and moving into more space than she had to offer. The man controlled her at work, but she worried he might try to control her home life too, and that scared her.

"Well now, boss, he asked me out, and I don't have any other plans." She smiled at him, ignoring the intensity of his gaze at her response, as his black eyes seemed to swarm with disapproval while his lips straightened into the blank expression he mastered so well.

She stood and reached for her robe, then jumped and squealed when he slapped her bare ass.

"You know what I think about you seeing him." His growl screamed ownership as he stood as well and towered over her.

Roxanne slinked around him and donned her robe, feeling somehow protected by it. Her phone rang in the other room, and she almost felt relief at the excuse to escape Jordan and the spell of ownership he seemed to be casting over her.

"Hello," she said, as she picked up the cordless, then looked at the box on the cradle that displayed the number.

Aaron Tipley's name, one of the executives from work, appeared in the small box along with his number. Roxanne frowned, wondering why the man would be calling her at home during the evening.

"Roxanne, there's a problem," her co-worker said, as Jordan appeared from the hallway wearing only his slacks.

Jordan padded barefoot to the nearest lamp and turned it on, flooding Roxanne's dining and living area with a shadowy light. He then proceeded to close each of her blinds on her windows, before turning to face her.

"What is it?" Roxanne watched Jordan scan her room, and realized what he was looking for when he walked over to the cradle for her cordless, and read the caller ID.

"I'm preparing month-end reports, just routine stuff," Aaron began, and Roxanne detected a note of nervousness in his tone. "One of our clients really fascinates me, the way he capitalizes."

Roxanne watched Jordan disappear around the corner of her dining room, and reappear a second later with shirt, socks, and shoes in hand. He sat in her easy chair opposite her, and continued to dress.

"I know it's not necessary to go through every account in such detail," Aaron continued, "but like I said, this guy really fascinates me. He invests in such a random pattern, and has accounts everywhere."

"Okay…" Roxanne tried to prompt him to get to the point. She understood digging into the files, something she had done on her own time many a night in order to learn the clients.

"Roxanne, I wouldn't have bothered you at this hour, but something is wrong here." Aaron sighed into the phone, and Roxanne pictured him leaning back in his chair and rubbing his fingers along the top of his strawberry-blond crew cut.

The man had served with the Marines, gaining an accounting degree courtesy of the U.S. government. She knew him to be all business, and wondered how he had managed to get his young wife to the point where she would have their first child in the near future. "The money in one of the accounts seems to have disappeared," he told her.

"What do you mean disappeared?" Roxanne glanced at Jordan as he slipped on his shoes.

"Well, we have a printout in the file of the most recent deposits, the last one being just a couple weeks ago. But when I pull the account up online, there's no money in there."

Roxanne sighed. "Put the file on my desk and I'll go over it when I get in tomorrow morning."

"I would have done that and not bothered you at home, but there's more."

"More?"

"Yes. This particular file has so many accounts that we don't manually check each one of them regularly. We rely on the printouts." Aaron had taken on that tone he often adopted that annoyed Roxanne, one of explaining something to her that she already knew.

"I'm aware of office procedure," she said.

"I decided to go through another file with an equal number of accounts." Aaron spoke faster, as if determined to convince her that his call at this hour had merit.

"That's a good idea." Roxanne felt Jordan watching her, and glanced up to see that he had finished dressing, and now leaned back, arms crossed, watching her.

"I found another account with the money gone from it."

"What? Are you sure?" Roxanne couldn't believe that their records could be so off base from that of the banks'. "What do you mean gone? You mean they are closed out."

"No, Roxanne, I don't mean that. I mean the banks in question show a zero balance when we show a balance in the thousands of dollars."

"Aaron, that's impossible." Her tone caught Jordan's attention because he leaned forward, studying her.

"What is it?" Jordan asked quietly.

"Roxanne, that's why I am calling you. I don't know what Hall would think of this if he saw it, but somehow these accounts need to match what we have in the files. I wondered if you had a bit of time to come into the office and look over these files with me." The urgency in Aaron's voice had Roxanne standing.

She knew very well what Jordan would think if he found money missing. He would blame his employees, and wreak havoc on the office until someone resolved the problem. She guessed Aaron worried his job could be on the line.

"Okay, give me thirty minutes and I'll be there."

"Good, and thank you." Aaron sounded noticeably relieved. "I'd just as soon put this in order without Hall knowing about it."

Roxanne couldn't have agreed more that the situation would be better if Jordan didn't know about it. And she wondered how she would pull off the impossible as she stood to return the cordless to her cradle.

"I need to take a shower," she mumbled, and left Jordan sitting in her living room.

Roxanne slipped into jeans and a short-sleeved T-shirt after showering, and then ran a blow-dryer over her hair until it remained slightly damp. She grabbed her briefcase and headed toward the kitchen when Jordan's voice stopped her.

"What's wrong at the office?"

Roxanne turned to see Jordan standing in her living room, once again appearing to be the successful businessman. Only the look in his eyes reminded her of how their relationship had altered. She watched him take in her attire as he approached her.

"Tipley is having some problems with a few accounts," she summarized, and held her footing when Jordan stopped within inches of her.

"A problem with a few accounts," Jordan repeated, and slid his fingers through her damp hair, then gripped and pulled her head back until she met his gaze. "What is the problem?"

"Jordan..." Roxanne began, but realized the sooner a few guidelines were set the better. "He is having some problems with a few accounts, and he called me because he is worried you will go on a warpath if you discover discrepancies in the morning. Now you're going to go home, or wherever it is you wish to go, and I'm going to the office to handle matters."

"Do you make a habit of covering everyone's asses at work?" Jordan loosened his grip on her hair, and moved his fingers to her cheek.

"No," she said, and realized she smelled cum on his fingers. "What I mean is, there aren't that many mistakes to cover up."

Roxanne stepped around Jordan to grab her purse then moved to the back door.

"Go see what the problem is." Jordan followed and then pulled the door behind the two of them, assuring it was locked as he did so. "I'll be there shortly."

"Jordan, no." Roxanne turned in her yard, and Jordan walked into her, wrapping his arms around her waist. "Aaron called me because he doesn't want you to know there's a problem. He didn't realize you were here when he called. And if things had been different, you wouldn't know about this. Now let me go do my job."

Jordan lowered his head and kissed her lips, then trailed kisses to her ear. She stood motionless, briefcase in one hand and purse in the other, unable to move and wondering how her body could possibly want this man again so soon.

"I'm going to go take a shower," he whispered. "Be good."

And with that he turned her toward her car, and slapped her ass gently before she could get out of reach. Roxanne wondered what he meant about being good.

Chapter Four

ﻬ

"Any luck?" Aaron Tipley peered into Jordan's office.

Roxanne glanced over her monitor and smiled at the nervous-looking young man who fidgeted in the doorway. Every executive that Hall Enterprise employed did a good job with their accounts, but Roxanne knew from experience that Jordan could make them feel their work barely made par. It made perfect sense that Aaron wouldn't want to see Jordan right now, and she watched his eyes look over the office, making sure Jordan wasn't there.

She leaned back in her chair and rubbed her eyes. "Not yet," she sighed. "I've contacted both banks and am waiting for a call back after they do some research."

"I just don't know what happened." Aaron shot a glance down the hall, and then back at Roxanne. "But I really appreciate you coming in last night and taking a look."

"To be honest with you, I thought I could find the problem." Roxanne stifled a yawn.

"And I kept you out too late, so now you're exhausted." Aaron glanced down the hallway again, and then dared his way toward Roxanne's desk. "I'd like to make it up to you, if you'll let me. My wife suggested I offer to take you to lunch."

"Well, how sweet of you."

Roxanne's phone buzzed and she hit the intercom button. "Yes, Dorothy?"

"Mr. Uphouse is on line one. Do you still want me to take a message?"

Roxanne frowned at her phone. "I never—" she broke off in mid-sentence. Jordan had told Dorothy to take a message if

Roger called her. And then he intercepted her messages. Roxanne picked up her pen and began tapping it in irritation. The man had a lot of nerve trying to control her like that. "Go ahead and put Mr. Uphouse through, Dorothy."

"Will do, sweetie," Dorothy said in her chipper tone. "And do you know when Mr. Hall will be in?"

"I'd say after three sometime," Roxanne said, and then noted Aaron hovering at the edge of her desk as she pushed the button to accept Roger Uphouse's call. "This is Roxanne."

"Well, there is the busy lady," a friendly male voice said through the phone. "I began to wonder if you were avoiding me."

Roxanne silently cursed Jordan. "Now I would never avoid our largest account," she said, putting equal cheer in her tone to match his.

"Good. I'm glad to hear that." Roger immediately got to the point. "I'm sending a car to your office. Your receptionist has already told me that you are in for the day working on files, and I plan to take you away from that. We'll have lunch here in my room—call it a business lunch, if you will."

Roxanne grinned and glanced at the clock on the wall. Mr. Jordan Hall deserved nothing less than her being the perfect employee, after the way he confiscated messages, and attempted to speak on her behalf. Her job description included seeing to the client's needs and wishes, and she planned to do just that. "What time should I expect your driver?"

"I'll send him right over."

After hanging up the phone, Roxanne smiled at Aaron. "Duty calls," she said.

"Not a problem." Aaron tapped her desk once, and then backed up to the doorway. "I'll make sure Dorothy transfers the calls to me, if we hear about those accounts."

"Good idea." Roxanne glanced at her screen then saved the file she had open. "And give me a call if we do hear anything. I'm curious to know who made these withdrawals, and when."

Roxanne grinned as she thought how Jordan might react to news that she was out of the office on business with Mr. Uphouse. She glanced out the tinted window of the plush limousine that had arrived for her. Dorothy would tell Jordan, if he asked, that Roxanne was with Roger Uphouse, and Dorothy didn't know when she would return. She tapped the sides of the computer laptop that Jordan kept in his office for meetings such as these, and felt a surge of nervous excitement.

Take a deep breath and relax, Roxanne told herself.

She was simply doing her job. There had been times in the past when a client would call, wanting to do lunch, and Roxanne would find herself dining the afternoon away. Today would be no different. She stared out the window as the limousine turned into the circular drive and slowed at the entrance to the luxurious hotel. The driver hopped out and beat the bellboy to the car door, opening it for Roxanne. She stepped out and smiled.

"The lady will go to Mr. Uphouse's suite," the driver said to the young man in uniform, who nodded briskly.

Roxanne found herself being escorted through the exquisite lobby, and then up the elevator to the floor Mr. Uphouse had mentioned on the phone. Roxanne followed the bellboy to the end of the hallway, and then was left alone after the employee rapped on the double doors to the suite.

Roger pulled the door open and stepped to the side. "Excellent, you're here. I've taken the liberty of having lunch laid out for us. Please, come in."

"Oh my, there's enough food for an army here," Roxanne laughed as she noticed the extended dining room table, with a variety of meats, pastas, salads, breads and desserts sitting in fine china, with a carafe resting in a silver ice bowl to the side.

"I didn't know what you liked." Roger's comment sounded like an apology. He gestured with his hand at the laid out table. "I had room service bring a sample of everything."

"Well, I hope you're hungry." Roxanne searched for a place to put her briefcase and laptop. "The food doesn't leave us any room to sit," she giggled, still feeling nervous.

"We have plenty of room." Roger grinned and reached for her arm. "I thought we would eat in here. You aren't nervous, are you?"

Roxanne felt her cheeks warm, and decided it was all Jordan's fault for making her feel she had anything to worry about. Roger had arranged a wonderful lunch, and she had the opportunity to spend time with a nice man in a beautiful suite. She wouldn't let her nerves, created by an overly obsessive man, ruin her time there.

Roger pushed open French doors and escorted her into a large family room. A circular table had been set for two with sparkling china and crystal, and white cloth napkins. Roxanne felt her heels sink into the thick carpet as she allowed Roger to guide her to the table, and then sat when he pulled out her chair.

She set her briefcase and the laptop on the chair next to her and then took in her surroundings. Roger walked over to an entertainment center and pushed a few buttons, and some light jazz began playing.

A large screen television housed in the middle of the entertainment center reflected her image back at her in its black screen. Two large fern plants sat on top of the casing. A couch and two reclining chairs faced the television, with a glass oval coffee table in the center of the room. Roxanne noticed another set of French doors, and guessed the bedroom might be on the other side of them.

"Would you like me to make your plate for you?" Roger pulled the carafe from the ice. He grinned down at her, and Roxanne felt herself relaxing.

"I think I'll make my own," she said, picked up her plate, then reached for Roger's, handing it to him after he poured wine for both of them. "This is such a treat. Not what I usually expect for a business lunch."

"Well then let's just put business aside for the moment, and enjoy the food and company." Roger took his plate from her, then ran his hand down the back of her head, running his fingers through her hair, and then slid his hand down her back as he walked her toward the food.

A rather familiar gesture, not what she'd expected from a man she barely knew. She wouldn't let her defenses get the better of her, though. Jordan had put caution in her, and it was unwarranted. Roger Uphouse was a client. And he was offering her a luxury she didn't often enjoy. She was going to have fun this afternoon, and the hell with Jordan Hall.

She couldn't believe how good everything tasted. And Roger proved to be wonderful company. She found herself laughing with him over his anecdotes, and feeling very at ease by the time she finished eating.

"So I had my taste of ranch life, but discovered I preferred business," Roger said as he slid his plate to the side and reached for his wine. "When I learned a trick or two about the market, I just couldn't leave it alone."

He stood and then extended a hand to her. "Let's move to the couch," he invited, and Roxanne grabbed her wine and stood, not taking his hand but patting her belly instead.

"I'm not sure I can move after all that wonderful food. I think I just gained ten pounds." She pretended not to notice he had wanted to hold her hand, and decided if they were to get cozy on the couch, it would be a good time to turn the conversation to business. She moved to the couch and situated herself at one of the corners, then turned her body so she faced him. "I'd love to hear what made you choose such a diversified market for many of your accounts."

"We should make time to go through each account thoroughly, and I'll explain it to you." Roger didn't join her on the couch, but instead set his wineglass on the coffee table, and then sat at the other end of the table so that he faced her. He took her legs and turned them, so that she found herself suddenly facing him, with his legs on either side of hers. "But right now I don't feel like talking about business."

"Oh?" Roxanne felt a chill from nerves run through her, and took a sip of her wine.

"Has Hall told you anything about me?"

The question threw Roxanne, and she felt her grin fade. *Just to stay away from you*, she thought, but quickly gathered her composure. "Jordan has kept me briefed on your accounts as long as I've been with Hall Enterprises."

Roger smiled. "I'm not talking about business." He ran his hands along the outside of her legs, halfway up her thighs, and then reached to take her wineglass and set it next to his. "In the past when I've been in town, I've made requests of Hall to provide me with a special type of entertainment. Your boss is well-connected, and has always been able to find me a lovely escort. But this time, after having lunch with you the other day, I decided to see if the possibility existed of spending time with you instead."

Roxanne felt her food turn uneasily in her stomach, and a rush of heat passed through her as she stared at the man sitting in front of her. "I am no whore, Mr. Uphouse," she said very quietly, and stood abruptly as anger consumed her.

"It's Roger, and I never thought for a moment that you were." Roger also stood, meeting her growing outrage with a calm smile. "I'm not implying that I pay for your services."

"Oh, so you thought I would put out for free?" Roxanne turned from him and walked to the table to grab her briefcase and laptop. "Do I come across as some easy slut to you?"

"Hardly," Roger said with a laugh, and she turned to glare at him. The man had moved in behind her, and took her hands in a firm grip. "I see an incredibly intelligent and sexy lady, who shares common interests with me, and who could be a lot of fun to spend time with while I'm here on business."

Roxanne blinked as hurt mixed in with her anger. She had seen interest in the man's eyes from the first time they met, but hadn't expected him to be so forward about his desires. Roxanne knew many men and women away on business often sought out a casual partner for sex. She wasn't so naïve to think otherwise. And casual sex could be great. She realized his comment about wanting her over a prostitute had taken her off-guard, and she forced herself to relax. Men had propositioned her many times in the past. She took in a deep breath, and exhaled quietly before meeting Roger's gaze.

"Well, thank you." She managed a smile.

Roger's grin broadened, making him look boyish. "I guess I should have approached the topic differently. One thing a paid escort can do is make you lazy when it comes to making arrangements, so to speak. The last thing I wish to do is offend you."

Roxanne studied the man in front of her. His natural ease with people added to his good looks. She could see how he would do well in business with his ability to smooth his way through a conversation. She found her anger ebbing, and relaxed as she pulled her hands from his.

"Every now and then I run into a lady who has a natural fire like you do," Roger continued before she could speak. "I see the spark in your eyes. And I imagine you would be the type of lady who would enjoy an alternative type of sexual play."

Roxanne forgot to breathe. Alternative type of sexual play? The anger had abated, but she raised an eyebrow in question. "Alternative sex? Now what do you mean by that, Roger?"

Roger brushed her cheek with a finger, and then drew a line past her cheekbone, down her neck, and then ran his finger over her nipple. His boldness surprised her, but she managed to keep her expression blank as she stared at him.

"I can pay a lady to play with me. And many of them are very good. But there isn't the electricity that can occur when I meet a lady who will abide by my wishes, and submit to me when I tell her to."

"Submit to you?" Roxanne questioned. "You mean like you want me on my knees?"

"Oh yes." Roger gripped her rib cage in excitement. "And when you don't do as I say, then I can punish you."

"You can punish me?" Roxanne didn't smile, although for some reason she found Roger's behavior amusing. "Do you mean you would spank me, or something?"

"You'd like that, wouldn't you?" Roger gripped her hair with his free hand, although she could sense hesitation in his touch. He didn't pull, but merely held on, as if the act were staged. "And maybe I'll tie you up, and do nasty things to you. Have you ever tried nipple clamps? I brought some with me."

Roger grew more daring, and his hand moved from her rib cage to cup her breast, gingerly, barely touching her, as if testing them for size.

She didn't flinch, and she didn't step away from him, although the look of excitement over sharing the news of his toys made him look like a schoolboy asking if she would come out to play. Roger lowered his head, as if he would kiss her, but Roxanne placed a hand on his shoulder, and wasn't surprised that her gentle push had him taking a step backward.

"You're an incredibly attractive man, Roger," she began, and turned from him to pick up her briefcase and laptop. "And I'm sure we could have a wonderful time playing, but I really think we need to keep our relationship at the professional level."

Roger let out a notable sigh, and turned from her toward the couch, then sat on the edge of the backside of it as he watched her. "We would have a wonderful time playing. Are you sure you don't want to just try it?"

"I'm sure, but you flatter me with your offer." Roxanne almost felt sorry for the crushed expression she now saw on the man's face. He ran his hand through his brown hair, tousling it and allowing a few more gray streaks to appear.

"Please don't get the impression that I think of you as a hired escort, but I would be willing to buy anything for you that you wished. Would you at least consider it?" His forehead wrinkled when he looked up at her. And she smiled at how defeated he looked.

"I'll let you know if I change my mind."

"I guess that's fair." Roger sighed and then pulled a cell phone from his shirt pocket. "I'll call to have the limo ready for you. At least let me walk you to the lobby."

Roxanne nodded, and allowed him to escort her to his car. She couldn't help wondering how a man, who so easily accepted defeat, could be dominating during sex.

Either Roger didn't tell Jordan about their luncheon date, or Jordan had decided not to rub the awkward afternoon in her face. Either way, she didn't hear anything about it. The rest of the day flew as she focused on her accounts, and saw little of Jordan. Of course since she arranged his schedule for him, she knew he was with Roger most of the time, which was fine. Jordan was already distracting her dreams. It was a lot easier to get work done without him distracting her at work, too.

She was glad when the weekend arrived, and she could put work behind her for a while.

* * * * *

"And then you just left?" Joanie sat on the edge of her bed, with wedding apparel scattered around her, and appeared to glow as she grinned at Roxanne.

It was Saturday, and Roxanne had made time to stop by and visit Joanie in order to catch up on their lives. Joanie had eagerly shown Roxanne her bridesmaid dress, as well as invitations, napkins, and catalogs full of flower arrangements that Joanie had yet to decide upon. The two of them sat among the clutter, while Roxanne brought her best friend up to date on her own life.

"Roger walked with me to the lobby, and then to his limo." Roxanne rubbed the lacing that trimmed one of the flowergirls' dresses between her fingers as she rested against the headboard of Joanie's bed. "He really didn't strike me as the kind of man who would be into BDSM. He didn't appear to have an aggressive bone in his body."

"And you want aggression," Joanie said, nodding as if concluding Roxanne's thought.

Roxanne frowned and studied Joanie for a minute. "Why would you think I would want an aggressive man?"

"Oh, Roxanne," Joanie laughed, and tossed the dress that she held in her lap to the other side of the bed.

She turned and crawled toward Roxanne, until Joanie was on hands and knees over her, with her face mere inches away. "Because you like it wild, just like me," she whispered. "And because our men need to be strong enough to handle us, and keep us happy."

Roxanne grinned, and ran her fingers through Joanie's blonde hair until she had a handful, then held on. She watched Joanie's eyes close then open again, this time appearing a brighter blue than the second before.

"Roger certainly didn't have what it took to handle me," Roxanne said. "I think he liked the thought of being kinky, but acting it out made him hesitate."

"I hate hesitation." Joanie made a face.

"So do I." Roxanne tugged on Joanie's hair, and then let it go.

The two of them sighed, collapsing on the bed next to each other. Roxanne stared up at the ceiling.

"My timing is always perfect," David, Joanie's fiancé, said from the other side of the room. "Two women lying on my bed — and beautiful women at that."

Joanie giggled and Roxanne couldn't help laughing as well. She'd known these two for years now, and also knew the two of them enjoyed an adventurous sexual lifestyle. The summer before she'd been able to watch Joanie have sex with two men at once. It had been her best friend's fantasy, and David loved Joanie enough to give it to her. Roxanne turned to see David leaning against the doorway, arms crossed, grinning at the two of them as they lay sprawled over ruffly dresses and catalogs.

"We haven't seen much of you lately," David said, moving into the room and sitting on the edge of the bed next to Joanie. He ran his hand up her leg. "You must have a new boyfriend."

Roxanne's old boyfriend, Jeffrey, had been David's best friend. She wasn't sure she was ready to share with these two her recent encounters with Jordan.

"I've just been swamped at work," she said quietly, which wasn't exactly a lie.

Joanie turned on her side to face her. "You are seeing someone, aren't you?"

Roxanne studied her friend's pretty face for a moment, knowing her friend earned her living counseling others, although that hardly made her a mind reader.

"No. Not exactly." She chewed her lips, suddenly at a loss of words at how to explain Jordan.

I've just been fucking my boss hardly sounded good.

"Not exactly," Joanie prompted.

Roxanne looked at the two of them while they stared at her expectantly. She knew they both only wished the best for her. Sighing, she looked back up at the ceiling.

"My boss is giving me a bit more attention than usual," she conceded, not wanting either of them to think less of her for having sex with her boss.

"You're fucking your boss. Way to go, girl," David said, laughing easily.

Joanie made a face at him, and Roxanne couldn't help but roll her eyes. But she smiled. David had such an easy way of looking at things.

"Okay. Yeah. I'm fucking my boss." It was surprising how easy it was to say it. She grinned at the two of them.

"I've seen Jordan Hall." Joanie wagged her eyebrows. "You could do a lot worse."

"How many times have you done him?" David asked. "And don't leave out any of the kinky details."

"David!" Joanie sounded horrified, and gave her fiancé a playful punch in the arm. She then turned to Roxanne, raising her eyebrows. "Well? How many times have you done him?" she asked quietly.

Roxanne couldn't help but laugh. "Twice. Once at work, and once at my house."

"At work! Woo-hoo!" David laughed along with her. "We might have to have this guy over for dinner."

"I don't think we're at that point." Roxanne chewed on her lip, not sure what point she was at with Jordan. "I'm not sure he's right for me," she added, and then hesitated. Her friends waited silently, allowing her to sort her thoughts. "He's trying to control me, and that is definitely not what I want." There. She'd said it.

"I see," Joanie said quietly.

She turned to look at her friend. "I hate it when you say that."

But Joanie didn't smile. "You're more serious about him than you want to admit."

"I am not." Roxanne shook her head adamantly. "He tries to tell me who I can see. If I give him an inch, he'll turn me into his slave or something. I don't want that."

Roxanne gasped and jumped when her phone, still clipped to the waist of her jeans, rang once.

Joanie collapsed on Roxanne as she started giggling. "Saved by the bell."

Roxanne unclipped her phone and looked at the number as it rang a second time. Her gut twisted at the sight of Jordan's number. Why would he call her on a Saturday? She wondered if he wanted to see her, and then immediately chastised herself for having such thoughts. The man was trying to control her life, and that wasn't what she wanted.

"What's wrong?" Joanie looked concerned.

"Nothing." Roxanne realized her expression must have shown her feelings. She pushed the button on the phone and then brought it to her ear. "Hello."

"What are you doing?" Jordan's baritone sent chills through Roxanne.

"Nothing," Roxanne said again, and then cleared her voice when it cracked. She also moved to a sitting position, and began straightening her clothes.

"Oh? Where are you?" Jordan's tone sounded challenging, as if he suspected she was doing something wrong.

Roxanne licked her lips. She couldn't be doing anything wrong, because she had no rules to follow with this man. He didn't own her.

"I'm at my girlfriend's house." Roxanne sucked in a breath, and glanced at Joanie and then at David. Both watched her with serious expressions.

"What girlfriend?" Jordan asked.

"I'm at Joanie Anderson's house. I think you may have seen her in the office once or twice." Roxanne closed her eyes, and realized she had just tried to gain an approving response with this man.

"I'm leaving a business luncheon now, and thought I would stop by your house. When can you be there?"

Roxanne swallowed as her heart fluttered with the knowledge that she would see Jordan. She wondered if Jordan would fuck her. Of course he would, he always fucked her when they were alone.

Dear Lord. She was turning her boss into a fuck buddy. She was out of her mind!

"I can be there in about thirty minutes." Again Roxanne realized she had just submitted to Jordan. She needed to quit doing that if she didn't want him to control her.

"Good. See you soon." And with that, Jordan terminated the call.

Roxanne lowered the phone slowly, and then pushed the button to end the call. She glanced up at Joanie who watched her warily, and Roxanne offered a reassuring smile.

"I've got to go," Roxanne offered.

"That was your boss, wasn't it?" Joanie asked.

"Yeah. He wants to meet me at my house." Roxanne shrugged and then finished straightening her clothes. "I guess he needs to see me about something."

"Hey, Joanie, let's go peek through the windows." David nudged Joanie, a shit-eating grin on his face.

Roxanne felt her cheeks flush as heat raced under her skin. She quickly slid to the side of the bed, not able to look at either of them at the moment.

"Did you see how she jumped when he called her?" Joanie spoke to David behind Roxanne's back.

"Yup," David said, standing also and moving to the doorway. "If you're seeing him, we need to have him over. You realize I need to approve of this guy."

Roxanne looked at David and realized he was serious. "I'm not seeing him," she insisted.

"You're not seeing him, and he already has you this trained?" Joanie giggled and slid off the bed, then moved to cuddle into David.

"He does not have me trained." Roxanne put her hands on her hips, and stared at Joanie and David, who both stood grinning at her. She forced herself to remain calm and explain the situation to them. After all, she considered these two good friends, and knew they only wanted the best for her. "He told me he had just finished a luncheon meeting and that he wanted to stop by my house. I'm sure there's something he needs to discuss with me. That's all."

"Uh-huh." Joanie offered her a friendly grin. "I think you like him more than you want to admit."

"I…" Roxanne fully intended to deny again any type of relationship with her boss, but she met Joanie's gaze, and then looked at David. "Our relationship really is just about business. It's not like I'm falling in love, or anything."

Joanie left David's side, still grinning that stupid grin, and gave Roxanne a hug. "If it doesn't mean anything, then why are you running when he calls?"

"I am not running," Roxanne said, and heard the whine in her voice and cringed. She sighed and patted Joanie's back. "Well, maybe I am," she admitted. "And I don't know why. It's just something about him. He demands things."

"Like what?" David asked.

"Like wanting to know what I'm doing, and who I'm with."

"David does that." Joanie released Roxanne and stood facing her. "But he does it because he cares, and is watching out for me."

"I don't need to be watched out for." Roxanne scowled at both of them.

"Sounds like this Jordan Hall thinks differently," David said, and then moved back from the doorway, gesturing with his hand that the ladies should exit the room. "I think you should get going so you aren't late."

"Yeah, I better," Roxanne said, but then hesitated. "And what does it matter if I am late? He can just sit and wait for me."

"It matters because you want to please him." Joanie followed Roxanne out of the bedroom, and spoke from behind her. "Sounds like maybe you have finally met a man who is strong enough for you."

"We'll see," Roxanne muttered, sighing, and then hugged her friend goodbye.

She hadn't been home since that morning, and guessed she wouldn't have much time before Jordan showed up. Just thinking about the fact that she would see him soon sent electric tingles through her.

"Jordan Hall, you're going to make me crazy," she said, shaking her head while driving home.

She couldn't wait to see him, and didn't want to see him all at the same time. The closer she got to her house, the more her body screamed with need.

God! The last thing she needed to do was beg him to fuck her the second he walked through that door.

Roxanne didn't know whether to be relieved, or disappointed, when she made it home, and Jordan wasn't there.

She kicked off her shoes in the direction of her bedroom closet then turned toward the hallway to check her messages. Thoughts of changing into something a bit more revealing entered her mind—show a little cleavage, maybe a tighter pair of jeans.

No. She wouldn't do anything to imply she wanted him. But damn, did she want him.

Chapter Five

solo

Jordan snapped his cell phone shut and slid it into his shirt pocket, then glanced around the still crowded banquet hall. Luncheons like this always bored him, too many arrogant assholes eager to give speeches on how successful they were. Jordan had no need for any of them. But since he was the most successful broker in the tristate area, he had to make an appearance, and let all the suck-ups kiss his ass. He scowled at the still mingling group.

Jordan had considered bringing Roxanne to the affair, but he'd known it would be a bore. Besides, the gossips in the crowd would go nuts over the most eligible bachelor in the business world showing up with his personal assistant as a date, although she was so much more than a personal secretary.

Roxanne wasn't ready for that yet. He needed more time with her alone first. The phone call he'd had with her just now confirmed that—she didn't trust him. He began moving for the elevator as he mulled over the conversation he'd just had with her. She'd sounded reluctant to tell him where she was, and what she was doing. But it was more than that, something in her tone made him think she'd just been doing, or saying something that she didn't want him to know about.

Obviously she was content to live her life without him. That bugged him. No. It did more than bug him. He wanted her to think about him, wonder what he was doing, be happy to hear his voice on the other end of the phone.

She'd been on his mind for a while now, but fucking her had been like releasing a gate that had held back all of his feelings for her. Sure he'd thought about her over the months, watched her, craved her, but now… Now he *needed* her…and he would do what it took for her to need him too.

The woman would not lie to him, he'd see to that. But she had definitely been up to something that she hesitated in telling him about. Secrets would not be accepted either. Jordan felt an incredible urge to get the hell out of there and to Roxanne's immediately. If she was with another man…

"Oh, there you are." The female voice behind him made him cringe. "Jordan dear, I thought you might have slipped out on us."

Jordan masked his feelings and turned around to face Mrs. Elaine Rothchild as she approached with her oversized, artificial-looking breasts that didn't bounce, in spite of the strut she put in her walk.

"Matthew and I were just talking about you." Elaine slithered up to Jordan, drowning him in her too sweet perfume.

He managed a gallant smile, although he wanted to curl his lip at her and run.

"You aren't leaving, are you?" she purred.

"Unfortunately, my dear, I have another pressing engagement that I need to attend." His smile came easier at her crushed expression. "I do believe my secretary keeps my schedule booked to keep me out of trouble."

Elaine giggled, and ran sculptured pink fingernails through her blonde curls. He noticed the pink polish matched her lipstick, which he felt had been applied a bit too thickly.

Jordan had almost made it to the hallway where the elevators were, when Elaine slipped her arm through his and began walking with him. He allowed her to escort him down the hallway, noticing the perfect line of gray hair when he looked down at her that had grown from her scalp before the blonde hair took over.

As soon as they were away from the banquet crowd, Elaine turned to face him and ran one of her long nails up his shirt.

"You know Matthew and I have a very open marriage. Did you know that, Jordan?"

"No." Jordan realized a tall fern plant standing next to the elevator doors blocked their view from the banquet door. At least no one could see Miss Fake Boobs coming on to him. He managed a crooked smile that he hoped appeared amused. "I guess I didn't know that about you two."

"Well, it's true. And I know my husband would do anything to secure a position with your company." Elaine ran her fingernail back down his chest and hooked it in the waistband of his slacks. "I would do anything, too."

"Oh?" Jordan could feel Elaine's hard tit press against his chest when she reached to tap the down arrow button next to the elevator. Roxanne's full, soft tits came to mind, and he felt his body respond at the thought. Elaine must have felt his dick move too, because when the elevator door slid silently open, she looked up at him with a mischievous grin and almost tugged him into the elevator.

"Oh yes, Jordan. Anything you want." She leaned against the back wall of the elevator, grinning while she watched him push the button for the lobby.

Jordan knew Matthew Rothchild had just undergone a scandal with the company he was with. More than likely, the man had nothing to do with the scandal, but exposure like that could tarnish a good broker's reputation. Jordan wouldn't risk adding a man like that to his staff. Mathew was shit out of luck, and there was nothing Jordan would do to help him out of his bind. Jordan had his own company's solid reputation to keep in mind.

The elevator doors slid closed, and Elaine pushed herself away from the wall. She pressed into Jordan, mashing her implants against his chest, and cupped his dick with her bony hands. He knew that even soft, he could impress a woman with his size, and Elaine was no exception. She smiled hungrily at him. "Matthew told me I could take you up to our room if I wanted," she whispered.

Jordan wondered how many men Matthew tried to pawn his wife onto, and decided he couldn't blame the man for trying to be rid of her for at least an hour or so.

"That's not likely to happen." Jordan politely put Elaine at arm's distance.

The elevator doors opened and he walked into the lobby, leaving the woman pouting in the elevator.

Fresh air helped clear his nostrils of the sweet perfume he had endured the last couple of minutes, and he waited patiently for his car to be brought around. Glancing at his watch, he realized the allotted thirty minutes that Roxanne had told him it would take to get to her house had now passed.

The valet stopped Jordan's Porsche in the circular drive, and after Jordan handed the kid a five, he slid in behind the wheel just as his car phone rang. Jordan picked up the business line.

"Jordan here," he said, as he shifted into first gear.

"Ralph here, boss." Ralph Layette had a scratchy, deep sound to his voice, making him sound, in Jordan's mind, just as he appeared—like a bulldog who smoked cigars. The man was a good old boy, and a damn good accountant. Jordan had put Layette on his staff shortly after he opened Hall Enterprises, and he trusted the man with his life. "You got a minute?" Ralph asked.

"Yup. What's up?" Jordan turned onto the street, and switched the phone to speaker.

"We've got a discrepancy on some of the accounts, all overseas. I've been tracking it for a while, and thought it was time to bring it to your attention." Layette's rough voice filled the small car through the speaker. Jordan knew about the discrepancies already, thanks to his "on-top-of-it" assistant, but he thought Roxanne had resolved the problem since she hadn't mentioned anything to him since the night she went into the office to help Tipley. "Our three largest accounts—Uphouse, which you handle, and Rantom and Curry, which Boswell handles—all seem to have errors in their files. I've done a little poking around."

Jordan knew Layette often took the liberty of going over the accounts that the younger brokers supervised. Jordan had never assigned the job to Layette, but the man kept an eye on things and that was just fine with Jordan. Of course, it would get the dander up of any of the young brokers if they thought they had a babysitter. But Layette liked to feel he had a hand in everything. The man didn't make a show of going over all the accounts, often staying late or going in early to make sure all was in order. The way Jordan saw it, there was never any harm in double-checking everyone's work.

"What did you find, old man?" Jordan accelerated as he hit the on-ramp for the freeway, and glanced at the digital clock on his dash. Roxanne should be at her house right now, waiting on him.

"I checked the codes to see who last had activity with each account. Oddly enough, your personal assistant has recently been accessing files with all three of these accounts. Do you have her assigned to overlook overseas files now?" There was a touch of disapproval that Jordan didn't miss in Layette's tone. And Jordan knew the man had strong convictions about women in the work force.

"Tipley contacted Roxanne about a problem with one of his accounts, and I know she is looking into it," Jordan said.

Layette grunted into the phone, and Jordan thought he heard papers rustle. "Speak your mind, old man." Jordan didn't hide his smile.

"How well do you trust Miss Isley?" Ralph Layette asked, then immediately cleared his throat.

"I trust Roxanne." Jordan didn't hesitate. He knew how much the woman cared about Hall Enterprises, he could see it in her enthusiasm for her work. "Why do you ask?"

"I ran into Uphouse last night at one of the downtown bars," Layette began. "He told me he had spent time with Roxanne."

"I took her with me when we met Uphouse for a business luncheon." Jordan frowned. "Is that what he meant?"

"Well, boss, he didn't mention you being there." Layette chuckled.

The wrinkles in between Jordan's eyebrows increased. "What did he mention?"

"Just that he had her up to his room for a private luncheon yesterday."

Jordan slammed his steering wheel with his fist. He had specifically told her not to see that man. Jordan straightened in his seat as his entire body tightened with controlled irritation. He accelerated and whipped the Porsche into the left lane so that he could pass the car in front of him, then whipped the car back to the right lane, glancing at the large green sign that passed over him telling him he had three and a half miles before his exit. Well, Layette didn't know Roxanne had defied orders, so that wasn't the man's reason for telling him about Roxanne's personal life.

"And?" Jordan couldn't hide the irritation in his tone, and sucked in a breath to remain calm. "What else did Uphouse say?"

"Not a lot. Got the impression he liked her. But then I guess what man wouldn't." Layette snorted, as if no more needed be said on that subject.

And the man was right, Jordan thought. What man wouldn't be attracted to Roxanne?

Layette continued without prompting. "But I'm thinking that Uphouse is our largest account, and also one of the accounts with discrepancies. Your little assistant has access to all of our accounts, and has recently gone through every account with problems. Now someone is doing something to screw up things. And personally, I don't think it's happening by accident. There are a handful of accounts with balances that don't match up. Someone is making withdrawals, and not documenting them in the files."

"Roxanne is not doing anything to jeopardize Hall Enterprises," Jordan barked, not liking where Layette headed with his line of thinking. "Someone may be jacking with accounts, but it sure as hell isn't her."

"Okay, boss," Layette said quietly, backing down. "I'll keep checking."

"You do that." Jordan hit the button on his dash, and turned off the speakerphone, which also terminated the call.

His day had gone from bad to worse. Jordan agreed with Layette, someone was fucking with his clients' accounts. And Jordan would make sure whoever it was never worked in the industry again, that was for damn sure. But Layette had Roxanne figured wrong. The only thing that woman was guilty of was defying his orders.

Jordan reached the exit that took him to Roxanne's house, and decelerated when he hit the off-ramp. He merged into local traffic, and cruised the few blocks to her street. Pushing the button on his door, which opened his window a few inches, he let the air run through his hair. Best to cool down a little bit, and not storm into her house on a rampage. Roxanne had some news to share with him, but the best thing to do would be to see if she would offer the information voluntarily. He hadn't spoken to her in a couple of days, and so would give her the benefit of the doubt that she hadn't had opportunity to explain to him why she had gone against his wishes and seen Uphouse anyway.

There was also the issue of her sounding a bit evasive when he had asked what she had been doing when he called her earlier. Granted at the moment that seemed a bit trivial, but Roxanne needed to come to the decision on her own that she would do best if she answered to him, and him only.

Jordan pondered over his decision to have Roxanne. There had been women before, but bachelorhood suited him, and he had made it clear in all previous relationships that there would be no plans to walk down the aisle.

One or two women in his past had inspired him to seek out their complete loyalty. The women hadn't had what it took, though. Jordan tried to pin down what exactly he saw in Roxanne that made him feel she was different, and why it had become imperative that he have her loyalty. The answer came to him like a brick upside the head, jarring his senses with its painful reality.

Dear God, he couldn't be falling in love with her, could he?

"No fucking way," he muttered, denying the reason that came to him too easily.

Jordan knew he had never experienced love. Not as an adult. Not for a woman. There had been some hard-core, serious cases of lust, but not love.

Roxanne might be the sexiest woman he had ever laid eyes on, and she definitely had a keen eye in the business world, not to mention a way about her that made people feel at ease. But all that meant was that he had made a damn good choice in hiring an accountant and making her his personal assistant.

He thought about how she could fuck, how erotic her reactions were to his demands on her, and surmised he had fallen into another case of serious lust. And this case simply demanded that he have her complete loyalty. Jordan blew out a relieved breath of air, convinced that lust was the core of his need to possess Roxanne.

He managed to relax his body as he pulled his Porsche behind Roxanne's Probe in her narrow driveway. He stopped the engine and got out of the car then approached her house, noticing the front door stood open. He couldn't see into the house through the glare of the screen door, but took the open door to mean she expected him and so left it open. He felt calm, and began organizing his thoughts as he pulled open the glass door and stepped into her living room.

Roxanne glanced at her wall clock hanging across the room on her dining room wall, and realized it was almost four in the afternoon. The day had disappeared without her realizing it. She had left to visit Joanie after breakfast, and the two of them had lost hours discussing Joanie and David's upcoming wedding. If only the conversation had stayed on that and not swayed over to her confused love life. Love? What was she thinking? She wasn't in love with Jordan Hall. For crying out loud, he was her boss! Not to mention he was pushy and demanding—definitely not the man for her.

If she could only convince her body of that. Just thinking about him raised her body temperature, created a yearning that started deep in her gut and surged through her like a fever.

She picked up her phone to call her voice mail, and plopped down at one of the chairs at her dining room table. She felt the moisture between her legs as she sat, and slid a finger up her shorts so she could dip it in the cum lodged between her pussy lips. With one hand, she punched in her code to retrieve her messages, while she sucked the cum off her finger on her other hand. Glancing up, Roxanne's heart felt as if it had just exploded when she realized Jordan stood just inside her front doorway.

Roxanne pulled her finger from her mouth. "How come I never hear you enter my house?"

"Taste good?" Jordan walked across her living room, forcing her to lean her head back as he approached so that she could see him.

Even dressed casually she was an incredible sight. Her flushed cheeks, and her eyes sparkling with sensuality. Her lips had puckered into a delightful circle as she looked up at him.

Jordan took her wrist then lifted her hand to his mouth and sucked on the same finger. He pulled her from her chair in order to get her hand to his mouth, and she tossed her phone onto the table next to her. Her free hand pressed against his chest, the warmth of her touch scalding his senses.

Jordan unnerved her, and she knew he would be able to sense that if she didn't control her feelings. He read people well, and she wouldn't have him always taking the upper hand with her. Roxanne got her footing, and pulled her hand free from his grasp.

"Do you like how it tastes?" She turned from him, needing space.

"You know I do." Jordan wrapped an arm around her, and pinned her against his chest. His free hand slid down her shorts and he slipped a finger easily into her pussy. "You are soaked, my dear. Did the thought of meeting me here get you that excited?"

Roxanne knew if she told him that it did, they would be naked and entangled within minutes. That didn't sound like such a bad idea, but she had a feeling he wished to meet her here for other reasons, and she wanted to know what they were.

"I guessed you wished to talk to me about something that happened at the banquet you attended today," she said, and squirmed with no success to be free from imprisonment next to this virile man.

"The banquet was boring as hell," Jordan grunted. "Why are you so wet?"

"I'm horny." Roxanne saw no reason to lie about the obvious, and again she struggled to free her back from being pinned to his chest.

This time Jordan let her go. Roxanne took several steps away from him, moving to the other side of the table, before turning to face him.

"So why do you pull away from me?" Jordan watched her, his displeasure obvious when she put distance between them.

Suddenly she was on the defensive, trying to justify her actions and how she felt. Roxanne couldn't allow him to put her in such a position every time they were alone together. Just standing near him made it difficult for her to think. She had to move just to stay focused.

"So that we could talk." Roxanne waved at the air between them, as if implying this mutual space made conversation easier. "You wanted to meet me here, so tell me why."

Jordan didn't speak. Roxanne felt that mutual space grow heavy in the lingering silence until she glanced up toward Jordan's face. His dark eyes appeared to glare down at her, and she crossed her arms, shifting from one foot to the other, until she could take it no more. She met his dark gaze head on.

"Well, say something," she demanded. "Why are you staring at me as if I've done something wrong?"

Roxanne squealed when Jordan took one long step to get around the table, and then lifted her into the air with little effort. She hit his shoulder just below her rib cage, and felt air blow out of her with a huff. Her hair fell across her face, and she didn't quite know what to do with her feet, as she hung upside down over Jordan's shoulder.

"What the hell?" she stammered, staring at her floor as Jordan carried her through the room.

It took Jordan only a few seconds to carry her to her bedroom and then toss her on her bed, where she landed with a bounce.

"I may be staring at you, but it's you who gives the impression of having done something wrong," Jordan whispered in a tone that Roxanne wasn't sure she had ever heard out of him before.

She froze in the middle of her bed and stared at him as he bent over and met her gaze.

"How have I given you that impression?" Roxanne's voice squeaked and she cursed herself for acting like a scared fool in front of this intimidating brute. She let embarrassment fuel her anger. "I haven't done anything wrong."

Jordan straightened, standing in the middle of her bedroom and staring down at her while she sat on her bed. "What were you doing when I called you earlier?"

"What I do when I'm on my own time is none of your business." She'd never raised her voice to her boss before, but damn it, he was out of line. She stood up quickly, poking her finger into that rock-hard chest of his. "I'm not on the clock, boss."

"This has nothing to do with work," Jordan scowled, his black hair and dark eyes giving him the look of a wild animal, on the prowl, ready to pounce. "When I called you, the tone you used implied you didn't want me to know what you were talking about."

Roxanne threw her hands up in exasperation. "She's getting married. We were discussing wedding stuff."

"And there's nothing else you want to tell me?" He knew he sounded unreasonable. The news that she'd been with Roger Uphouse had thrown him. But he couldn't just broach that subject lightly. "You weren't talking about anything else?"

She should have looked confused. But she didn't. He was hounding her about her visiting her girlfriend, and there was nothing wrong with her doing that. But he hadn't expected her expression to suddenly turn contemplative. She'd sounded so hesitant on the phone, but he'd guessed it was simply because she wasn't expecting him to call her over the weekend. Now however, he wondered what else she hid from him.

"Enough, Jordan. If you want a doormat, go find someone else," she began, focusing on his chest.

Jordan pulled her to him, wrapping her up in his arms. "And if I want you?" he whispered.

It felt so damned good in his arms.

She needed to answer him. She should tell him then he would respect her, wouldn't be so demanding, wouldn't try to control her every action. He needed to show her that he loved her.

Her throat had constricted into a tight knot, his hard body pressing against her making it hard to think, to sort her thoughts into words.

So she said nothing, and focused on his heart beating, matching the throbbing that was growing by the minute between her legs.

Chapter Six

❧

Jordan's cell phone rang and he took a step backward, releasing Roxanne, then pulled his phone from his pocket.

"Hello," he said firmly into the phone.

She stood within inches of his broad, muscular chest, and made no attempt to move from him. Roxanne could smell the man in front of her. Jordan smelled of deodorant, a faint touch of cologne and possibly aftershave, as well as laundry soap, the combination of which made up the smell that was his own.

But something sweet mixed in with those scents. Roxanne had worked alongside Jordan long enough to be familiar with how the man smelled every day. Today however, something smelled different about him.

"Once you set up your PIN, you should be able to access any of your accounts from the Internet," he explained, and then nodded silently, concentrating on the caller.

Roxanne listened as Jordan explained how to access accounts to one of their clients, and absently traced a line down the front of his shirt. He wrapped an arm around her and pulled her to him so that her head tucked under her chin. What an incredible feeling of safety and comfort, Roxanne thought, as he maintained a protective grip on her. She could get real accustomed to Jordan and his control-oriented form of affection.

Her thoughts went to the comments Joanie and David had made before Roxanne left their apartment, that Roxanne might have finally met a man who was strong enough for her. Did that mean that she wanted to be controlled? She pondered this thought and, at the same time, half-listened to Jordan walk the client through a transaction.

Jordan finished the call and snapped his cell phone shut, leaving Roxanne's whirlwind of thoughts hanging there, unresolved.

"I don't think I'm asking too much wanting to know what you're doing with your time." Jordan's tone had softened, and he stroked her hair with his fingers.

"You want to know where I am, and who I'm with?" Roxanne asked, looking up at him as his fingers moved to stroke her cheek. She wondered how he would feel if she made the same demands of him.

He didn't respond, but the slightest movement at the edge of his mouth could have been interpreted as the beginning of a smile.

Roxanne realized she wanted some kind of acknowledgment from him. She wanted Jordan to express how he felt about her. Maybe Joanie had been right, and Roxanne did want to please this man, but in return she wanted Jordan to let her know he was pleased. And she wanted the same respect from him.

Jordan's silence left her thoughts in turmoil, and she fought for words to tell him what she needed from him. But Jordan seemed satisfied with her understanding of his demands, and lowered his head to brush her lips with his. The man's scent consumed her, intoxicating her, and she felt desire rise inside her.

Something else triggered her attention though. Among the well-known smells that made up this man, Roxanne smelled something sweet, something unfamiliar, and her fogged senses took their time in acknowledging it. When she realized what she smelled, her insides revolted and a taste of bile rose in her throat.

Perfume.

Jordan Hall smelled like another woman's perfume.

Roxanne placed her hands on his chest and pushed, when he would have deepened their kiss.

"What is that smell?" She asked the first thing that came to mind, surprisingly enough since the rest of her thoughts seemed wrapped in turmoil, unable yet to be voiced.

Jordan simply stared at her, his dark eyes glazed with passion. He didn't seem to understand her question, and Roxanne felt her heartbeat increase and a small sweat break out underneath her shirt.

"Jordan, why do you smell like a woman's perfume?"

Again he simply stared at her, although the haze of passion cleared from his eyes. The man was so damned unreadable sometimes. But his silence on this matter was not acceptable.

Roxanne pushed herself free from his arms, took a step backward, and then crossed her arms across her middle. She felt sick to her stomach, and Jordan seemed to take up too much space in her bedroom.

"Well?" she demanded.

"I don't smell like women's perfume," he said flatly.

The air in her bedroom seemed to be disappearing. Roxanne breathed quickly through her mouth as she stared at Jordan. He made no attempt to reach for her, but appeared larger than life as he stood before her. Roxanne could definitely smell the perfume now. It seemed to stand out over all other scents, a sweet, rose-type perfume, and it made her want to gag.

She couldn't believe his nerve. He had entered her home, full of questions, demanding answers, and he'd just left another woman's company. Jordan wanted her to voice her loyalty to him, but apparently he didn't see it as a two-way street. Anger rose within Roxanne, and she could taste the bile that churned in her stomach.

"How dare you," she hissed. She clenched her sides with her fists, and pressed her crossed arms against her middle. "How dare you stand there and tell me that you don't smell like perfume. The smell of that shit is about to make me sick."

"Then I suggest you calm down." He'd never seen her get so angry, so quickly. She had quite the temper, but her outburst wasn't warranted. "I won't have you implying what I think you're implying."

"Calm down?" She wanted to smack him. "You demand that I come home. You want to know who I am with, and where I am but yet you offer no explanation as to your own whereabouts."

"You know where I was." Jordan's calm manner fueled her anger.

"What I want to know now is who you were with." Roxanne glared at him.

"I went alone. You know that also. And I left alone." He thought of his brief meeting with Elaine Rothchild, but that was hardly worth mentioning. "If I'd taken a date, you would have known that, too."

"You're lying," Roxanne yelled. She pointed toward her bedroom door. "Out! I want you out of my house."

Jordan grabbed her hand that pointed to the exit. Roxanne tried to swing at him with her free hand, balling her hand into a fist and aiming for Jordan's face. The man was taller, faster and stronger than she was, and in the next second he held both of her hands and pulled her to him.

"You don't tell me what to do," he whispered into her hair. There was no way he could walk away from her. She was outraged over something, but she wouldn't push him away. He needed her, and walking away wasn't an option. "I'm not going to leave you."

Hot tears seeped from Roxanne's eyes and burned trails down her cheeks. She felt deflated. Jordan would offer her no explanation, and she knew he was lying to her. She felt confused and humiliated.

"Yes. You are. I want you to leave, Jordan. Please." She couldn't stop the tears, and she wouldn't look at him.

Jordan let go of her hands, and Roxanne stepped backward until she sat on the edge of her bed. "Please go," she begged, unable to stand for another moment that he could reach inside her and rip her heart out so easily. Yet she swore it felt like it had just split in two.

Jordan turned and left her room, and Roxanne didn't look up, or move, when she heard her front screen door open, and then close. After the sound of his Porsche faded, Roxanne fell back onto her bed, pulled her knees to her chest then cried until she fell asleep.

* * * * *

Dark shadows spread across Roxanne's room when she awoke. She glanced at her alarm clock, and blinked at the green glare of the numbers. It was just past five a.m.

Roxanne let out a long, heavy sigh as she watched the bubbles began to foam up under the faucet of her tub. She tested the water with her foot, and then grabbed a washcloth and her razor. What a mess everything had turned in to.

She had no doubts at this point that Jordan had been with another woman before coming to see her. And she'd lost the entire weekend thinking about it.

Roxanne stood from the soapy water, and released the long snakelike hose of the showerhead, then brought it down as she sank back in to her hot, sudsy water.

The pain from the knowledge that Jordan was a player consumed Roxanne and cut deeply. She let out a choked sigh, and sunk deep into the suds-filled water as she rinsed shampoo from her hair.

Jordan had shown up at her house the other day on a mission. She could see that clearly now as she replayed his actions from the moment he had entered her home. It was just like a guilty party to hide their guilt by trying to find some wrong action in their partner. Jordan had begun accusing her of wrongdoing from the first moment they were together. And Roxanne had done nothing wrong. She needed to view the weekend as a blessing. Roxanne rinsed the conditioner, and the soap from her body, then lathered her legs and began shaving.

Joanie and David had observed that she needed a strong man to match her personality. And maybe they were right. Roxanne had learned something about herself, and in the future, she would look for that trait when considering a man as a potential boyfriend. She had learned, too, that Jordan was not that man. Roxanne wouldn't be manipulated by a cheater—or a player.

She'd enjoyed an alternative sexual lifestyle with Jeffrey, her previous boyfriend. There was nothing wrong with bringing someone else into the bedroom as long as both parties agreed to it. But being with another woman behind her back was completely unacceptable.

If Jordan had another woman, and had asked her to join them, at least he would have been honest about it. Roxanne wasn't sure she was ready for something like that. She'd had some sexual fun with Joanie and David when she'd been with Jeffrey, but that had been different. Joanie was her best friend. And Joanie loved David. She'd never worried that Jeffrey fucking Joanie would make Jeffrey want to leave her.

In the end, she'd lost Jeffrey anyway. But it had been to work, not another woman. She still missed him. But that was another world. And Jeffrey wasn't coming back. So she'd moved on, dug into her work, took on life with a new energy.

And Jordan had always been there. Maybe he'd been watching, waiting. She doubted he knew anything about her sexual adventures in the past, but then she didn't know a lot about his previous sexual experiences either.

That was the problem. Jordan hadn't appeared the least bit guilty. A woman had been close enough to him, more than likely rubbing herself all over him, to leave the scent of her perfume so strongly on him. Yet he'd been inclined to deny it.

"It would have been better if he'd just been honest," she said to herself, watching the suds run off her arm.

She let out a heavy sigh. "Oh well. I guess it's best that I found out now, as opposed to later."

With new resolve, Roxanne once again rinsed and then stood as she let the bathwater out. Today she would take on life without Jordan in her personal space. The man would remain her boss, and she would continue to give Hall Enterprises her best show. But she would not date Jordan, and she would never, ever have sex with the man again.

Roxanne toweled dry, and walked to her bedroom to find clothes for the day. She didn't like the painful emptiness that seemed to consume her, and although she tried to tell herself she simply needed to eat since she'd fallen asleep without supper the night before, Roxanne knew that the pain inside her stemmed from loss.

She dressed, applied makeup, and did her hair, then left the house without eating breakfast and headed for her office two hours before she was required to be there.

* * * * *

"How long have you been here?" Roxanne poured herself a cup of coffee she didn't want, and turned to give Aaron Tipley her attention.

The man appeared freshly shaved, with a crisp white shirt and tie that knotted just under his Adam's apple. His expression showed worry, Roxanne observed, and dark shadows that weren't usually under his eyes seemed prominent this morning.

"I got here about thirty minutes ago." Aaron stood in the doorway to his office, having moved there when Roxanne had unlocked the two glass doors to Hall Enterprises. He waited until she had her coffee, and started to move through the secretarial pool toward him, before he turned to reenter his office. "I didn't sleep well last night."

"I never heard the response from the bank," Roxanne said, and now took the position that Aaron had just held, standing in the doorway to his office. "Did you find out who made those undocumented withdrawals?"

Aaron sifted through the neat stacks of paper on his desk until he found what he searched for, and handed a piece of paper to Roxanne. She entered his office and took it from him.

"The bank shows three small withdrawals from a source in Nebraska." Roxanne frowned at the printout of recent withdrawals from their client's account. "Who would be making withdrawals in Nebraska? Isn't this client based out of New York?"

"Yes." Aaron ran his fingers over the top of his crew cut, and glanced at his desk. "I woke up this morning wondering about my other account that shows a discrepancy."

"How so?" Roxanne looked up from the printout, and focused on the young man who stood staring at his desk. "Do you think maybe the balances being off in the different accounts might be related?"

Aaron met her gaze, and bit his lower lip. "I figured I'd come in early this morning to see if I could find out."

Roxanne placed the printout she'd just studied back on Aaron's desk. "I'll help you. You check your other account, and I'm going to take a look at the other files that aren't balancing."

Adrenaline surged through Roxanne as she turned to leave Aaron's office. She turned down the hallway toward Jordan's office, and flipped the light on as she entered the large room. If they found a connection between all the files that had money missing, then someone had managed to tap into Hall Enterprises' client base and was stealing money out from under them. It wouldn't take long before clients grew aware that the money in their accounts didn't match the printouts Hall Enterprises sent them. That would mean scandal for Hall Enterprises, and could ruin Jordan. Roxanne would not let that happen if she could help it.

The clock on the wall showed just a bit past seven. Some of the other brokers could be showing up soon and Roxanne decided it best to keep a low profile on her actions for the moment. She had no idea who could be stealing from these accounts, if in fact there was a connection. But she didn't want to give someone the time to cover their tracks if they found out she was on to them. Best to compare notes now on the files she supervised and look into the other files later.

Although the workday hadn't started, the London banks were well into the afternoon, and Roxanne opened her first file and flipped through pages until she found the bank number that held the accounts she had marked incorrect for Uphouse.

"I need to verify who made withdrawals on this account over the past thirty days," Roxanne explained, after giving her verification numbers so the officer would know she was who she said she was.

The officer in charge of the accounts, who Roxanne had spoken with several times before, didn't take too long to answer. "Yes, here is the information you want. Shall I fax?"

"Please. I need to have names of who made the withdrawals, and their location. Will the fax show that?" Roxanne asked.

"Aye, that they will," the London clerk said. "Got it going out to you now. Anything else I can do for you today?"

"No, and thank you." Roxanne said her goodbyes, and then moved to stand over the fax, wondering what she would find out.

Half an hour later, Roxanne sat at her desk, staring at the printout. Two other brokers had arrived, and milled about in the secretarial pool, as the smell of fresh coffee trickled down the hallway to Roxanne. Another cup of coffee would be a good idea. The office would be busy with a new workday in thirty minutes or so, and she needed to use every minute well in order to sort through the information in front of her. All of which made absolutely no sense.

"What did you find out?" Aaron had buzzed her on her phone, and Roxanne sat at her desk, nursing a fresh cup of coffee as she cradled the phone between her shoulder and ear. "I got information on my other account, but it doesn't match up."

"Where did the withdrawal occur?" Roxanne had experienced the same thing, and had felt a twinge of disappointment that the withdrawals didn't come from a source in Nebraska.

"The Johnson file has a ten thousand dollar discrepancy," Aaron began, and Roxanne decided to start scribbling notes. She wrote as he continued, "The bank sent me a printout of the most recent withdrawals, but that showed nothing. We went back over ninety days before I found the unaccounted for withdrawals. They were done in thousand dollar increments, all from Reno, Nevada, and all within a week's time."

Aaron sighed into the phone, and Roxanne glanced at her calendar to verify the time frame for ninety days ago. "What were the dates of the withdrawals?" she asked.

Aaron gave them to her. "All of them happened right after we did our quarterly audit, and that is why they didn't show up until now."

Interesting, Roxanne thought to herself. This would make it appear that whoever took the money, knew when Hall Enterprises did their audits.

"Good work, Aaron," she said into the phone. "I want you to put the files up now, unless you have other work to do on them."

"No," Aaron hesitated. "But what are we going to do about this?"

Roxanne didn't have a clue at the moment, but she knew one thing she did need to do, and that was to keep this as quiet as possible. "I want you to make sure you don't mention this information to anyone at the moment. Go about your day, and handle business as usual. I'll talk to you more about this later."

She glanced at the wall clock, and noticed it was almost eight o'clock. As if on cue, chatter filled the outside office, as a couple of the secretaries arrived for work.

"Okay," Aaron said. "I do have a busy day ahead of me."

Roxanne hung up her phone, and flipped her calendar pages to show her daily schedule. She had scattered meetings throughout the day, but nothing until later that morning. She stood and stretched, and then walked around Jordan's desk to verify his schedule. A yellow post-it note had been attached to his day planner. Roxanne pulled it free, and read the block print.

"I've cleared my schedule for the day, and won't be in," the note read. "You are free from two this afternoon on, and I wish to see you at my house at two-thirty."

Roxanne stared at the note. He hadn't signed it, and it didn't say whom it was for, but Roxanne knew the note had been left for her. She felt the coffee churn in her stomach, and suddenly felt queasy and tired.

Jordan wanted her to come over to his house. And he had cleared his schedule? Roxanne couldn't remember the last time Jordan had ever missed a day of work. The note didn't say that he would be in meetings all day, but simply that he had cleared his schedule. She continued to stare at the block print, reading meaning into the words, as she moved back to her desk, and flopped down in her chair.

Had her kicking him out Saturday night upset him that much?

Nothing Jordan had to say would matter right now.

And she reminded herself, she hadn't wanted a relationship anyway. After Jeffrey, she didn't want to endure the pain again of losing another man.

Not to mention her plate was full. Work with Hall Enterprises kept her busy, and she had Joanie to keep her social life full. Jordan had always been a man she had watched from the corner of her eye, but she never had illusions of anything happening with him. In a short time, she'd let her feelings toward Jordan blossom. But now was the time to call it quits before she got in any deeper with him.

Roxanne crumpled the note in her hand, and tossed it in the wastebasket, ignoring the pang of regret that made her eyes burn.

* * * * *

"I have Mr. Uphouse on line three, Roxanne." Dorothy sat at her desk, and pointed to the phone when Roxanne turned to face her.

"Did he say what he needed?" Roxanne placed the forms she had just completed with one of their clients in the processing in-basket.

She turned her attention briefly to Linda Rickmeier, a middle-aged housewife who had returned to the workforce after all her children were in school. "Let me know if you have any questions entering the data," she said to the woman.

Linda looked up from her computer screen and smiled. "I think I've got it now, but thank you."

Linda had been with them for several months now, and Roxanne had to commend Jordan on giving the lady an opportunity, since she had no previous office skills. So far, Linda had proven that she could do the job.

"He asked to speak to Mr. Hall, but when I told him he was out for the day, he asked for you," Dorothy offered, and Roxanne left Linda's desk and started for the hallway.

"Okay, let him know I'll be with him in a moment," Roxanne said, and left the secretarial pool for her own desk.

The office phone rang again, and Roxanne heard Dorothy answer as she entered Jordan's office.

"This is Roxanne, may I help you?" Roxanne rubbed her burning eyes. Although the morning hadn't been busy, she felt she had already put in a full day's work.

"Hello, good looking," Roger Uphouse said into the phone. "I sure do admit it's a pleasure to get to speak with you again."

Roxanne leaned her head against her hand and closed her eyes. "Well, thank you, Mr. Uphouse. What can I do for you today?"

She knew the man held many accounts with the firm, and she would speak with him many times because of that fact, but she wouldn't let him feel he had any right to treat her any differently than he ever had.

"Oh darlin', you know what you can do for me." Roger chuckled into the phone, and Roxanne felt a headache coming on.

"Mr. Uphouse," she began.

"Call me Roger, and I apologize." Roger's tone softened, sounding almost wounded. "You distract me, my dear. I'm sure you know that, but my reasons for calling are strictly business."

"What can I do for you?" she asked again, wishing for the first time since her workday had begun, that Jordan was here at work so he could deal with the man.

"I've gone over the papers that Jordan left with me after our luncheon the other day," Roger began. "I admit at the time, thoughts of you had me pretty distracted, but my personal secretary and I have some questions about some of the figures. There are some discrepancies, and I need some answers."

Roxanne felt her stomach tighten.

Chapter Seven

စာ

"Let me pull your account up on my screen," Roxanne said, as she turned to face her computer. "Maybe I can give you answers now."

"No. I wish to conduct business in person." Roger used a tone that Roxanne recognized as one of a businessman with power. His words didn't allow room for argument.

"That's fine, Roger." Roxanne did not want to see him again, but she knew he had a right to have his questions addressed as he saw fit. She turned to face Jordan's desk. "Let me get Mr. Hall's schedule, and we'll get you in to see him."

"Aren't you qualified to handle my account?" Roger asked.

"Well sure," Roxanne stopped, just as she was ready to stand, and reclined in her seat again. "I assumed you would want to see Mr. Hall since he handles your accounts personally."

"If you aren't qualified to handle my accounts, then of course I will see him." Roger said through the phone. "But darlin', I would much rather conduct business with you."

Roxanne cringed. Jordan wouldn't be happy if she handled one of his accounts without talking to him about it first.

"Since Jordan isn't in the office at the moment, I'm sure you and I can set up a meeting time, and I will make him aware that you have questions."

"You do that, sweetie. I understand your needing to answer to your boss. My flight leaves later today, ah yes, here it is…" Roger hesitated a moment, and Roxanne heard papers shuffling. "I'm leaving town at four this afternoon. How does lunch at that nice club we went to the other day sound to you?"

Roxanne buried her head in her hands when she realized her dreams of a long lunch hour had just gone up in smoke. And to make matters worse, she would need to contact Jordan to make him aware of the luncheon. Regardless of how much she'd avoided having to call Jordan for any reason today, this was business, and the man was her boss.

"I'll meet you there at noon," Roxanne resigned.

"Won't hear of it. My car will be there to pick you up at that time. And you let me handle the reservations, young lady," Roger said, making the business meeting sound more like a date.

"As you wish," Roxanne said. "I'll see you then."

She hung up the phone and leaned back in her chair, wishing more than anything for the day just to be over.

"Going to lunch with Uphouse, are you?" Ralph Layette stood in the doorway to her office, and Roxanne jumped at the sound of his voice.

"How long have you been standing there?" she countered, frowning as she leaned forward.

"Long enough to hear you making a date with one of our largest clients." Ralph Layette sounded like a disapproving father, and Roxanne wasn't in the mood for it.

"Roger Uphouse has questions about his account," she countered, and didn't hide the fact that she didn't like the tone the older accountant had just taken with her. "Now if Mr. Hall was here, he would handle the matter. But as you can see…"

She didn't get her sentence finished. Ralph Layette entered the office and pointed a finger at her.

"You watch your step, missy," he snarled, looking like a bulldog as the wrinkles deepened in his forehead. "Jordan may have a soft spot for a pretty smile, but I'm here to let you know I'm keeping my eye on you."

"You do that." Roxanne would not be bullied. "And while you're at it, make sure you keep an eye on the quality of your own work, Mr. Layette."

Roxanne stood and met the man face-to-face. She would be damned if this old coot would intimidate her. It was bad enough to have to deal with sexual harassment from one of their largest clients, but she would not allow this old fart to make her feel unqualified to do her job.

Layette stared at her a minute longer, then turned and marched out of the office. She heard his office door close, and knew he would sit behind his desk and light a cigar, violating the nonsmoking policy of the building. She had half a mind to arrange for a sprinkler system to be installed in the man's office. She turned and slammed her hand on her desk, and then brought it to her mouth quickly when she felt the sting against her palm. This was not turning out to be a good day.

* * * * *

Jordan Hall leaned back in his chair and rubbed his eyes. He had been up and on the run since very early that morning, and it felt good to be home, and to just sit.

"Will you be eating lunch here today, Mr. Hall?" Millie stood in the doorway of his den, wiping her hands on a dishtowel.

"I don't think so, Millie. We had a late breakfast at the business meeting I just finished." Jordan smiled at the motherly look his housekeeper gave him. "And I might grab a bite to eat later, when Roxanne arrives."

"How about if I prepare some sandwiches for the two of you," Millie offered. "Or maybe I could thaw out a couple steaks, and you can show her your skills on the grill."

Jordan laughed. Millie had nagged him to find a wife as long as she'd been in his service. He knew his over-concerned housekeeper would be underfoot the entire time Roxanne was there if he didn't give her something to do.

"That would be fine," Jordan said. "And then, my dear, you may have the afternoon off."

"Oh, I see how it is to be now." Millie turned from the doorway, and headed back toward the kitchen. "You think this old woman would eavesdrop if you don't shoo me away," she called out.

"Hell yes, you would," Jordan muttered, stood, and then walked over to the wall-length windows that overlooked his backyard.

As much as he would like to plan his afternoon meeting with Roxanne, Jordan forced his thoughts to the morning he had spent with a potential new client. The Bradfords were old money, generations thick out of New England. Paul and Roberta Bradford had heard of the successful Midwestern broker, and had flown into Kansas City just to see Jordan, and discuss the possibility of him managing a few of their accounts.

"I thought I'd start you out with several accounts I have overseas that are just sitting there," Paul Bradford had told Jordan over breakfast that morning. "If you do well with them, we will consider turning more over to you."

It had been worth clearing his morning to spend time with the Bradfords. Jordan had assured the man he could double his money before the year was out. The morning had proven productive, and Jordan had several contracts to drop off at the office. Of course, he had wanted to see Roxanne first thing that morning, since he figured she would have time to cool off, and they could speak reasonably to each other. But there hadn't been time to do much more than leave her a brief note.

"Mr. Hall, I just noticed you didn't gather your messages when you got home." Millie interrupted his thoughts, and he turned around to face her. "I took the liberty of listening to them for you."

She entered his den, and extended a couple of slips of paper. Jordan reached for them, and glanced at his housekeeper's neat cursive writing.

"I didn't realize you weren't here this morning." Jordan glanced at the top slip.

He'd forwarded his cellular phone to his home voice mail, so he wouldn't be disturbed while meeting with the Bradfords. Layette had called and wanted Jordan to return the call as soon as possible.

"I spent the morning shopping for material to make curtains for the back sun-porch." Millie looked offended. "You said I could decorate the porch any way I wanted, remember?"

"Yes. Of course." Jordan smiled, and squeezed the plump woman's shoulder. "Did you find material you like?"

"Oh yes, the perfect pattern." Millie smiled up at him, and patted his hand as it rested on his shoulder. "Well, there you have your messages. I think your girlfriend is one of them."

She turned and left his den, and Jordan fished through the slips of paper, until he found the message from Roxanne.

"What?" He almost shouted, and then turned to search for his shoes.

She had left a brief message saying she was having lunch with Roger Uphouse because he had questions about his accounts. Jordan pulled his shoes on and felt his blood pressure soar. Like hell the man had questions about his account. And this was the second time Roxanne had met the man without Jordan present. She was playing with fire, and Jordan was going to put an end to it here and now. He stormed out of the house without saying a word to Millie.

Jordan's cell phone buzzed as he backed out of his driveway, and he pushed the button to send it to speakerphone.

"Where have you been?" Layette's brusque tone didn't faze Jordan.

"I had a meeting with a new client this morning, old man," Jordan said, and shifted into gear. "Got to pay the bills."

"When will you be in the office? We need to talk."

Jordan drove through his quiet neighborhood, doing his best not to speed. He had no idea what time Roxanne planned on meeting Uphouse, but he had every intention of speaking with her beforehand.

"I'm headed there now. Roxanne and I are going to have a short meeting," Jordan offered.

"She isn't here," Layette said. "Your personal *secretary* left just a bit ago with Roger Uphouse, and that is what I need to talk to you about. Do you know why she's meeting with him?"

"Do you know where they were headed?" Jordan didn't hesitate in hitting the gas as he entered the on-ramp to the Interstate.

"Dorothy would know. But Jordan, there's something going on here, and I don't like it."

"Speak your mind, old man," Jordan said, and then reached to pull his personal cell phone out of his glove box to call Dorothy and find out where Roxanne went.

Jordan put his speakerphone on mute, and half-listened as he called Dorothy, who informed him that Roxanne had left about half an hour ago to have a business luncheon with Mr. Uphouse. Roxanne hadn't mentioned where they were going, but had told Dorothy she could be reached by cell phone, if needed.

"I find it peculiar, however," Ralph Layette said through the speakerphone, "that the files with discrepancies have all been accessed by your personal secretary. And after contacting the banks where the accounts are held, I learn that she has been in contact with all of them. I'm not aware of any policy that gives her liberty to access information on my accounts."

"What are you saying, Ralph?" Jordan switched to the fast lane, and accelerated.

"Jordan, someone is taking money from your accounts. And you have a secretary out wining and dining with one of our wealthiest clients. Don't you find it a bit odd that a woman on a secretary's salary, who has no authorization to be meddling in these accounts, has accessed accounts that now show money missing?"

He ignored Layette's comment about Roxanne being on a secretary's salary. It was no one's business that she was one of his best-paid accountants, and worth every penny of it. But the old man's last words got Jordan's attention.

"How much money is missing?"

Jordan listened as Layette did some quick calculations. "We have over $150,000 unaccounted for."

* * * * *

Roxanne stood in the parking lot outside her office building and stared at Roger Uphouse. "I'm sorry you made the trip over here. I won't be needing a ride."

His long, chic, black Rolls idled behind him, and he stared down at her with an amused expression on his face.

"My dear, I assure you that you are quite safe in my hands." Roger raised a hand to her face, and brushed a strand of her hair back that the breeze had moved.

Roxanne took a step backward, crossing her arms over her chest, unwilling to let him think for a minute that his actions appealed to her.

"I tried to call you to let you know that I could meet you at the restaurant," Roxanne began. "But the hotel clerk told me I'd just missed you. Since your account isn't one that I normally handle, I don't have access to any of your personal phone numbers."

"Let me remedy that." And Roger pulled a card from the inside pocket of his business suit. "Now you have my number. And please, since I'm here, allow me to escort you to the restaurant."

Roxanne had wanted to take her own car just in case she needed to get away from him. She believed that Roger Uphouse had found some discrepancies—she had found them herself. But she couldn't convince herself that he didn't have some hidden agenda as well. She narrowed her gaze and stared at him.

"I need your word that this is just a business luncheon," she said.

Roger sighed. "I got off on the wrong foot with you the other day, and for that I sincerely apologize. Yes, we have business to discuss. I understand you don't usually handle my accounts, but I believe I'm right in that you are more than qualified to do so."

"Yes, I am," Roxanne said, wondering if the man simply flattered her, or if he realized she could do the job.

"Very good." Roger opened the door to his Rolls, and his chauffeur hopped out from the driver's side, and hurried around the car to assist. Roger ignored him, and held the door for Roxanne. "Shall we go discuss business?"

Roxanne relaxed during the ride to the restaurant. The Rolls had a very comfortable ride, with enough room that she didn't feel crowded by Roger. And lunch proved to be just as enjoyable as her first luncheon had been with him, before he had propositioned her, and turned into a louse. Roxanne had to remind herself a time or two that she had a low opinion of Roger Uphouse, because throughout the meal he proved quite the gallant gentleman.

"We're aware of the discrepancies you mentioned." Roxanne reached down for her briefcase, and pulled it to her lap. "I brought the printout I have from the bank. We're tracking the matter as we speak."

"I knew you would be on top of things." Roger leaned back, and smiled at her. "I told my secretary just this morning that I had no worries with my money in your hands."

"Mr. Hall will be pleased you feel that way." Roxanne felt pleased that she had put the man's mind at ease all by herself, and also very relieved that neither Roger, nor his secretary, had noticed all the discrepancies. It would only be a matter of time, though, before they did, which meant she didn't have much time to resolve the problem.

Roger leaned forward and took Roxanne's hands in both of his. "I can't apologize enough for acting the way I did the last time we were together." His smile made his green eyes twinkle, and Roxanne noticed how attractive he was. "I don't have much time before my flight leaves, but I'd be honored if you would spend that time with me. I'd like to know you better, because what I see right now, intelligence and beauty, has me more than intrigued."

"You made me feel like a whore the other day," Roxanne told him, not even remotely interested in his flattery.

As good-looking as he was, he wasn't in the same league as Jordan.

"Then let me make it up to you today." Roger rubbed his thumb over the top of her hand, and she lowered her gaze to watch the action. "We can go shopping, take a walk in the park, anything you like."

"I don't think so." She wanted to tell him to go hire an escort if he wanted to see the sights, but she would keep the conversation on a professional level, even if Roger wasn't. "I need to head back to the office."

"Tell them you're working with their most valued client." Roger nodded to the waiter as he passed by, and the man placed a velvet pad on the table with the bill for Roger to sign. "You captivate me, Roxanne. And I simply can't let you slip through my fingers so easily."

Roxanne studied Roger's face. His soft brown hair, with wisps of gray, had been combed to the side, but fell over the top of his forehead. He had broad cheekbones and a full mouth, with lips that appeared soft. There was a rugged look about him, as if he spent a fair amount of time outside. His hands were soft and smooth though, and Roxanne guessed he'd lived a life of leisure.

There was little doubt that he could probably find women to entertain him without much problem. But she wouldn't be one of them.

"No, Roger. Now if our business is done, I need to get back to work." She slid the chair back just enough to show she was ready to leave.

Thoughts of Jordan Hall suddenly consumed her, and she remembered that he expected to see her at two that afternoon. Granted, she had no intention of keeping the date with him, but she couldn't help wonder what tactic Jordan had planned if she was to show up.

Roger stood and held his hand out for her to take, then slid her chair back as she stood. "I can only imagine that Hall Enterprises doesn't do well without you there," he said, and slid his hand down her back, to rest just above her rear end, as he escorted her toward the exit.

Roxanne waited until they were through the main doors of the establishment and then shrugged his hand off of her. She didn't like this man. No matter that he brought in so much money for Jordan. The man was a creep.

Jordan should be the one with Roger, explaining the accounts. And she'd tried to reach him. Even when she hadn't wanted to talk to him, she'd tried to let Jordan know she was going with his client to lunch—a client whom Jordan had forbidden her to see.

"Mr. Hall runs a smooth business," she countered. "But I do have my responsibilities."

"Yes, I'm very impressed with him. But don't deny that you have a hand in keeping that business running as it should."

Roxanne didn't deny it, simply because she believed it to be true. But she didn't feel a need to agree either. Roger escorted her out into the sunny afternoon, and the Rolls seemed to appear as if on cue. The chauffeur parked the vehicle, and once again hopped out and moved around to open the door for them. Roger paid the man no attention, but focused completely on Roxanne. He turned her to face him, and ran his hands up and down her arms.

"I hear Kansas City has some beautiful museums. Accompany me, and I'll have you back to your office before your workday is out." Roger moved one of his hands to her back, and before she realized his intent, he pulled her close and kissed her forehead. "Please," he whispered.

"Take your hands off me." Roxanne pushed him back, glaring at him. "I don't care how successful you are, or how much money you bring in for Hall Enterprises, you won't touch me like that again."

"Roxanne." Roger's tone was smooth, but she noticed his gaze harden. "Come with me. You won't regret it."

"I'm afraid that she might." Jordan Hall's voice, shattering the moment like an ice pick through glass, startled Roxanne and she jumped.

She stared up into the outraged expression on her boss's face. "Jordan," she gasped, and her heart began pounding.

But Jordan didn't look at her. His gaze fixed on Roger Uphouse, and she watched his mouth turn into a flat line.

"Well there, Jordan." Roger sounded surprisingly calm, and Roxanne turned her head to focus on him. "I can't say your timing is appreciated."

"I'm sure it isn't," Jordan responded with a calm that ran a chill through Roxanne. She looked from one man to the other, and got the weird sensation that she was about to experience a showdown.

"Roxanne and I were just making plans." The calm, gallant exterior that Roxanne had witnessed throughout lunch seemed to fade from Roger's face. She watched a smooth hardness overtake him, and realized this man would be as good as Jordan when it came to cutting deals and manipulating a situation as he saw fit.

"I believe I made it quite clear that Roxanne would not be included in any of your plans." Jordan spoke quietly, and although she recognized the anger consuming him, overall his body appeared relaxed, and to any onlooker, Roxanne realized it would appear the three of them chatted easily.

Testosterone began to clog the air as she stood between the two men, however.

"Roxanne is a consenting adult." Roger matched Jordan's tone. "I wish her to accompany me. Surely there isn't any harm in that."

"I..." Roxanne was ready to protest, make it clear that Jordan didn't speak for her. She wouldn't accompany him, and that was final.

"My millions are worth an hour or so of your time, my dear." Roger grabbed her arm.

Before she could even step back to avoid his grasp, Jordan stepped between the two of them, and faced Roger head-on.

"Your millions be damned. Touch her again and you can find another accountant," Jordan hissed, and Roxanne stared at the muscles that stretched Jordan's shirt. "I've made it quite clear that you weren't to have any contact with her without my consent. And I will not be ignored."

The silence only lasted for a second, but to Roxanne it seemed to last forever. She stepped around Jordan, and Roger immediately met her gaze.

Roxanne had half a mind to storm away from the two of them and take a cab back to work. Jordan's show of ownership had to be controlled. She had kicked him out of her home over the weekend, yet he here stood, informing another man that she would not accompany him. That should upset her. Yet part of her realized Jordan knew about Roger's particular kinks, and Roxanne saw that he was here trying to protect her, standing here as her knight in shining armor, albeit rather tarnished.

"Roger, I think you should leave," she said quietly, and watched Roger Uphouse study her for a moment. "You'll be notified within a day or so once the discrepancies are in order. Otherwise, our luncheon meeting is over."

"Very well," Roger sighed, and without another word he climbed into his Rolls. The silent chauffeur shut the door and moved without a word around to the other side of the car.

Roxanne watched the classy vehicle move toward the exit. Jordan's presence at her side seemed to grow, and Roxanne realized suddenly that she was at his mercy for a ride back to the office. She could call a cab but somehow she knew she would have to throw a fit to do that, and at the moment she'd had enough scenes.

"Let's go." Jordan's hand on her back accompanied the command, and Roxanne decided to save her comments for later, and walked with her boss across the parking lot to his car.

She realized after a few minutes of being in the car with Jordan that they weren't headed toward the office.

"I need to get back to work," she said without looking at him.

"You have a two o'clock appointment to see me," he reminded her. "We're going to my house."

"I want my car." Roxanne wanted to tell him that she'd had no intention of keeping that appointment, but felt bringing that up while confined in the close proximity of his car might not be the best idea.

"You can get it later."

"Quit making all of my decisions for me." Roxanne glared at Jordan but he simply turned his attention to her briefly, didn't say a word, and then returned his focus to the road.

Roxanne wanted to smack him for his silence. How could she argue with him if he didn't speak? At the same time though, she wanted to give herself a good bashing for feeling so turned on by him. Every inch of her tingled with Jordan sitting so close to her in the compact car. She had a feeling she would be in big trouble once they were alone at his house.

Chapter Eight

❧

Jordan glanced at her as he turned onto his black paved driveway and pushed the button for his garage door to open. She had a look of complete bewilderment on her face, and he enjoyed watching her lips part as her jaw fell open as she stared at his house.

"This is your home?" she whispered, and then looked around quickly when they entered the garage and the garage door slid down behind them.

"Yup." He turned off the engine and opened his door to climb out. "Let's go inside and then you can explain to me why you were with Roger Uphouse, for the second time, when I made it quite clear that you shouldn't see him."

Jordan took a second to glance at her, before stepping out of his car and into the heavy shadows of his garage. She scowled at him and he felt a wave of desire race through him. He'd have fun taming his outraged beauty, and he bet himself that he'd have her calm, and in his arms, within the hour.

Jordan was pleased to see that Millie had left and that two steaks thawed in the refrigerator. Maybe he'd grill them for Roxanne for supper later, but for right now he was ready to spar with his lady.

He led them through the kitchen, aware of Roxanne's quiet steps behind him, and decided his den would be a good place to start. He would hear her arguments and take it in a business-like fashion, and then wait for her to start fuming. Jordan couldn't place his finger on what it was that he liked about watching her work to prove her point, but something about Roxanne all worked up sure did get to him.

Jordan stopped at his desk, turned and faced her, and leaned against the smooth, cherry oak finish.

"Roger had questions about his accounts. If you'd bothered to come in to work, you would have seen him and I wouldn't have been doing your work for you." Roxanne studied his expression, but when he didn't flinch, she felt she needed to make her point more clear. "We are not a couple, Jordan. I work for you and that is it."

Jordan pushed himself away from his desk and she felt the urge to take a step backward, but she'd be damned if he'd bully her for one minute. She held her ground and kept her arms crossed.

The room grew very quiet, other than the continuous muffled tick-tock of the grandfather clock that stood in the corner. Outside the day appeared sunny and bright, but here in Jordan's study, Roxanne felt a chill, like a nasty thunderstorm brewing.

"Business or not, you weren't supposed to see him. Yet now you've seen him twice." Jordan spoke quietly, adding to the threatening calm that filled the room.

He moved closer and Roxanne's heart began pounding in her chest. For the life of her, she couldn't look away from that dominating gaze. She stared up at him, her mouth going dry. The man was trying to intimidate her and she wouldn't allow it.

"Maybe it's that you enjoy the certain kink he likes to partake in," Jordan continued, and moved even closer until he hovered over her.

And if she did, damn it, he wouldn't be able to stand her doing it with Roger Uphouse. He had no problem with rough sex, but his partner needed to be consenting. And he wanted his partner to be Roxanne.

Roxanne turned and walked away from him.

"I had no problem handling Roger," she began, with her back now to Jordan.

Roxanne held her head high, shoulders square, looking at the surroundings of his yard outside the long windows.

"The man is a gentleman, and knows how to respect a lady's wishes." She sounded way too calm.

"Do you have any idea what kind of perversions that man is into?" He'd find out right here and now if she shared an interest in these perversions.

Hell. He wanted to know everything about her—what was on her mind right now, what it would take to have her back in his arms.

Jordan's body brushed up against her backside, grabbing both of her wrists before she could stop him. He bent her over the table, so that her body covered the documents she had just observed. He pinned her wrists to the table, his blood surging through him while he looked down at her submissive position.

"And did the lady wish to be tied up and used?" Jordan leaned forward so that she felt the heat of his breath on her cheek, and in her hair.

He pressed against her rear end. His feet were planted on the floor next to both of hers, so she couldn't move her legs. Holding her like this excited him. His dick throbbed as he stared down at her. Controlling everything around him had always been important to him. Now he saw how he needed confirmation of that control too. He needed to know that Roxanne wanted to be with him, that she wanted him, and that she regretted making him leave her over the weekend.

The thought that someone else might do this to her, that another man would control her, made his blood boil. Anger surged through him just thinking that Uphouse might have tried something like this with her.

"I don't ever want to be used," she told him, the coolness of the desk against her cheek doing nothing to calm the fire that rushed through her.

Roxanne couldn't move. She closed her eyes briefly to try and regain control of the way her body responded to the vulnerable position Jordan had put her in, but the moistness between her legs saturated her pantyhose.

"But you would spend time with Uphouse. And don't tell me that he didn't make it clear what he wanted."

"He did not impress me. He had questions about his account, and wanted to discuss them. That was it."

"He propositioned you, didn't he?" Jordan pressed his body against her just a bit more. "And his offer didn't appeal to you?"

"No!" Roxanne realized her one-word response didn't cover both of his questions, but damn it, it was getting real hard to concentrate with him pressed against her like this, holding her, controlling her.

Jordan switched positions with the skill of a master and quickly took both of her hands in one of his, so that now he held her pinned with her hands stretched above her head. She tried to move but his feet and legs still pinned hers and she couldn't straighten.

Slowly he ran his hand down her ass. Reaching the end of her skirt, he slid it up, exposing her.

Roxanne opened her eyes, and lifted her head as far as she could, straining to focus on him.

"Oh God." Her insides boiled over, heat surging through her like a wildfire, out of control.

Never had she seen a more intense look on his face, his expression controlled, lined with raw, carnal lust.

His fingers moved over her skin, reaching under her pantyhose, and then slid them over her bottom and down to her thighs, leaving them bundled there, a natural restraint. Then with skilled movement, he slid his fingers between her legs.

She quivered from his touch, his fingertips barely grazing over her skin, yet igniting a fire in her that made her ache to move. She wanted to turn around, get out of her clothes, be free to attack him and demand he fuck her right there on the spot. Yet curiosity and excitement had her holding still, wondering what he would do next.

Jordan slid his fingers inside her, the moist heat that greeted him enough to make him crazy with need. His fingers glistened with her cum when he pulled them out. She was smooth and so damned fucking hot that all he could do was admire her while stroking the sensitive skin from her pussy to her ass. The sight of her curvy rear made his cock rage in his pants for freedom.

"I thought you just told me that what he offered didn't appeal to you," Jordan whispered, aware that his voice had become more gruff.

"Nothing about him appealed to me," she said on a sigh, placing her cheek against the cool wood, then opened her eyes when she felt Jordan's fingers brush her lips.

"Then why are you so wet?" Jordan asked, and slid a finger into her mouth, so she could taste the richness of herself.

The finger slid from her mouth as smoothly as it had slid in and out of her. Tasting herself somehow intensified her lust, made her head spin while need rushed through her.

Roxanne heard the slap the same instant that she felt it.

Jordan spanked her ass just hard enough to offer a quick sting. She sucked in a breath of air and opened her eyes wide, lifting her head and straining to look at Jordan as he brought his hand down on the other side of her bottom.

"Jordan," she gasped, as heat spread flushed over her skin.

She could see him standing over her, with one of his arms pinning her hands above her head, while his other hand rested free in the air, palm down, ready for another strike.

His gaze locked on her rear, while she waited with bated curiosity for him to spank her again. The slightest amount of pain mixed with intense pleasure was hotter than she had ever imagined it would be. It was on the tip of her tongue to ask him to do it again.

Roxanne could feel how hard her nipples had become as they pressed against the wooden table. Her body stretched over the hard surface and her legs were close together, straight, with her feet planted on the floor. She was so exposed, with her clothes bundled around her waist, and her pantyhose restricted around her thighs. When Jordan slipped his fingers inside her again, heat rushed through her body straight to her pussy, which burned with an ache she was sure she would die from if he didn't fuck her soon.

"Oh," she cried, as he pushed deep within her and then pulled free when an orgasm coursed through her so hard she thought she might pass out.

Once again he ran his fingers from her pussy to her ass, coating her with her own fluids.

"Did Roger do this to you?" Jordan asked, his heart thudding in his chest while he looked down at her smooth ass.

He loved how she didn't move, didn't protest, and appeared to be waiting to see what he'd do next. More than anything he wanted to know what was in her heart, her thoughts, that she wanted this intimate moment because she wanted him.

"No," she whispered.

"But he propositioned you?"

"Yes," she admitted, trying to spread her legs to allow him better access.

"And why did you tell him no?" Jordan asked.

"He doesn't appeal to me," she whispered.

"I see."

Jordan thrust his fingers deep inside her and she cried out, lifting her head, arching her back, as she climaxed for the second time. Roxanne squeezed her eyes shut, realizing she could never tell Jordan no. More than anything at that moment, she wanted him inside her, and she bit her lip so that she would refrain from asking him to make love to her.

Telling him to fuck her wouldn't let him see everything she felt at that moment. All he would see was that she would submit to him. And as important as she saw that was to him, there had to be a deeper understanding with this relationship. She needed mutual trust, respect, compassion for each other's feelings.

Jordan released her hands and immediately Roxanne pulled them down so that they rested flat on the table on either side of her head. She meant to push herself up, but found she didn't have the immediate strength to do so. Jordan removed his fingers from inside her and then quit touching her altogether. She felt his legs move from either side of hers, and realized he had stepped away from her. Slowly she pushed herself off the table, and felt her skirt crumple down her hips, but with her pantyhose gathered at her thighs, movement was still very restricted.

"Turn around," Jordan ordered, although his tone was quiet.

Roxanne didn't need to have intelligent thought to know that the man was as aroused as she was. She stood and turned around so that her warm rear leaned against the hard edge of the table, then she reached to pull up her pantyhose, and wondered how she could find the strength to tell this man no.

Even if he hadn't actually been with another woman, there was a reason for him smelling like perfume that he hadn't shared with her. She had a right to know that reason. But training this man, who was hell-bent and determined to have her complete submission, might possibly be the challenge of a lifetime.

"Take your clothes off," Jordan said, and she noticed his tone had grown husky.

He saw her hesitate, and knew he didn't have her compliance. A stubborn gleam in her eyes brought him pause. His heart constricted. There was no way he would be able to have a relationship with her if he didn't have her complete submission.

"No, Jordan." She reached down and pulled her pantyhose back over her hips, and then slid her skirt down.

"You can't fight this," he murmured, and approached her with a predatory look in his eyes.

Jordan pinned Roxanne with the table behind her as he approached. He pressed his body against hers, and his hand came up to cup her cheek.

"Why would you tell me 'no'?"

"I won't be one of many," she whispered, and she closed her eyes. "And I have no idea how many women you have. You want my complete loyalty, for me to share everything I do with you. I must have the same in return."

The phone rang and Roxanne jumped. She took a deep breath to still her overheated nerves, and listened to it ring a second time before Jordan released her and moved to answer it.

"Jordan here," he said a bit too harshly, and then listened to the party at the other end. "I should be there within thirty minutes," he said then hung up.

"Are we headed back to the office?" She didn't look at him but focused on straightening her clothes. Her hands shook and she prayed she would be able to concentrate on her work for the remainder of the afternoon.

"Yup." Jordan sounded terse and didn't say another word as he left his den.

She wanted him to open his heart to her. And damn it, that was a fair request. He just wasn't sure he knew how to do it. And that bothered him—no, it terrified him. All of his life, performance was all that was needed to show loyalty. No one had ever asked more of him. His father hadn't asked for love, simply perfection. He'd never let another woman get under his skin enough that they'd demanded anything more from him than sexual satisfaction.

And up until now that had been fine. Life had been good. He'd reached the top of his ladder and enjoyed his social ranking, and the respect and appreciation of being the best at what he did.

Hell, how many businessmen could tell a millionaire client to go fuck themselves?

Jordan had reached the top of the hill. Yet he still wanted more. He wanted Roxanne. Now he needed to figure out if he could meet her expectations and demands in order to have her.

Damn it. How the hell had he gotten himself into such a predicament?

And why did it matter?

Because you love her, the little voice inside of his head annoyed him.

There was work to do, matters that needed his immediate attention. Roxanne would work by his side and somehow, at a later time, he would figure out how to gain her complete submission. He would have her and on his terms.

* * * * *

Roxanne had no problem keeping her mind off the events that had occurred at Jordan's house. After enduring a silent and brooding ride with Jordan back to the office, she found herself quickly submerged in her work.

"I can't believe it's five o'clock." Dorothy, the office receptionist, opened her bottom filing cabinet drawer and reached for her purse. The phone rang one more time, and she reached for it.

Linda stood up in her cubicle and turned to Roxanne. She'd been hovering over the files that were housed in the secretarial pool for the last hour, going through each file to ensure paperwork was in order. It was refreshing to spend time among these ladies, their knowledge of the business limited to their individual tasks, and therefore their stress almost nonexistent. Roxanne smiled at her and watched as she ran her hands over her dress.

"Thank you for walking me through these files," Linda said, and offered Roxanne a warm smile. "I promise I'll get the hang of it."

"You're doing fine," Roxanne assured her. "It takes a while to pick up on everything."

Linda sighed and nodded. "Now it's home to get supper on the table for everyone."

Dorothy turned from her desk to face Roxanne, and Roxanne looked her way.

"Joanie is on line two for you. I'm sorry, I hadn't set the phone to voice mail yet," Dorothy apologized.

"It's okay." Roxanne smiled. "At least it's not work-related. I'll take it right here."

She closed the file she'd been going through and shut the filing cabinet.

"You have a good evening, Dorothy. And you too, Linda." Roxanne watched as the two ladies headed toward the glass doors to leave. "I'll switch the phones over, Dorothy," she called out, and Dorothy mouthed a "thank you" as she left the office.

Pedro Romero, the payroll clerk, still hovered in his cubicle, and Roxanne moved to Dorothy's desk to forward the phones then picked up the line to speak with Joanie.

"Hi, sweetie, how was your day?" Joanie's chipper tone made Roxanne smile. She leaned against Dorothy's desk and stared at the empty cubicles. She could see Pedro's back and knew she would have to go tell the college boy that it was time to go home. He had been known to get lost in his work and forget to leave for lunch.

"I'll tell you about it later," Roxanne mumbled, as the events at Jordan's house came to mind and at the same time a warm flush rushed through her. She crossed her legs as she felt a pressure build and realized how horny she was.

Damn the man for being so bullheaded, yet making her crave him all at the same time.

"That doesn't sound good," Joanie said. "Well, I called to see if you wanted to go to dinner with David and me. We thought of asking you and your boss."

Joanie giggled and Roxanne leaned back a bit on Dorothy's desk to get a clear shot down the hallway. Jordan was in his office, as were several of the other accountants. Roxanne leaned forward and blew out a puff of frustration.

"That wouldn't be a good idea." Roxanne stared at the toes of her pumps.

"Hmm. Sounds like supper might be a good idea then." Joanie continued talking, but her voice sounded muffled and Roxanne figured that her girlfriend was telling David what Roxanne had just said. "How about if we meet at Senorita's, downtown. I hear the rain is out of the forecast and we could eat outside on the patio."

"That sounds good," Roxanne agreed. "I should be able to get there by six-thirty. Will that work for you two? I would love to head home and shower first."

"Sounds great." Joanie repeated the time to David. Roxanne could hear him say something in the background but couldn't catch his words, but they made Joanie laugh. "We'll have a table ready. See you then."

She sighed as she turned to hang up the receiver. Her friend had found true happiness with David and Roxanne wondered if there would ever be a man in her life who would make her feel that content.

"And who are you running off to see this evening?"

Jordan's question surprised her and she hopped off Dorothy's desk, then turned to face him. He stood opposite her with his arms crossed, looking rather disgusted, and she frowned at him.

"It's after five. My work for the day is done, boss. But if you want to dock the personal call from my pay, that is your prerogative," Roxanne said, knowing she hadn't answered his question.

A groan from down the cubicles caught Roxanne's attention, and she turned in the direction of Pedro. "Pedro," she called out. "It's after five. Go home."

She turned, walking around Jordan and down the hall toward his office to get her purse. Jordan was on her heels. She reached down to grab her purse and shut down her computer.

"Roxanne." Jordan had to know if she had a dinner date with another man.

He'd overheard her talking on the phone, sounding at ease and comfortable with whomever she talked to, and a surge of jealousy had rushed through him. He didn't like it. He had no right. But he couldn't stop himself from getting up and finding out who she was talking to. The fact that she wouldn't tell him made him want to lock her in his office until she shared every detail of her plans. Hell, who was he kidding—he wanted her to spend her evening with him.

She glanced up at him.

"Tell me who you're seeing tonight."

Roxanne slid her purse under her arm as she walked toward him.

"It's none of your business what I'm doing tonight." She glared at him when he didn't move from the doorway. "Don't make a scene, Jordan," she hissed. "I'm going out with Joanie tonight."

"And who else? You said, I'll see you two." Jordan didn't budge.

"I'm meeting Joanie and David for dinner downtown. May I leave now?"

Jordan didn't move right away but stood there staring down at her. His gaze traveled across her face and then moved lower. Roxanne had her hand on her hip and a scowl on her face.

More than anything he wanted to go with her, meet her friends, learn more about her while she laughed and relaxed after work. Some downtime would be excellent. And having Roxanne at his side would only make it better.

"Please move," Roxanne said, her voice quavering.

Jordan didn't move from the entrance of his office, but watched Roxanne leave the office and enter the elevator without glancing back. Once she was out of his sight, he crossed the hallway toward Layette's office. He had a major problem on his hands and focusing on Roxanne right now would be a distraction he couldn't afford. The woman had ignited something inside him that he hadn't experienced before. More than anything, he felt the need to claim her and make damn sure she knew where she belonged.

But she wasn't going anywhere, and business matters demanded his immediate attention. Jordan knew if he didn't have such a gaping problem with his accounts he would have tore after her. The woman wanted a commitment from him that he didn't know how to give. But maybe if he spent more time with her she would see what she meant to him.

Jordan entered Layette's office and sank into one of the comfortable leather chairs that faced the man's well-polished desk. The plush office smelled of lingering cigar smoke and the dark furniture reminded Jordan of his father's office.

This room, with its masculine furnishings, always took Jordan back to a time otherwise forgotten. It was as if, between these walls, deals could be cut among men that couldn't be dissolved through simple litigation. The atmosphere of this office displayed a mind-set of a generation gone by, where the shake of a hand had as much merit as ten signatures and five lawyers did today.

Jordan steepled his hands in front of his face, resting his elbows on the wide armrests, and pursed his lips against his fingers. Layette entered the office and walked over to the glass cabinet that housed a minibar. He pulled down three glasses and poured a finger of whiskey into each. "I've arranged for Joe Dixon to join us," Layette said, focusing on his task.

Jordan sniffed the whiskey before swallowing the shot, and then winced. He placed the glass on Layette's desk and declined a second shot. He needed his head clear to manage matters, and unlike Layette, who had mastered the art of drinking and cutting a perfect deal, Jordan preferred to do business without the alcohol.

"Is this the detective you mentioned to me earlier?" Jordan asked, and watched the older man walk behind his desk.

Ralph Layette turned to straighten a framed picture of downtown Kansas City at the turn of the century. Jordan remembered the old oil painting hanging in his father's study and knew that Layette cherished the picture more than he would ever admit.

"It's very important that we determine who is taking money from these accounts without letting the public know that there's a problem." Layette didn't turn around as he spoke. "I know you realize this, Jordan, but the scandal could ruin you. Someone is stealing from Hall Enterprises and Dixon will be able to dig in places that you and I can't dig without eyebrows being raised. He will be our tool of discretion."

"And how will he do this?" Jordan didn't like the thought of bringing someone in from the outside. The more parties that knew the money was missing, the more people Jordan had to keep an eye on.

A cell phone that sat on top of a pile of papers on Layette's desk began buzzing and Layette turned to pick up the phone.

He glanced at the number displayed and then answered it with a gruff acknowledgment. A minute later he ended the call and dropped the phone back on the desk.

"You can ask him yourself," Layette said, and moved to leave his office. "He's here now."

Jordan stood and followed Layette into the hallway. "We'll meet in my office," Jordan said, glancing at the man who stood on the other side of the glass doors, waiting to be let into Hall Enterprises.

The scent of Roxanne's perfume captured Jordan's attention as he passed through the doorway but he couldn't let his thoughts stray to what she might be doing this evening while he plotted to capture a thief.

Chapter Nine

ဆ

Sounds of laughter and steady conversation mixed with the clicking of silverware against china when Roxanne entered Senorita's. She sat next to Joanie, greeting the two of them with what she hoped was a relaxed smile.

"Strawberry margaritas for both of you?" David wagged his finger at the two of them once the waiter had come to their table.

"Sounds yummy." Joanie looked relaxed in her pale pink blouse and matching skirt.

"Sure. With salt." Roxanne nodded to the waiter who jotted down their order then hurried off.

Minutes later she sipped at the drink, feeling the strength of the alcohol immediately. Maybe she should just get good and drunk tonight, anything to clear her head of Jordan. His silence when she'd made it clear she wanted from him what he wanted from her — honesty in what he did, where he went — had hurt her more than she wanted to admit.

Jordan wanted her submission, her undying loyalty, but he wouldn't offer the same. And she didn't want him to submit to her. She didn't want a weak man. That much she knew already. What she wanted was honesty, respect, appreciation of the fact that she was intelligent, and not some stupid bimbo to use and then discard.

"Roxanne, are you with us?" David waved a chip in the air and Roxanne blinked and then smiled.

"I'm sorry, David. I'm with you." Roxanne tried to recall what they had just been talking about.

Her thoughts kept straying to the nonchalant way Jordan had acted when she left the office. She took another drink of her margarita, the tequila in it floating to her head. Nothing she wanted mattered to Jordan and it pissed her off.

"What were you thinking about?" Joanie asked, and then sucked the last of her margarita through her straw.

"Oh, nothing," Roxanne lied. "It's just been a long day at work."

She wouldn't put a damper on their evening by telling the two of them she had allowed her boss to turn her into a sexual play toy. And that is exactly what had happened. She wouldn't deny how Jordan affected her physically. Dear God. Just thinking about some of the things he'd done to her warmed her more than what the alcohol could possibly do. But great sex wasn't enough to create the foundation for a good relationship. And so she'd put an end to it. If only it didn't hurt so much. She took another gulp of her drink. There wasn't enough alcohol in it though to numb her pain.

Roxanne watched Joanie study her for a moment, and knew her psychologist friend could see through her lies. Roxanne smiled and hoped Joanie wouldn't press the issue. Now wasn't the time for her to dump her personal problems on her friends. Roxanne wanted to enjoy the evening and not end up crying on her friend's shoulder.

David leaned forward. "Well, I had just suggested the three of us get naked and get in a pile," he said quietly, so the people in the booths on either end of them wouldn't hear.

"Oh, you did not," Joanie scolded, and moved to kick him under the table.

"Ouch," David cried out, and this time a couple of kids at a nearby table did turn, and then giggled.

The waiter showed up then with several steaming plates of fajitas complete with all of the fixings. Suddenly there was food everywhere, and again Roxanne envied her friends' happiness when the two of them helped each other prepare their plates.

And she was glad when they turned the chatter toward something easy.

Try as she did, eating simply wasn't an option, the churning lump in her gut not letting her put her personal problems to the side. David talked about his work, rambling on about things going on in his office. Joanie added comments about her day, and the two of them supported each other, offering support and agreeing with what the other said. A true bond lay between them. And although she knew they were her friends, at the moment she felt like running home to her bed and crying her eyes out that she didn't have the same camaraderie with Jordan. Hell, they weren't even close.

No. She wouldn't cry over the man. Being with her friends was a good idea. The last thing she needed to be was alone right now.

"Let's go," Joanie finally said. "If I have another drink, I won't be able to walk out of here."

"Can't blame a guy for trying to get you drunk," David said, winking at Roxanne.

They paid the bill and then left the restaurant to walk toward their cars parked on the street. It was still light out, but streaks of orange and pink ran across the sky as the setting sun painted a beautiful picture along the Kansas City skyline. Roxanne slid her arm around Joanie's, and the two walked amiably with David bringing up the rear.

"Is it okay if I come over for a while?" Roxanne asked quietly. "I'm not in the mood to be alone tonight."

"Of course." Joanie squeezed Roxanne's arm. "You can stay the night if you like."

They reached Roxanne's Probe first, and David's black Nissan was parked just a few parking places more down the street. Joanie turned to her fiancé and released Roxanne to wrap her arms around his waist.

"I'm going to ride with Roxanne," she told him. "We'll meet you back at the apartment."

"Okay," David said, and then kissed Joanie while Roxanne watched. "Don't dawdle, you two."

The two women climbed into Roxanne's car, and Joanie waited until Roxanne had pulled into the street before speaking.

"You going to tell me what's bothering you?" she asked.

Roxanne turned to see the concerned look on her friend's face. She smiled, and returned her attention to the traffic.

"I could tell you all the problems at work," Roxanne said, but then felt an incredible urge to unload all of her frustrations about Jordan on to her friend.

"Why don't you tell me about this boss of yours," Joanie said quietly.

Roxanne laughed, but then felt dampness in her eyes, and rubbed them. She would not cry over that man.

"He wants so much from me," Roxanne began. "And he won't give me the same in return. Not to mention I think he's seeing other women."

"He's dating other women?" Joanie asked. "Did he tell you this?"

"Well, he sure didn't deny it." Roxanne remembered his stubborn silence, and anger consumed her all over again. "I just don't get him. He moves into my space, and tells me what I can and can't do like he owns me. But then for some reason he feels he doesn't have to follow the same rules."

"So how did you find out he was seeing other women?" Joanie asked.

"He came over the other day, and reeked of some other lady's perfume." Roxanne gripped the steering wheel, as an image of Jordan's unreadable face appeared in her thoughts. She wondered what he was doing tonight, but then pushed the thought away in frustration.

"So you confronted him about it," Joanie prompted.

"You're damn right I did," Roxanne declared. "He had just finished berating me about who I spent my time with. Can you believe it?" Roxanne turned to glare at her friend, feeling the outrage all over again. "And he just stood there. He made no attempt whatsoever to try and deny anything. It was like he could do whatever he wanted, but I was supposed to follow his every rule and demand."

"So let me get this right," Joanie said. "You told him you could smell the perfume, and then accused him of being with another woman? Or did you ask him if he had been with someone else?"

Roxanne watched as David's Nissan whipped around in front of them. She glanced over her shoulder to check for cars, and then focused on the rear of David's car, as she followed him to the other lane.

She frowned as she considered her friend's question. "What's your point?" Roxanne asked.

"Well, if you told him he had been with another woman, and he hadn't, you might have pissed him off, and he kept quiet out of anger," Joanie explained, sounding very much like the therapist she was. "But if you asked him if he had seen another lady, and he didn't answer, that would imply guilt to me, and he is taking time to consider a good alibi, or another means to respond to your question."

Roxanne sighed. She tried to remember the details of their conversation in the bedroom, but all that stuck out in her thoughts was the smell of that perfume, and the hardened expression Jordan had offered her.

"I don't remember." Roxanne blew out a hard sigh of resignation. "None of it matters now anyway. It's over."

They pulled into the parking lot of Joanie and David's complex and Roxanne parked in a stall next to David's Nissan. The sun still lingered but cast long shadows from the cars, and the pink in the sky faded into a darker blue. Roxanne made sure her car doors were locked after Joanie was out on her side of the car, and then moved around to the front of her vehicle to join her friend.

"I don't want to think about Jordan tonight," Roxanne said quietly, as David approached.

"Well then, we shall do our best to distract your thoughts." Joanie smiled, and tossed her long blonde hair behind her shoulder.

"And how shall we distract her thoughts?" David came up behind Joanie, and tugged on her blonde strands, pulling Joanie's head back so that she stared up at him.

David planted a passionate kiss on her mouth, and Roxanne watched the two lovers. David opened his eyes, before pulling back from Joanie, and met Roxanne's gaze.

"Always the voyeur," he said, and chuckled.

"Sorry." Roxanne grinned too, and redirected her attention to the cars in the lot, as she started walking toward their building.

"You can watch anytime you want," David teased, and tugged on Roxanne's hair, then fell into line between the two women, and wrapped an arm over Roxanne's shoulder, pulling her to him in a brotherly fashion. "So what do you two ladies have planned for the evening?"

"Since I have Roxanne all to myself for the entire evening," Joanie began, and looked around David to smile at Roxanne. "I thought she could help me with some wedding decisions."

Roxanne saw the enthusiasm in her friend's face. Joanie had wanted her advice on several matters. Roxanne wasn't sure if planning the ceremony where these two would commit to each other for the rest of their lives would help her take her mind off Jordan, but she wouldn't let her personal life dampen her best friend's enthusiasm.

"That sounds like the perfect night to me," Roxanne smiled at her friend.

David let go of the two women and unlocked the door to their apartment. Joanie and Roxanne made a beeline to the bedroom, made themselves comfortable, and spent the next hour or so going through catalogs, and discussing miscellaneous items that Joanie had on her list of things to do for the ceremony.

"I can't believe how much preparation is involved in planning a wedding," Roxanne said, and tossed a magazine she'd been looking through to the floor on top of a stack of magazines already there.

"Want something to drink?" Joanie asked, and closed the magazine she'd been reading.

"If you want," Roxanne said, glancing around at the stacks of wedding paraphernalia that cluttered the bedroom.

"Let's take a break from all of this." Joanie looked around her room too. "How about we go out to the patio, see what David is doing. He's probably forgotten we're here by now."

"It's more like I figured I'd been forgotten." David had obviously overheard them, and greeted Joanie in the kitchen with a swat to her rear. "She just uses me," he added, doing his best to look like he was pouting, but his grin gave him away.

"I really do envy you two with how happy you are." Roxanne accepted the bottled water that Joanie gave her and then followed her girlfriend out to the patio.

"You're a hell of a catch," David told her, moving the lawn chairs around so they could all sit and face each other. "Is that boss of yours still giving you grief?"

"Well, thank you. And I'm not sure what to make of him, to be honest with you." She quickly shared his reaction to her phone call with Joanie before she'd left work. Maybe the best thing to do was unload on these two. "He asks me all of these questions, but then goes silent when I ask him questions."

"So you ask him where he's going and what he's doing?" David asked. "And then he tells you it's none of your business?"

"Well, no," Roxanne said, shaking her head. "I've never asked him to share the details of his day."

"Then what do you ask him?" Joanie wondered.

"Well, maybe I don't ask him questions." Roxanne knew all of this would be too confusing to explain. Hell, she didn't get most of it herself. "He won't share anything with me."

"That's not easy for a guy to do," David said, seeming to understand what she didn't.

"You and Joanie don't seem to have a problem with it," Roxanne argued.

Joanie laughed. "You have to work hard to gain perfection." She ran her foot up David's leg, grinning. "When you find it, you go after it until you get it."

"We don't know this guy is right for her, though." David turned serious, always the protector. "I still think I ought to meet the guy. If he's just playing her, then we don't want our girl hurt."

Roxanne let out a staggered sigh, appreciative of his friendship but frustrated at the same time.

"I'm not sure that there is any reason to meet him," she said, the pain in her gut returning with a vengeance. "I won't chase him if there isn't any reason to."

"If you can't live without him, that sounds like plenty good reason to me." Joanie spoke softly, reaching out to touch Roxanne's hand. "It might hurt a little fighting for him, but if he's worth it, you'll be happy you did in the end."

Roxanne nodded but didn't say anything, fearful she might start crying if she did.

Shortly after that she left, the evening getting late. She would face Jordan again tomorrow at work, and a good night's sleep would only help.

The night air felt good, and the sky was clear and black. Roxanne turned up the radio on her ride home and forced herself to sing along, clear her head. She didn't hear her phone ring, but felt its vibration against her side, and her stomach did a flip when she guessed Jordan was checking up on her. But it wasn't Jordan's number that displayed on the small phone's screen.

"Hello," Roxanne said.

"Roxanne, where are you?" The hushed voice spoke so quickly that Roxanne didn't recognize the caller.

"Who is this?" she asked.

"Oh, sorry," the male voice continued to speak in rushed whispers. "This is Aaron Tipley."

"Why are you whispering?" Roxanne wanted to know.

Aaron sounded strange, but the man got excited easily, and his hushed whispers simply aroused Roxanne's curiosity.

"I hope I'm not interrupting anything."

"Nope. I was just heading home." She held the phone with one hand, so she could look over her shoulder as she merged on to the Interstate. Traffic was light this late in the evening, and within seconds she had accelerated to the speed limit, and adjusted the phone between her shoulder and ear.

"I'm in Nebraska," Aaron said, and then continued quickly. "I brought up my own computer and found a cheap motel room, since I didn't have time to authorize anything through the office."

"What the hell are you doing in Nebraska?" Roxanne frowned, suddenly worried that Aaron had done something stupid. "What are you doing?"

"I'm tracking our thief," Aaron told her. "And I think I need your help. How soon can you be here?"

"What?" Roxanne almost shouted into the phone, and her smile disappeared.

Chapter Ten

🔊

Roxanne stood up and stretched while continuing to stare at the glow of her computer screen. She rubbed her lower back, and then picked up her cell phone to make sure the charge and signal were still strong.

After convincing Aaron that it would be foolish to make a three-hour drive from Kansas City, across the state line, to the small Nebraska town where Aaron had set up camp, she had gone home and signed on to her computer so she could catch up on the work Aaron had accomplished while she'd been at Joanie's.

She'd talked to Aaron on the phone several times over the next couple hours, and learned the accountant had discovered that a withdrawal of ten thousand dollars had occurred earlier that day from an account that had not yet been touched. He had confirmed with the banker, whom Aaron had managed to get out of bed and convinced to work with him, that the withdrawal had been made in the small town of Auburn, Nebraska. While working with the banker over the phone, the two men became aware of a second transaction from another account at Hall Enterprises. The withdrawal had been made from the exact same location.

"I couldn't wait," Aaron had told her on the phone. "I tried calling you, but just got your voice mail. And I even tried contacting Mr. Hall."

"And you couldn't reach him?" Roxanne again wondered what Jordan was doing that night.

"No. I got his voice mail, too," Aaron had explained.

Roxanne stared at her wall clock, and rubbed her eyes. It was almost one in the morning and Aaron hadn't called her in almost an hour. She had tried to reach Jordan twice but he apparently had his phone shut off. Roxanne knew he forwarded calls to his home voice mail whenever he turned off his cell phone, and she felt aggravation peak when she couldn't reach him.

"You own a damn company," Roxanne mumbled to herself, as she walked barefoot into her kitchen. "I should be able to reach you when I need you."

The glow of her refrigerator lit up her dark kitchen briefly, and Roxanne remembered the times Jordan had managed his way into her home without her knowing. She reached for a bottled water, and then turned to look around the kitchen. She walked toward her living room and took in the contents of the quiet and dark house before accepting the fact that she was alone in her home. Jordan had not sought her out that evening. But that was okay, he needed to quit trying to control her life, and maybe he finally had seen that she would be happier without him.

Roxanne settled back in front of her computer, and moved her mouse to make the screen reappear in front of her. The monitor buzzed to life just as someone knocked on her front door. Roxanne turned quickly to look at her closed curtains.

"Who in the hell could be here at one o'clock in the morning," she mumbled, and wondered if it was Jordan.

If it was Jordan he wouldn't knock. He would come on in like he owned the place.

Unwelcome tingles crept down her spine. She was too jumpy after playing detective all evening. Entering the living room, she flipped on the porch light and pulled the curtain aside an inch from her living room window. She didn't recognize whoever it was who stood at her door. But she knew one thing — it was not Jordan.

Roxanne slipped the chain lock into place then opened her front door an inch to see a small and very pregnant lady standing in the glow of the porch light.

"Roxanne?" the woman asked.

Roxanne slid the chain back out of its lock, and pulled the door open to stare at a young woman who stood clutching a purse to her protruding belly. "May I help you?" Roxanne could tell the woman was very upset, and obviously had been crying.

"Roxanne, I'm Jeannette, Aaron Tipley's wife. He's been arrested, and I need your help."

"Aaron has been arrested?" Roxanne pushed the screen door open and beckoned Jeannette inside.

"He just called me from a jail in Nebraska." Jeannette started crying and Roxanne hurried for a box of tissues.

Returning with an extended hand, Roxanne offered the tissues, and then switched on a nearby lamp. "Please sit down and tell me what's happened," Roxanne said, and placed a hand on Jeannette's back to guide her to the couch.

Roxanne sat at the other end of the couch but then jumped up and began pacing as she heard Jeannette's story.

"He didn't call me until he was halfway to Nebraska," Jeannette Tipley explained. "I told him it was too dangerous for him to go alone, but he insisted that if he acted immediately he could find out who was stealing money from his employer."

The woman dabbed her eyes and then looked at Roxanne as more tears streamed down her face. Roxanne grabbed more tissues from the box, and handed them to her.

"He told me he had the location pinpointed where the thieves were, and he could prove it through his printouts and that he planned to go to the police. He promised me that he wouldn't go after the bad guys without seeking out help," Jeannette continued through sobs.

"Well then, what went wrong?" Roxanne glanced at the clock and saw that an hour and a half had passed since she had spoken with Aaron. "When did you last talk to him?" she asked.

Jeannette hiccupped and placed a hand on her large belly. Roxanne followed the movement with her eyes, and watched as Jeannette glanced at her watch. The young woman was pretty, her pregnancy making her glow, even though she was upset. She had short brown hair that curled under around her neck, and loose strands that she'd tucked behind her ears. Soft brown eyes appeared doe-like as they filled with fresh tears.

"I guess it was about forty-five minutes ago." Jeannette looked up at Roxanne. "He said you could help. You can prove that he was working in Hall Enterprises' best interest, and not stealing from them."

"Stealing from Hall Enterprises?" Roxanne stared at Jeannette, not believing what she had just heard. "Who says he is stealing from Hall Enterprises?"

"That is what he is being charged with," Jeannette wailed. She adjusted the strap on her maternity jumper, and then shifted on the couch as if she wasn't comfortable. "They came to the motel room where he was and arrested him. He called me from the jail."

Roxanne was confused and sat down on the coffee table in front of Jeannette. "The police went to his motel room? How did they know he was there?"

Jeannette put her hands over her face, and shook her head.

"This is really all too much for me," she whimpered. "I'm sure that I don't make any sense."

"We'll get this all worked out," Roxanne reassured her, and ran a hand over Jeannette's head. "I think the first thing we need to do is contact the jail. Let me figure out all the details."

Jeannette lifted her head, and smiled at Roxanne for the first time. "Aaron said you could solve everything," she said. "He told me that you pretty much run the company."

Any other time, Roxanne would have enjoyed such a compliment, but at the moment she had a distraught pregnant woman to deal with, a co-worker in jail in another state, and a boss who was missing in action. Not to mention it was the middle of the night, and Roxanne began to feel that she would be lucky if she got any sleep that night at all.

It took over an hour to gather information from the small-town jail in Auburn, Nebraska. The night clerk appeared unfamiliar with any recent arrests, and Roxanne had to repeat Aaron Tipley's name to the woman several times. Jeannette paced behind Roxanne as she spoke with the night clerk, which made Roxanne feel even more apprehensive about her ability to handle the matter in a calm fashion.

"I'm sure we simply have to work our way through the red tape until we find out where the mistake occurred," Roxanne tried to reassure Jeannette while on hold with the jail.

The clock on the wall now read two-thirty in the morning.

"The mistake is that they arrested him." Jeannette stopped pacing, and put her hands where her hips probably were.

Roxanne studied the pregnant form and then attempted a smile at the distraught lady. "You might do best to try and get some rest," Roxanne suggested. "This can't be good for your baby for you to be so upset."

"How can I sleep?" Jeannette held up her hands in a display of defeat. "My Aaron is up in some small-town jail, and the people who work there don't even know that he's there," Jeannette wailed.

The clerk chose that moment to come back on the line, and Roxanne gestured for Jeannette to be quiet as she adjusted the phone to her ear.

"I have the information you requested," the clerk said through the phone. "Now tell me again who you are?"

"This is Roxanne Isley," Roxanne said. "I am an employee with Hall Enterprises, where Mr. Tipley is employed."

"Well, it seems that Hall Enterprises is listed as who is pressing charges," the clerk told Roxanne. "I suggest you contact your employer in the morning. The charges are felonies. Mr. Tipley isn't going anywhere."

Roxanne couldn't believe her ears. She didn't dare repeat out loud what she had just been told. The last thing she needed was a very pregnant woman going into hysterics in her living room. She thanked the clerk and hung up the phone.

"What happened?" Jeannette fixed her bloodshot eyes on Roxanne. "What did they say?"

"We can't do anything to help him until business hours start in the morning." Roxanne offered the partial truth. "The best thing for you to do is to get some sleep."

"No," Jeannette wailed. "I want my Aaron home."

Roxanne feared the hysterics would start anyway, and approached Jeannette, then placed her hands on the woman's shoulders.

"Jeannette, your husband needs you to be there for him." Roxanne stared the scared-looking woman in the eyes, and hoped her own tone sounded reassuring. "But both of us need to get some sleep so that we can tackle all that bureaucratic paperwork in the morning."

Jeannette nodded but didn't look convinced. "I'm not sure I can sleep without my Aaron," she mumbled, sounding defeated.

"Would you like me to give you a ride home?" Roxanne asked. "I can pick you up in the morning, and we can figure out what we need to do to get Aaron out of jail at that point."

Roxanne stumbled into her bed shortly after three-thirty in the morning and wondered if she would be able to sleep at all that night. It made no sense to her why Hall Enterprises would press charges against Aaron Tipley. And try as she did, she still could not reach Jordan.

The alarm clock buzzed and simultaneously early morning radio chatter filled Roxanne's dark bedroom with too much energetic noise. She groaned and almost fell out of the bed when her blankets twisted around her legs.

Roxanne slapped at her alarm clock then ran her fingers through her hair as she shuffled to the bathroom. A hot shower and coffee didn't do a lot to wake her up but Roxanne had a lot to accomplish and she needed to get started.

The bright morning sun blinded her as she sipped more coffee while walking to her car. Jeannette's car still sat in front of her house but Roxanne wanted to make a quick trip to the office before contacting her. No one had arrived at work when Roxanne let herself in twenty minutes later.

While the computer buzzed to life, Roxanne strolled to Jordan's desk and fingered the papers that lay about. A card caught her attention and she picked it up for a closer scrutiny.

"Joe Dixon. Private detective," Roxanne whispered, as she fingered the engraving on the card. "Well now, Mr. Hall, what have you gone and done?"

"What are you doing here, Miss Isley?" The gruff voice behind her had Roxanne turning with a start.

Roxanne put her hand to heart and felt it pound through her blouse. "You startled me, Ralph," she said to the older accountant. "I thought I was the only one here."

"I bet you did." Ralph Layette didn't smile, and crossed his arms as he leaned in the doorway to Jordan's office and appeared to glower at her.

"It's been a crazy night," she began, and turned the card over in her hand. "And I haven't been able to reach Jordan. Do you know where he is?"

"He's been busy." He made no attempt to elaborate.

Roxanne's eyes burned, and she felt anxious to gather information and get this mess worked out. The last thing she had time for right now was Ralph Layette's piss-poor attitude.

"I don't have time for this, Ralph. Tell me where Jordan is. I need to talk to him right now." She crossed her arms, matching his stance. "I've been dealing with a very pregnant, distraught lady, and I need some answers."

She could've sworn that Ralph almost smiled at her comment. But his words didn't sound pleasant. "I'm sure Jordan will contact you when he's ready."

Roxanne glanced at her watch. "I realize it's early, but I need to talk to him now. Did you know that Aaron Tipley was arrested last night? The police told me that Hall Enterprises pressed the charges."

"Yup." Ralph pushed away from the doorway, and looked smug. "Once we put our guy on the matter, the situation was wrapped up pretty easily."

"But they arrested Aaron Tipley," Roxanne almost yelled, not liking Ralph's manner, and feeling grouchier by the moment. "Where is Jordan?"

"I do believe he's been in contact with the police." Ralph took a couple of steps toward Roxanne and she could smell cigar smoke as he approached. "Now, missy, are you going to tell me what you're doing snooping around Jordan's desk?"

"Snooping?" Roxanne narrowed her brow at the man. "I work here, Ralph, and I am not in the mood for your condescending tone. We've got to figure out why Hall Enterprises would have pressed charges against Aaron so that we can get him released."

Ralph laughed, and Roxanne felt an uncomfortable chill race through her. The man looked almost menacing as he pointed a finger at her.

"Look, missy," Ralph growled, "you may have wrapped your legs so tight around Jordan that he can't see straight, but I am not quite so blind. I've been onto your little act for a while now, and the gig is up. You hear me?"

"How dare you talk to me like that," Roxanne hissed, and instantly felt a dull throb in her temple.

She worked on too little sleep, and although Ralph Layette had never been overly cordial with her, he had never used such a demeaning tone with her before. His actions made no sense and his words were rude. "My personal relationship with Jordan is none of your damned business, and if you can't help me with a work-related issue, then I will thank you to leave this office immediately. And once I have the authorization to do so, I will see that you are written up for such sexual slander."

"Lady, you've got some nerve." Ralph Layette didn't budge from his spot several feet inside the office. "I've done nothing wrong and have been loyal to this company since the day it opened its doors."

She didn't have time for this.

"I'm sure you've got work to do, Ralph. I suggest you get busy on it." Roxanne turned and walked around the other side of Jordan's desk, intentionally ignoring him.

Ralph had moved in on Roxanne without her realizing it, and he now took her by the arm and pulled her from Jordan's desk.

"Step away from there, missy," he instructed in a tone that reminded her of a detective off one of the old-time seventies cops and robbers movies.

"You will not touch me!" Roxanne snapped angrily as she yanked her arm free of Ralph's grasp. She pointed a finger in his face and fought to keep herself from doing a little manhandling of her own. "This is my office, too. And I have every right to be in here. You need to be in your office handling matters pertaining to work. Now go!"

Ralph smiled and rocked up on his tiptoes, then crossed his arms and appeared immune to her rising temper. His actions only infuriated her more. He nodded toward the card she held in her hand.

"You going to call him?" Ralph asked, obviously ignoring her instructions to get busy.

Roxanne took another look at the card she held in her hand. "This is the investigator you hired to find out who was stealing the money?"

"Yup." Ralph sounded smug.

"Well he did a crappy job," Roxanne snapped. "He nailed the wrong man, and now there's a huge mess to muddle through. Not to mention the real thief is probably laughing at us right now."

Ralph held up his hands as if in surrender but his grin appeared almost amused. "It's your story, lady, but you can tell it to the police."

"I plan on it," Roxanne snapped, and marched around him to her own desk. "Where is Jordan?"

"He's with our man there," Ralph said, and nodded at the card.

"Jordan is with this Joe Dixon?" Roxanne sat at her desk and reached for her phone. "Well, I tried to reach Jordan all night last night and he isn't answering his calls. So maybe this Mr. Dixon can shed some light on why they have Tipley in some small-town jail cell."

"You go ahead and make that call." Ralph strolled to the office door. "I'm sure Dixon would love to hear from you."

Chapter Eleven

🙠

The phone rang several times before voice mail answered. Roxanne listened to the baritone voice explain office hours and how important her call was. She hung up, frustrated.

Roxanne stood and reached for her coffee cup. She walked over to the cabinet and small sink area along the wall in Jordan's office and went through the motions of making coffee. Ralph had moved to the doorway but continued to stand there. She wished he would go away.

She remembered Jeannette Tipley and knew that she would be looking for her soon. Roxanne needed a plan, and she needed one soon.

"Are Jordan and this detective up in Nebraska right now?" Roxanne asked as she prepared the coffee. She didn't bother to turn around.

"Last I heard. I wouldn't go running to Mr. Hall crying though," Ralph said. "I doubt he's going to listen to you, or any arguments you might have. He's got the facts now. Keep to doing what you do best, making coffee, and whatever other services you offer Jordan. Let the men handle solving the mess this office is in."

Roxanne fought for energy she barely possessed at the moment to remain calm, and not to fly at the bastard who stood behind her tossing insults. Taking the man on would only make matters worse and would make it harder for her to think. She watched the coffee drip into the pot.

"If you don't have any work to do, Ralph, then take the day off. Otherwise get the hell out of my office and get to work." She barely kept her cool but was proud of herself for not screaming at him. He wasn't worth it.

Roxanne wasn't sure if Ralph grunted or used profanity. But when she turned around with her steaming cup of coffee he no longer stood in the doorway. She blew on the hot drink and walked back to her desk. It was time for action, she told herself, and sitting there trying to wake up was only wasting time.

She left Jordan's office and walked down the hall to Aaron's office. She didn't see Ralph but the smell of cigar smoke through his closed door led her to believe the man had returned to his office. Once she flipped on the light and walked to Aaron's desk, she saw the light on the phone and realized Ralph was making a call.

Was he calling Jordan? Would he answer for Roger and not for her? Roxanne felt a sudden urge to be quick with her search and scanned Aaron's desk for any sign of what caused the young accountant to head up to Nebraska in such a rush. After several minutes, Roxanne realized her search was futile.

"Ralph?" Roxanne tapped on the man's office door and then opened it when he didn't answer.

"Hold on a moment," he said to whoever he spoke to on the phone.

Roxanne watched him push the hold button and then stare up at her as if she were a rude interruption. She gathered her strength to stare down the man and show him his crass behavior didn't daunt her.

"I'm headed up to Nebraska," she began and watched his mouth twist in what might be considered a smile. "I'm not going to get any answers here so I might as well head to the source of the problem. Since neither Jordan nor I will be in the office today, until either of us returns, you are in charge."

Roxanne could tell he didn't like that comment at all.

"Young lady, I—" Ralph began.

Roxanne held her hand up to silence him and continued speaking when he sputtered instead of commenting.

"Whether you like it or not, I am acting office manager in Jordan's absence. Now with both of us out of the office I trust you can run a smooth ship." Roxanne enjoyed the annoyed expression that quickly crossed the older man's face. She smiled coldly at him and turned to leave but then looked at him over her shoulder. "Feel free to let Jordan and this Mr. Dixon fellow know that I will find them once I get to Auburn."

Roxanne left the office walking tall, and feeling she had put the arrogant, pompous ass in his place, but by the time she reached her car she felt deflated again. Why wouldn't Jordan contact her if he knew Aaron had been arrested? She wouldn't accept the fact that their personal relationship would hinder his work. That wasn't Jordan.

Roxanne sat in her car for a minute with it idling, wondering what she would say to Jeannette when she called her. In her present state of mind, Roxanne just knew that if the woman broke down crying, Roxanne would start bawling right along with her. Roxanne needed advice and she needed to be thinking clearly. She knew where to turn, and picked up her cell phone, then punched in the auto-dial number for her best friend.

"Joanie, are you busy?" Roxanne asked when her friend answered the phone.

"I haven't left for the office yet," Joanie answered. "What's up?"

There was no way she could answer that question in just a few words. She let out a sigh, doing her best to organize her thoughts.

She kept wondering who Ralph Layette had been speaking to when she entered his office.

"Is everything okay?" Joanie's tone suddenly turned serious when Roxanne didn't respond right away.

Roxanne had to smile at her best friend's intuitiveness. Joanie was certainly in the right field.

"No, counselor, and I need your help." Roxanne decided to start driving, and switched her phone to her other hand, then rested it between her shoulder and cheek. "How much time do you have? I have a serious problem and need some professional advice. I know you're a sex therapist, and this isn't actually your area, but do you have a minute?"

"My first appointment isn't until nine. What's wrong?" Joanie asked.

Roxanne started explaining the problems that Hall Enterprises had with someone stealing cash from their client's accounts.

"I stumbled onto it while preparing the accounts for one of our largest clients who was in town this week," Roxanne explained. "He also found a few discrepancies and I had to walk him through them and then assure him that we were in the process of clearing up the problem."

"And he accepted that?" Joanie asked.

Roxanne remembered the lunch she'd had with Roger Uphouse and how Jordan had intervened in the parking lot. At the time, she'd thought that Jordan didn't want her seeing any other men. Now she wondered if Jordan had thought her guilty, and simply wanted her away from their client. Roxanne's head spun as she tried to keep the facts straight and not let her mind draw inaccurate conclusions based on her feelings. There were so many reasons why Jordan might not be answering her calls right now. No matter that he'd arrested the wrong man—and she was sure Aaron wasn't guilty. That didn't mean that Jordan might think she was guilty of some crime.

"I think that Mr. Uphouse was a bit preoccupied with trying to ask me out," Roxanne confessed, and then filled her friend in on the details of her time with the man and how Jordan had saved her from Roger's kinkiness.

"But when I realized Jordan was seeing other women, I broke it off with him." Roxanne continued with her explanation. "During all of that, Aaron Tipley started doing his own digging into files, and trying to figure out who the thief was."

"Did you and Jordan continue working together on the problem with the money disappearing after you broke it off with him?" Joanie asked.

Roxanne had reached the Interstate and made a quick decision to run by her house and grab a few things before heading north.

"Of course," Roxanne told her friend. "But then Aaron contacted me after I got home from your house. I was up almost all night last night, and now I need to go to Nebraska."

"Nebraska? Why are you headed there?" Joanie shrieked, obviously stunned.

Roxanne filled her friend in on the recent happenings, and Joanie listened without a word.

"Joanie, none of this makes any sense. And I'm not getting any answers sitting here. I need to go up there. Aaron is relying on me." Roxanne had reached her house and noticed Jeannette's car parked in front. She needed to get Jeannette so she could have her car—shit.

"You're right, it doesn't make sense," her friend agreed. "So now you're going to this town in Nebraska? What are you going to do there?"

"Well, I need to contact Jeannette first," Roxanne explained, and at the same time dreaded making the call to the very pregnant lady. "I know she'll be upset when I tell her that I'm headed north. She'll want to go with me but I really would rather do this alone. I have no idea what to expect, and I swear, Joanie, she looks ready to have that baby at any moment."

Roxanne entered her house and immediately went to her closet to grab a small suitcase she kept there. "What do you plan to do once you get to Nebraska?" Joanie asked.

Roxanne paused in the bathroom, hastily grabbing a few things, and then plopped down on the closed toilet lid. She took a deep breath, her head spinning. "Now I see why you're the best in your business," Roxanne chuckled.

Joanie's tone grew serious. "You can't just drive up there without a plan. I understand that you're panicking, and I would be too in your shoes. But right now you need to focus on a specific plan and you need to stick to it."

"You're right," Roxanne agreed, and stood once again as she dropped items from her bathroom cabinet into her small bag. "I know what I'm going to do once I get up there, but I doubt you'll like it."

"Tell me anyway," Joanie encouraged.

"I'm going to find out who Aaron Tipley thought was stealing money from our client's accounts and then I'm going to go after that person myself."

* * * * *

Jordan Hall stood with his arms crossed, just inside the small conference room at the Auburn, Nebraska, police station. Two police officers, along with Joe Dixon, sat around the table, the only piece of furnishing the room had to offer, and stared at a small thirteen-inch television screen. Jordan studied the screen as well, and listened to the recorded interview with Aaron Tipley. The young man appeared distraught, and fidgeted in his chair, continuously looking around the room, and then down at his hands.

The quiet whir of the old VCR, playing the tape of Aaron being interviewed after he was brought in, reminded Jordan of the budget this station had to work with in handling this arrest. Jordan wondered what he was doing here. He stared at a good accountant, who should be behind his desk at the moment, doing his job.

The police officers and the private detective Layette had hired discussed Jordan's affairs while watching the tape. Jordan didn't participate in the conversation though. There was a big hole in this entire mess. Something wasn't right.

"We checked out the location Tipley says those people were at," a young man in uniform said, looking away from the television and glancing at Jordan.

Jordan guessed the man not much older than Tipley, with the standard-issue crew cut, and a knick on his chin where he'd cut himself shaving.

"There wasn't anyone there," the officer reported.

"I drove to Auburn because that is where the last transaction took place." Aaron's voice sounded tinny on the recorded tape. "Once I had the routing information, I couldn't reach my employer and so drove up here."

The police officer doing the interview scribbled something on a pad. "What phone number did you use to try and contact your boss?" the officer on the tape asked Aaron.

Jordan watched the officers in the room stare at the TV screen. They had watched this recording last night and Jordan hadn't seen anything at that time that made the tape worth watching again.

"So who was on the phone?" Joe Dixon turned to face Jordan and glanced at the cell phone Jordan still held in his hand.

Jordan had left the room when his cell phone had rung. This small town had more pockets in it where his phone couldn't get a signal than any town Jordan had ever been in.

"Layette checked in," Jordan mumbled, not liking at all the way Dixon made him feel he had to account for his every action.

The detective nodded and then glanced to hear the comments of the two officers. Jordan studied Joe Dixon who was about the same age as Jordan's father, or how old his father would have been if he had still been alive.

Dixon was tall, slender, and well-built. His hair was silver, and he had pale green eyes that seemed to study everything longer than necessary. Jordan knew he had a very good track record as a private detective. He had studied up on Dixon during the time he had to kill the night before while they booked Aaron. The man had solved every case he'd been on for the past five years. Prior to that, he'd served thirty years on the Kansas City police force. His record was impeccable.

Dixon turned his attention back to Jordan.

"How is everything going at the office?" the detective asked.

"Sounds like things are going fine," Jordan said, deciding not to tell the detective that he had just found out that Roxanne was on her way up here.

Dixon stared at Jordan for a minute, and Jordan guessed the man thought he wasn't telling the detective everything. Well, he could just wonder about it. Jordan scowled, and felt the same sensation that had run through him more than once since they had arrived up here. They on a wild goose chase. He didn't know if Tipley was guilty or not. But if he was, Jordan had sure judged the young man wrong. And if he wasn't, then he'd go through hell and high water to make sure none of this went on the young man's record. Either way, there were still pieces to this puzzle that didn't make sense.

"How much longer are we going to be here?" Jordan asked, and the two officers turned their attention to him.

Dixon glanced at the two officers. He addressed the older of the two, a short thin man who wore wire-framed glasses. "I think we'll head out to find a bite to eat. You have our numbers if you find anything?"

"You want us to shake him up a bit?" the younger officer asked. "We can get a confession for you so you can wrap this up."

Jordan wanted to shake the officer up a bit. "No, let the man rest. He's been through enough." Jordan could tell the officers didn't like his response but at the moment he couldn't care less what they thought. "And let him call his wife. She's due to have a child soon, and probably worried sick about him."

The officers glanced at each other, but Jordan didn't wait to hear their comments. He turned and walked out of the small conference room and toward the front door of the station.

"You know the evidence against him is overwhelming," Dixon said once they were outside the police station. "We've confirmed that withdrawals were made from one of your client's accounts last night from a location here in town using a fraudulent card. We show up at Tipley's room and there is the account number to the exact same account. Why else would he be in this town?" Dixon waved his hand, gesturing as he looked up and down the street. "Do you think he's here to sightsee?"

"He didn't do it," Jordan mumbled, and left the detective standing there to walk over to his car. "And I won't have his life ruined by him sitting in that damned jail cell."

The town of Auburn, Nebraska wasn't that big. And Jordan knew if it wasn't for this ordeal, he would never have reason to be there. He had a room in the same motel where Aaron had been arrested the night before, which was the nicest place to stay in town. The community was small but it was a clean town and the people seemed friendly enough. None of that impressed Jordan right now however. His mood was dark and the scowl on his face matched how he felt.

Joe Dixon had told him they thought Roxanne was behind Aaron stealing money from the accounts. They had documented evidence of her being in contact with Aaron right around the same time several of the unauthorized withdrawals had occurred.

She had been in close contact with Roger Uphouse, and during the dates she had spent time with the man in person, someone had tampered with the accounts that reflected missing money.

It didn't sit right that she would have intentionally adjusted balances on any account. That simply wasn't characteristic of Roxanne. She had left him notes telling him of the discrepancies. She hadn't tried to hide them. Not to mention she wouldn't do anything to hurt him. No matter how difficult she was being right now, Roxanne cared about him. He knew she did.

But Dixon had shown him activity on the account that Layette had provided for him. Roxanne had been the only one who had accessed the accounts during the time in question. That knowledge left a sick feeling in his gut.

Then there was the handful of other accounts, all with money missing. And each time a discrepancy had been noted, it was Roxanne's personal login password that appeared as the person who had accessed the accounts.

Roxanne wasn't guilty. Jordan would stake his reputation on it. But proving her innocence was going to be damned hard to do while he was up here in this small town in the middle of nowhere. Jordan planned on telling Dixon he was headed home over breakfast.

"I think it would be a good idea to go over all the information we have while we're at breakfast." Dixon had caught up with Jordan and stood next to him as Jordan reached his Porsche.

"I can't imagine what else there is to discuss." Jordan didn't try to hide his contempt. "Personally, I don't think we're accomplishing a damned thing up here."

"I know it's frustrating trying to get all the pieces to add up." Dixon smiled and patted his shoulder. "You're a man of action, Jordan, just like your father. But if you'll allow me just a bit more time, I think we can wrap this up with the facts painted clear enough to satisfy all of us."

Jordan nodded and reached for his door handle. As long as the facts didn't paint Roxanne as guilty, he would be satisfied.

"I need to run by the motel room to gather all the files," Dixon said. "I hear there is a decent restaurant a few blocks from here and we can have a nice breakfast. How about if we meet there in about forty-five minutes?"

"That's fine." Maybe a shower and fresh clothes would help his mood, although he seriously doubted it.

An hour later he sat across from Dixon and listened to a cute, young waitress tell them about their morning specials. She caught Jordan watching her and smiled.

"You two aren't from Auburn, are you?" she asked.

The woman was short, with breasts that were a bit too large. The material of her T-shirt stretched tightly across her chest, and then fell just above the waistline of her jeans. Jordan got a glimpse of a tanned and muscular tummy. The woman was in good shape, although she didn't hold a flame to Roxanne. He wondered where she was at the moment. If she'd left Kansas City right after Layette told him she was headed up then she would be in Auburn soon.

Jordan returned the smile although he felt like scowling. "Just got here last night," he offered. "I think I'll have toast and coffee."

"Good man," she answered. "A heavy breakfast isn't good for the waistline."

The waitress ran her hand over her belly, showing just a bit more of that tight and well-tanned abdomen. There would have been a time when he would have enjoyed casually flirting with a waitress—it almost always resulted in much better service. All he could think of right now though was where was Roxanne. This town wasn't that big. He needed to call her, verify where she was, and make sure she came straight to him as soon as she arrived.

The waitress turned her attention to Dixon. "Do you see anything you like?" she asked, applying the same flirtatious grin to the older investigator.

"Sounds like I should definitely have the same." Dixon smiled, and Jordan watched the older man's gaze drop to the waitress's well-endowed breasts.

"I'll have everything over here to you two gentlemen in just a sec," she said with a smile, and looked from one man to the next. "Now you two let me know if there is anything else that you want."

Dixon watched the waitress walk away and then turned his attention to Jordan, still smiling.

"You get the feeling there's more here to order than what you see on the menu?" he asked.

Jordan didn't give a damn about the waitress and wished the detective wasn't so damned cheerful when there was so much to deal with at the moment.

The door to the restaurant opened, and Jordan turned his attention to the young woman who entered.

"I don't believe it," Dixon muttered.

The two men watched as Roxanne marched straight over to their table, and Jordan was sure he had never seen her so enraged.

Chapter Twelve

&

Roxanne took a deep breath to calm her nerves as she approached Jordan Hall. She had counted herself lucky after checking into the only decent motel the town had to offer, and then asked the motel clerk if Jordan Hall had a room there as well. The clerk had told her that she had just missed him, and then had leaned forward confidentially.

"Is he your boyfriend?" the clerk had asked while popping gum.

Roxanne had guessed the woman working at the motel to be no more than twenty years old at the most. The name tag on the uniform the lady wore said "Dana", and she was a bit too skinny with large freckles. Roxanne felt a protective urge race through her, and she wanted to tell the woman yes, that he was, and to quit drooling over him. But Roxanne blamed the emotion on lack of sleep and simply smiled at the lady.

"He's my boss," she had told the clerk.

"Well, you'll find him over at the diner." And the clerk had given her directions. "I'd jump his bones in a second. He's a hottie," the clerk had called after her.

Roxanne scowled at the brightness of the sun as she returned to her car, and headed in the direction the motel clerk had told her would get her to the diner.

Her reserve had quavered as she noticed Jordan's Porsche, and parked a few stalls from it. But she had driven up here to confront him and to get to the bottom of this mess. Joanie had advised her to be straightforward with Jordan and that was what she intended to do.

Aaron Tipley was in jail for no reason. His wife hadn't stopped crying since he'd been arrested. And Roxanne worried for the woman's health as well as for her unborn child. She intended to get to the bottom of this and get that innocent man out of jail and back to his wife.

"What in the hell do you think you're doing?" Roxanne hadn't planned on exploding the second she saw Jordan. But those were the first words out of her mouth.

"I think I'm getting ready to have breakfast," he said, and pulled out the chair next to him and patted it. "Sit," he instructed.

Roxanne slumped into the chair Jordan offered her and then sized up the man who was with Jordan. She held out her hand. "I'm Roxanne Isley, and you are?"

"Joe Dixon, I'd like you to meet Roxanne Isley," Jordan said, in a tone so pleasant that Roxanne wanted to laugh.

"Did you know she was coming up here?" Mr. Dixon apparently didn't see the need to be as chivalrous as Jordan.

"Yes," Jordan answered, wanting to advise the detective that he better treat her with respect.

"Well, this is rather interesting." Joe leaned back in his chair, crossing his arms over his chest while he stared at Roxanne. "Do you care to tell me what brings you to Auburn, Nebraska? Or have you been here a while?"

During the drive up there, she had rehearsed how she would handle these men. She had been cool and professional with Layette and she could be the same with the detective and Jordan. Roxanne took a deep breath and opened her mouth to speak, when a busty waitress bounced up next to her.

"Hi, sweetie," the waitress said, and beamed at her like they were best of friends. "Can't say I blame you for joining these two handsome men. What can I get for you?"

Roxanne wasn't sure she could eat a thing. Her mind was geared up for her confrontation and the switch in conversation left her at a lack for a response. She glanced down at the laminated sheet on the table that listed the items for breakfast.

Her vision blurred for a second and she couldn't think of anything that sounded good.

"Bring her some orange juice," Jordan spoke up.

"Have it here in a jiffy." The waitress bounced off.

Roxanne placed her elbows on the table and steepled her hands in front of her. All her fight seemed to drain out of her and suddenly she felt defeated and tired.

"I haven't done anything wrong," she said quietly, not looking at either man. "And neither has Aaron Tipley. I came up here to tell you that you've arrested the wrong man."

"You might do best not to say anything until you have an attorney," Dixon suggested.

Dixon thought she was lying.

She studied his firmly set jawline, straight nose, and gray, almost white, hair that was cut short. Overall, she found nothing about him that stood out, which was probably to his advantage if he made his living snooping around and gathering information for others.

"Here's your orange juice, sweetie," the waitress said, and Roxanne looked up at her and managed a smile. "Do you want to order anything to eat?"

The waitress placed a large glass in front of Roxanne and then put a tall, plastic pot of coffee in the center of the table.

"Bring her some toast, too," Jordan said, and for once Roxanne was grateful for him making the decision for her.

She waited until the waitress had walked away from the table and then stared at Joe Dixon. He poured himself some coffee and blew on the hot brew before glancing up and then raising a quizzical eyebrow at her. She felt her anger from earlier return and relied on it to fuel her energy level.

"There is no reason for me to have a lawyer, Mr. Dixon," she said quietly, and then enjoyed a cool sip of her orange juice. "I haven't done anything wrong and if you have any evidence then it would have to be fabricated."

Now he appeared amused. She wanted to slap that smug look off his face.

"How long will you be here in town, Miss Isley?"

"I drove up here to find out what the hell was going on." Roxanne heard her voice quaver and knew if she didn't calm herself quickly she would explode. The man acted as if she was a criminal. "And I have no idea how long that will take," she added, "but it would be nice to be back home soon."

"It won't go well for you if you try to run," Mr. Dixon said.

"Try to run?" Roxanne wanted to throw her juice in the man's face but she wouldn't stoop to childish behavior. She forced herself to remain calm. "Why would I run when I intentionally drove up here to find out why one of our accountants is in jail?"

She turned her attention to Jordan. "And I wouldn't have had to make the trip if you had answered any of my calls."

"I don't mind at all that you're here," Jordan said over his cup of coffee.

"Jordan has been advised not to respond to any of your phone calls." Joe Dixon offered the information casually and then leaned back when the waitress returned to their table.

"Toast all the way around," she said cheerfully and placed plates in front of each of them. "And here's a bowl of jams and honey so you all can just pick what you like. I'm right over there if there's anything else you want."

Roxanne didn't look up until the waitress had left them again. She stared at her toast and knew she couldn't take a bite of it.

"Well, since you seem to have taken the role of Mr. Hall's spokesperson," Roxanne began, no longer able to hide the venom in her tone, "maybe you can tell me why an innocent man is sitting in jail up here instead of being at home in Kansas City, and at work earning his living? You ask me how long I'm going to be here and then advise me not to run. First Aaron and now me. Mr. Dixon, do you make a habit out of arresting innocent people?"

"He has been booked on solid charges, ma'am," Joe Dixon said, and sounded less friendly than he had a minute ago.

The detective set his jaw, looking very much like he didn't want to discuss this with her. She glanced at Jordan. He met her gaze with eyes so black and penetrating that she felt her very soul being exposed for his perusal. She stared at him and managed to swallow but found all her thoughts had faded and a much more primal emotion had surfaced. She bit her lower lip until it hurt, and the pain helped clear her head just a bit.

"Do you think Aaron is guilty?" she asked.

"I have a feeling he had some help." Dixon spoke before Jordan could.

"No. I don't." Jordan didn't take his gaze from her.

She looked absolutely exhausted and more determined than he'd ever seen her. He was damned glad she was here, though. He didn't doubt she'd been going over every file, but her password showing up on the computers and her being the last to access the accounts in question, was incriminating her. At least with her by his side, he could keep her out of trouble.

"Jordan." Dixon sounded stern, reprimanding. "It's probably not a good idea to discuss this case with her right now." He focused on Roxanne. "I don't suppose you would mind answering a few questions."

Roxanne placed her glass of juice, now half empty, down on the table. She reached for her purse, pulled out a five-dollar bill and placed it on the table, then stood and stared at the two men.

Jordan stood also and picked up the bill to hand back to her. "I can pay for your meal, Roxanne."

"You aren't allowed to talk to me," she snapped. "You better sit down and be good before you get in trouble."

She ignored the bill he tried to return to her.

"I came up here to figure out why you arrested an innocent man," she snapped. "And obviously talking to the two of you is wasting my time."

She marched out of the restaurant. It didn't surprise her a bit to find Jordan on her heels.

"Jordan," she heard Joe Dixon call.

The fresh air felt good on her burning eyes. Jordan moved in alongside her as she headed toward her car.

"Shouldn't you get back inside before you get in trouble?" Roxanne wasn't sure where she would go now, maybe to the police station.

But she knew she couldn't talk to Jordan right now without exploding. The detective had made it sound like she was out of line for discussing this case. And she was too pissed and tired to hear the same from Jordan.

"Jordan!" Joe Dixon hurried out of the restaurant, his wallet in hand.

She turned to see the man try to stuff the wallet into his back pants pocket as he approached them. His expression showed his annoyance that he'd been walked out on.

Well, good! She was glad she wasn't the only one who was annoyed.

Jordan turned to confront his private investigator. "Do you think those cops downtown can do a better job of questioning her than you or I can?" he hissed at the man.

Joe Dixon wasn't daunted. He stared at Jordan, not answering immediately, and then turned his gaze to Roxanne. She could feel the testosterone running thick through the air. Roxanne wouldn't call these two friends but she had a feeling that the two men had known each other prior to Mr. Dixon being contracted to find Hall Enterprises' thieves. There was that relaxed air between the two of them. Neither was sizing the other up. They appeared to know and appreciate the other's abilities and now would counter each other over who would do what.

She studied both of them as they slowly turned their attention toward her. Both were casually dressed in jeans with haggard expressions lining their faces, although Jordan had a sex appeal that emanated from him, and Roxanne could feel the strength of it consume her like a strong drink.

She shouldn't have any feelings toward Jordan, yet just standing here, she wanted him. More than anything she would love for him to pull her into his arms, hold her, let her feel his hard body pressing against hers.

But all he had wanted was to use her, possess her like some kind of trinket, and then prance off to whichever woman he chose to be with next.

Not to mention that he hadn't called her the night before. She worked alongside him, almost as a partner, yet he hadn't deemed it worth his time to consult with her before going after Aaron. That showed her what he thought of her mind. All he wanted was her body.

Roxanne reminded herself of these facts as she stood so close to him that she could lean into him with the slightest of effort. That broad, strong chest was close enough that she could feel his power, smell his cologne.

"Miss Isley," Joe Dixon said, ignoring the question Jordan had just asked him. "I can appreciate that you're running scared right now but if you will talk to the two of us, explain everything to us, I'm sure things will go much easier for you."

"Until you get the notion out of your head that I'm some kind of criminal," Roxanne said, as she balled her hands into fists, "then I have no desire to talk to either one of you."

Roxanne turned around quickly, allowing her hair to fly over her shoulder, and yanked her car door open. She felt lightheaded for a moment from her quick movement and lack of sleep, but the car door braced her and she felt certain that neither man noticed. She slid into her seat behind the steering wheel and then slammed her car door shut.

"Jordan," she heard Mr. Dixon yell, as Jordan bounded over to his own car and then disappeared from her sight.

Roxanne didn't bother to watch what the private investigator did but started her car up and backed out of her stall and into the street. She could see Jordan's Porsche appear in her rearview mirror and knew that if he planned on following her that there was no way she could outrun him in her Probe.

Tears stung her eyes, yet she accelerated slowly, grateful for the small town and the few cars on the road during the middle of the day. At the end of the block she slowed and then stopped at the flashing red light that hung from wires above the intersection. Roxanne drew a blank when she tried to remember which way to turn to get back to the motel. She could see Jordan's Porsche idling behind her through her rearview mirror, and didn't want to just sit here and look like a fool.

"I can't believe he would think that I would steal from him," she cried out, and pounded her steering wheel with her fist.

The tears fell from her eyes, tracing a moist path down her cheeks. Jordan remained behind her as she slowly managed to find her way through the small town, and when she pulled into the motel parking lot, she noticed another car behind the Porsche enter the lot too. Roxanne guessed Joe Dixon had followed as well.

Roxanne parked and pulled her motel key from her purse and glanced at the number. She stared through tear-blurred vision at the green doors that lined the two-story motel. She felt more than drained as she got out of the car and started to walk toward the building.

"I'm going to talk to her alone and that is final," she heard Jordan say from behind her, but she ignored the rest of the conversation.

She had driven up here to help, to do what she could to get Aaron Tipley out of jail. But even in her current state of exhaustion, she knew that if she walked into the jail, more than likely they would arrest her too. She couldn't afford to end up in a jail cell when there was a thief running free and probably laughing at all of them right now.

Jordan reached her before she reached her motel door and tried to take her motel key from her hand.

"Leave me alone," she cried, and pulled her hand back so he couldn't take the key.

A strong arm wrapped around her shoulders and her face was smashed into Jordan's broad chest. His scent consumed her senses, and Roxanne felt herself grow weak. Jordan's hand slipped over her hand that held the key and took it from her without resistance on her part. "I have no intention of leaving you alone, lady," he whispered into her hair.

"You aren't going to do anyone any good when you're so upset," he continued as he unlocked the door, and with his arm still around her, led her into the room.

She didn't fight him and he guided her to the table next to the closed curtains and pulled out a chair for her to sit. She plopped down and all he could do for a moment was stroke her hair, wanting more than anything to ease her frustration, assure her that everything would be fine in no time. Unfortunately, he had no idea how long it would take to clear up this mess.

The door to the motel room remained open and Joe Dixon appeared in the doorway.

"So what Layette tells me is true then?" Dixon asked. "The two of you have some sort of relationship?"

"Yes." Jordan didn't hesitate. He had no desire to keep Roxanne a secret. Roxanne stood, not commenting, and headed toward the bathroom. He watched her go, wanting to go with her, comfort her. But unless she planned on crawling out of the window, she wasn't going anywhere. And regardless of Dixon and Layette's suspicions, he had no doubt of her innocence.

"Jordan, be very careful," Dixon said, still standing in the doorway. "We've discussed all of this and you agreed with me when you were thinking clearly, that what I said had merit."

Roxanne didn't quite understand Joe Dixon's words, but she didn't like the sound of them. She turned before reaching the alcove leading to the bathroom and faced the man in her doorway, silhouetted by the bright morning sun.

"I'm not sure what you are implying, Mr. Dixon," she said coldly, "but I will make one thing perfectly clear. Mr. Hall told you we had a relationship, not me. This man is pursuing me, not the other way around. I'm not trying to wrap my legs around anyone, and I am definitely not stealing the man's money."

The room was silent. Both men stared at her. She turned and left them to enter the bathroom, and felt a smug satisfaction in slamming the door on them.

Chapter Thirteen

ଔ

When Roxanne left the bathroom some time later, she was rather surprised to discover she was alone in the motel room. She stood in the middle of the room for a minute, somewhat disappointed that Jordan had left her.

"I guess your words hit home," she said to herself, and wandered over to peek out the window.

Roxanne pulled the drapes to the side far enough to notice Jordan's Porsche remained parked in the lot. She saw no one outside however, and let the drape fall with a sigh.

"So now what do I do," she mumbled, and walked over to where her bag and laptop sat.

She had packed so quickly prior to driving up there that she'd forgotten the plug for her laptop. She turned it on, and noticed the icon appear announcing the battery was low. Then to make matters worse, the room didn't have a cable hookup for the Internet. This trip to Nebraska, which at first had seemed like a good idea, now began to feel like an utter waste of her time. She needed to do something to get Aaron out of jail, but if she walked into that jail Roxanne feared she would be behind bars with him.

And that thought terrified her. Roxanne had always been the good girl. Even as a child she'd been crushed if her parents or teachers reprimanded her for the slightest thing. She'd been raised to carry her own weight, stand on her own two feet. For the life of her, she didn't see why Joanie thought she needed a strong man. She was strong on her own. And somehow she would muddle her way through this mess.

But it sure would be nice to have Jordan at your side while you figured things out.

"Well, damn." Roxanne stared at the laptop, virtually useless to her without Internet access.

Someone tapped on her motel room door and her heart started a mean pounding in her chest. She stood, trepidation coursing through her, and slowly opened it, peeking out into the bright sunlight.

"Hi, are you Roxanne?" The young lady smiled, and Roxanne remembered her as the waitress who'd served them at the café.

"I left money for my food." Roxanne would scream if she ended up in trouble in this small town for walking out without paying her tab. "Did the men I was with not pay my portion of the bill?"

Roxanne turned and looked around for her purse, as a knot formed in her stomach.

"Oh no," the woman said behind her. "The bill was paid, and you all left me a very nice tip. Thank you."

Roxanne quit searching for her purse and watched the woman place a bag on the table.

"One of the men you were with came back. Jordan Hall…that's it. He paid me nicely to drive over here and bring you breakfast." The young woman pulled a Styrofoam container from the bag, and also one long-stemmed red rose wrapped in pale green paper. "And he said to give this to you."

"He sent you over here to bring me breakfast?" Roxanne brought the rose to her nose and inhaled its fragrance. She didn't think Jordan capable of such a kind act and she held the flower to her nose, not sure what to say.

"You've got a keeper there," the woman said, and opened the container to show scrambled eggs and bacon with sliced toast on the side. "I thought you stormed out of there all upset. Is he sending you all of this to make up for being an ass?"

The woman looked at her, curiosity flaring in her expression.

"I guess you don't have strangers enter your restaurant that often and then make a scene," Roxanne said, and took a step closer to inspect the food.

"If there is new blood in Auburn, we locals notice them," the woman agreed with a chuckle. "Where are you all from?"

An idea struck Roxanne and she pulled out a chair, gesturing for the lady to sit. The woman did it willingly, and slid the food toward Roxanne. Roxanne wondered if maybe the woman would have noticed the thieves in town. But how could she approach such a subject with this stranger?

"Has any other stranger shown up recently?" Roxanne sat down opposite the woman, and picked up the pack of white plastic silverware. She ripped it open. "Possibly in the last couple days?" she added.

The woman chewed her lip, taking the question seriously and giving it some thought.

"You all are FBI, aren't you?"

Roxanne was taken back by the question. "Hardly," she muttered.

"Then why are all three of you here?" The woman leaned forward, putting her elbows on the table. "I doubt you know anyone in this town or you all wouldn't have been eating at the diner and staying here at the motel."

"You should be the detective," Roxanne said, and the woman grinned broadly at her.

"I've seen every *Murder, She Wrote* episode," the woman said with pride. She held her hand out across the table. "I'm Emily."

"Hi, Emily." Roxanne took the offered hand and was greeted with a firm handshake. Emily's hand was cool and soft. Maybe Emily would be able to tell her if any strangers had been in town. She decided on a friendly approach. "I'm Roxanne Isley, and the man who ordered this breakfast for me is my boss."

"Just your boss?" Emily asked, and ran a fingernail over one of the petals of the rose that Roxanne had laid on the table in between them. "Shouldn't we find something to put this in?"

Roxanne glanced at the rose, more concerned with learning about anything that could get Aaron out of jail. Her mind fogged as she stared down at the red petals wrapped in the green paper. She fought the exhaustion that dared to creep up on her and ruin possibly her only chance at gathering information.

"I'm not sure what this room has to offer," Roxanne said, and gave a feeble look at the contents of the motel room.

"You just sit there and eat," Emily instructed. She hopped up out of her chair, and Roxanne envied the woman her energy. "I'll call down to the front desk and see if they don't have a vase you can borrow while you're here. Now what was it you were asking me?"

Roxanne waited while Emily picked up the phone and told the person at the other end what room she was in, and that she had brought over flowers. Emily had plopped herself on the edge of the bed, and motioned with her head and a smile that Roxanne should start eating. She continued to talk to the motel employee in a calm cheerful drawl that made Roxanne think there couldn't be a soul in the town who wouldn't love the woman.

"They're sending a vase over to you," Emily said, and placed the phone on the cradle that sat on the small dresser next to the bed. "Now what were we talking about?"

Roxanne slid her eggs around in the Styrofoam container as she swallowed a bite of bacon. "I drove up here," she began, and then searched for the best way to begin her query. "A friend of mine is in trouble," she started again, and then glanced up to see Emily watching her with a concerned expression. "He didn't do anything wrong and I need to find out who really did do it."

"Who did what?" Emily asked, and her pretty blue-green eyes grew wide as she studied Roxanne with a look of pure fascination.

Roxanne sighed, and scooped a small amount of egg onto her plastic fork then stared at it. She wondered if she should share the entire story with this stranger. What harm would it do? But then maybe in her sleep-deprived state she wasn't thinking clearly. She swallowed the eggs and stared at the closed curtains.

"Someone up here stole some money," Roxanne began, deciding a vague summary might be best for the time being. "And my friend tracked them on his computer and then drove up here to find them. But now he is being charged with the crime and I need to figure out who really did it so I can get him out of jail."

"I don't know a thing about computers," Emily said, and pulled one of her legs up so that her knee pressed against her over-ripe chest. The woman's faded blue jeans moved easily with her, and Roxanne felt somewhat homely sitting next to the relaxed waitress. "But my boyfriend is a whiz with them, although he doesn't get off work until six. Maybe he can help," Emily offered, grinning.

"Thanks for the offer," she said in between bites. "But I'm sure by now whoever took the money has left town."

"But you are sure they were here in Auburn?"

"That is why my friend came up here," Roxanne explained, and pushed the Styrofoam container to the side of the table. She felt the weight of the food in her stomach and hoped eating hadn't been a mistake. "But now he is in jail and I can't even find out from him what exactly he did know."

"Why not?" Emily frowned. "They won't even let you visit him?"

She hated to admit that she hadn't even tried.

"They think I helped him steal the money." Roxanne watched Emily's expression to see her reaction to her words.

Emily's eyes grew wide. "Did you?" she asked.

"No." Roxanne answered a bit too loudly and then sank back in her chair, kicking her sandals off underneath the table.

"I believe you." Emily reached over and patted Roxanne's hand. "So if you go talk to your friend, they are going to take you in too? Do the cops know that you're here?"

"I'm not sure." Roxanne hadn't thought of that and glanced again at the curtains, wondering if she should expect them to show up at any minute to arrest her. "The men I was with at breakfast might have told them."

Emily scoffed at Roxanne's words and held up the rose wrapped in paper. "Why would a man send a lady a rose and then call the police on her?"

Roxanne didn't have an immediate answer for that one. Emily slid the Styrofoam container toward her, closed the cover, and then hopped up to deposit it into the small trash can.

"Well, it sounds to me like you need some help. What I could do," Emily began, and then turned to face Roxanne, "I mean if you are willing to let me help, I could go to the jail for you and ask your friend the questions that you want to ask him."

"Oh no," Roxanne said, and shook her head. "You don't need to bother doing that."

"So what are you going to do?" Emily asked.

Roxanne didn't answer right away. She really had no idea what to do at this point. She stared at the room, and the large bed covered with a royal green comforter beckoned her.

A knock on the motel room door made Roxanne jump. Emily studied her for just a second and then stood up, since she sat closer to the door, and opened it.

"Your vase is here," she said, and Roxanne sighed with relief that it wasn't the police arriving to read her the Miranda rights.

Roxanne unwrapped the rose and placed it in the vase while Emily chatted with the person at the door. After putting water in the vase, Roxanne placed the pretty flower on top of the dresser and fingered it a moment. Where was Jordan right now?

"Well, I'll get out of your hair," Emily said from behind Roxanne. "Here is my name and number," she added, scribbling it on to the pad next to the phone. "Call me if you can think of anything that you might need help with."

"Thanks for chatting with me," Roxanne said. "And if you think of anyone you've seen in the past couple days who wasn't from around here…"

"I'll let you know," Emily finished for her.

Roxanne grabbed one of her business cards from her briefcase and handed it to Emily.

"You're from Kansas City?"

Roxanne nodded and then held the door as Emily left the motel room, and walked across the parking lot. Roxanne noticed the Porsche wasn't out there before she shut the door and turned to stare at the empty motel room. Maybe a quick nap would help her to think more clearly.

Thirty minutes later, Roxanne woke out of a very deep sleep to the sound of her cell phone ringing. She stared at the local number that meant nothing to her.

"Hello," she said, stretching under the covers while she fought the sleep that had settled so deeply in her brain.

"Did I wake you up?" A female voice on the other end sounded cheerful, but concerned.

"It's okay." Roxanne had no idea who she was talking to. "May I help you?"

"This is Emily," Emily said. "And I know you told me I didn't need to help but I didn't have anything better to do so I went to the jail for you."

"What?" Roxanne stood up and stared at herself in the wide mirror that hung on the wall above the dresser. "Emily, that was nice of you but you didn't need to do that."

"Well, you're right." Emily chuckled. "Your friend has been released. At least I assume he was your friend since he was the only person they had there who was from Kansas City. I was told that he is headed back home."

Roxanne absently ran a hand over her hair as she stared at herself in the mirror and tried to digest what Emily had just told her.

"Aaron is out of jail?" Roxanne wondered if that meant they had found who really had taken the money. "Did they arrest someone else?"

"I didn't think to ask," Emily said. "But I thought you would want to know."

"Yes," Roxanne said quickly. "And thank you. I guess that means I can head home now, too."

"Well, it was nice meeting you," Emily said. "If you're ever up this way again, look me up."

"I'll do that and you do the same if you're ever in Kansas City." Roxanne added her goodbyes, and then clicked her phone off and tossed it on the bed. She scratched her head, staring at herself in the mirror. She looked like shit. A shower was definitely in order. She looked down at the rose, standing tall and elegant in its vase, and then noticed a piece of paper next to it. Picking it up, she stared at the familiar handwriting.

"Sleep, beautiful lady. I'll see you back at the office." It wasn't signed but she knew Jordan's handwriting by heart.

Jordan had been in her room while she slept. And she hadn't been asleep that long. He had stood in this room, possibly looking down at her while she slept, and had taken time to write her a note.

She couldn't believe she hadn't woken up. A warm tingle rushed through her when she wondered if he'd touched her or simply had decided to let her sleep.

There was a side to Jordan she hadn't noticed before, a compassionate side. Bending over to sniff the rose, she wished she could get inside that man's head, figure out his intentions — before he made her nuts.

There wasn't a cloud in the sky as Roxanne pulled into her driveway. She'd enjoyed an uneventful drive home, singing along to the radio, and even taking time to check in at the office and call Jeannette Tipley, who was full of tearful gratitude. "Did you miss me?" she said to Matisse, who all but tripped her as she walked through the house.

The cat meowed a scratchy meow until Roxanne sat on the edge of her coffee table and indulged the cat in a nice back massage.

Her cell rang and she left the cat to find it on her dresser in her bedroom.

"Roxanne, this is Aaron," the voice said through the phone.

"Aaron." Roxanne smiled. "Are you home?"

"Yes, and we need to talk." His serious tone caused Roxanne's smile to fade.

"That sounds good," she said. "I want to know everything that happened."

"I think it would be a good idea if we met somewhere public, and discreet."

Roxanne frowned but hurried into her dining room for a pad of paper and pen when Aaron asked her to write down an address.

"And Roxanne," he said. "Don't tell anyone you're going to meet me there."

Chapter Fourteen

ഔ

The first thing she noticed as she approached Aaron, who sat in the last booth along the wall of the sandwich shop, was that he looked very pale and agitated. She couldn't blame him since the man had spent the night in jail, and then more than likely came home to a very distraught wife. But she wondered why he had picked such a run-of-the-mill place to eat, in such a faraway location. Roxanne had driven almost forty-five minutes to the town of Gladstone, and then followed Aaron's directions to the fast food sandwich shop located in a strip mall.

"How are you?" she asked, and slid into the booth to face him.

"I've quit my job," he said, and stared at her with bloodshot eyes.

"What?" she asked way too loud, and then looked around the establishment. The place was empty since the lunch hour had passed, and the after-work rush hadn't arrived yet. Roxanne shook her head. "I can't believe it."

"Mr. Hall called me while I was on my way home," Aaron told her.

"I'll talk to him," she said. "Did he ask you to quit?"

"No." Aaron met her gaze and then sipped through the straw of a large soda pop. "But I did the right thing. The firm can't afford the scandal."

"But you didn't do anything wrong," Roxanne argued.

"No, I didn't," Aaron agreed. "But my wife and I agree that it would be best if we went somewhere else, a new firm, a new city—somewhere where no one will know that I spent the night in jail." Roxanne opened her mouth to protest, but Aaron held up his hand to stop her, and then continued with his explanation.

"Mr. Hall and I had a good conversation, Roxanne." Aaron attempted a smile, but his dry lips spread over his teeth making him appear weak after a long sickness. "He was the one who had me released from jail, the charges dismissed, and wiped from my record."

This surprised her, and she leaned back in the booth, crossing her arms, to hear the rest of Aaron's story.

"He didn't offer me all of the facts, and I didn't feel it my place to ask questions, but I think Mr. Hall never believed me guilty. It took a while to complete paperwork before my release." Aaron paused and sipped at his soda. "And there was a heated argument going on somewhere in the jail while I was there."

"Now tell me why you went up to Nebraska in the first place," she began, feeling a need to sort out everything from the beginning to the point where they were now.

Aaron snapped open his briefcase, which sat next to him on his side of the booth, and pulled out a paper-clipped group of papers.

"I printed what I found out, although the police arrested me before I could show it to them," Aaron said, and pulled a couple sheets from the group, then handed them to Roxanne.

Roxanne studied the printout of an account showing a withdrawal of thirty thousand dollars. She sucked in air as she realized how the amount disappearing from Hall Enterprises was growing to an ungodly amount.

"And what is this?" Roxanne studied the other piece of paper Aaron had given her.

Aaron's grin looked sheepish. "A friend of mine is a hacker," he began. "He was able to find out exactly what computer requested the transaction."

"And that is how you knew it was someone in Auburn, Nebraska?" Roxanne stared at the information printed on the sheet.

"Yes, and while I drove up there, he kept researching the matter and informed me that the computer used was one at their public library. I managed to reach Auburn before the library closed, but apparently I wasn't the only one tracking the transaction." Aaron paused, and Roxanne watched him as he looked around the quiet eating establishment.

A radio playing some modern rock station could be heard from the room behind the counter, and a teenage boy sat at a far table refilling salt and pepper shakers, otherwise the two of them were alone.

"And that is when you were arrested?" Roxanne prompted, and Aaron turned his attention to her.

"Yes," he said, and then looked down at his hands.

She imagined how humiliating that moment had to be for the young man, fresh out of the service, with a budding career ahead of him.

"I hate to see you leave over all of this," Roxanne reached out and patted Aaron's hand. "You're an outstanding accountant. This is Hall Enterprises' loss."

"That's exactly what Jordan Hall said." Aaron pulled his hand out from under hers, and ran his fingers through his hair. "I have an interview with a company out in Montana."

"We're going to miss you. Why Montana?"

He smiled for the first time since she had arrived. "Mr. Hall told me of a business acquaintance of his out in Montana who could use a good broker. So he is helping me find new work.

"But Roxanne," Aaron continued, "there's more that I need to tell you."

"Yes," Roxanne agreed. "We still have a criminal at large, and he is going to suck Hall Enterprises dry if we don't try and stop him."

Aaron leaned back on his side of the booth and crossed his arms over his chest. "Do you hear what you just said?"

Roxanne frowned. What had she just said? She repeated her words in her head, and then looked at him, confused.

"It's okay. I made the same assumption." Aaron smiled as if he were trying to help her figure out a puzzle.

She wasn't in the mood for guessing games. "What are you talking about?"

"The one comment I heard the librarian say that stuck in my mind, was that I was the only man who had been in the library that entire afternoon."

Roxanne didn't understand. "I know it's a small town, but you were the only man?"

"Yes." Aaron nodded, as if she were supposed to understand something at this point.

"I still don't understand what you're trying to tell me," Roxanne said.

"We know the computer at that library was used to make the illegal transactions from the Hall Enterprises accounts. But the librarian said no men were there."

"So the thief is a woman?" Roxanne concluded with her question.

Aaron nodded. "Must be," he said.

She didn't know why she had concluded their thief would have been a man. And as small of a clue as it was, they had more information now then they had before.

"You know with a few casual questions," Roxanne began, thinking out loud, "we might be able to gather more information about this woman."

"You mean question the librarian?" Aaron asked.

"Sure." Roxanne straightened on her side of the booth. "I bet we could determine an age, and maybe even a description if we ask the right questions," she added, her mind already churning with how she would go about doing this.

"You're right, but who is going to approach this librarian?" Aaron asked.

Roxanne stared at him as she popped the last bit of the cookie into her mouth.

"What I mean is that my wife will divorce me if I go back up there again," Aaron explained.

Roxanne grinned. "Well, we can't have that. I'll go back up there myself and see what I can find out."

"I'm not sure that would be a good idea," Aaron said.

"Why not?" Roxanne asked.

"I think they still believe you might be that woman."

* * * * *

Jordan sat behind his desk, still at work, later that evening, and listened as Layette and Dixon brainstormed over their latest facts. The dull throb of a headache had escalated into a long stretch of pain ranging from the middle of his forehead clear to the center of his brain. Jordan hadn't been home yet since returning to town, and he wasn't sure that sitting there much longer would accomplish anything more.

The printouts strewn across the desk in front of him made him so angry he felt a need to throw something. Over one hundred and fifty thousand dollars had been taken from random accounts in small increments. Jordan lifted one of the printouts to compare the dates to several of the transactions below. If he ever got his hands on the person who apparently was out to ruin him and Hall Enterprises, that person would not live to see the next day.

Jordan had worked very hard over the past decade to build a solid reputation and one of the most successful businesses in the country. He had respect among his peers, and had begun receiving national attention. At his age, not many men could make that claim. And he would be damned if some thief would take him down.

"Jordan?" Layette asked in a tone that made Jordan realize it probably wasn't the first time the man had tried to get his attention.

Jordan scrambled in his thoughts to remember what the two men had been discussing.

"Tipley is satisfied with the arrangement you've made for him," Dixon prompted.

Jordan noticed the man looked as tired as Jordan felt. "Yes, and I've made arrangements for him to have an interview at the beginning of next month. His wife is ready to have their first child, so in the meantime, I've granted him paternity leave."

"With pay?" Layette asked.

"Hell yes, with pay," Jordan grumbled, and frowned at the older man. "I've set Aaron Tipley up with a deal any man would jump at. I doubt he will be giving us any grief."

"Damn good thing," Layette mumbled, and stared down at an unlit cigar he held between his finger and thumb.

"I made it clear from the beginning that none of my employees would steal from me. I don't have that type of crew here." Jordan stood and looked out at the dark city through his window. "You sent me on a wild goose chase today and wasted my time. That won't happen again. I'll wish you two good night, and don't expect to hear from either of you again until you have something substantial to show me."

Jordan waited until the two men had left, and then walked into the outer office. He secured the alarm, and made a mental note that he would have to change the combination code on the alarm system. His thoughts strayed to Roxanne, and he wondered where she was right now. Both Layette and Dixon had commented on her absence from the office that day, and although Dorothy had confirmed that Roxanne had taken the day off, Jordan couldn't help but agree that it would have helped in her plea for innocence if she had made an appearance at work.

Jordan waited until he was on the road, and then picked up his cell phone and called Roxanne. She answered on the second ring. Well, at least she acknowledged his phone calls.

"Where are you?" she asked, instead of saying hello.

Jordan felt his insides tighten at the sound of her voice. She didn't sound like she was in a very good mood, but he had no doubts he could handle her.

"I was about to ask you the same question," he said.

"I'm standing behind my car, which is parked in your driveway. Now would you mind telling me where you are?"

Jordan had no idea why she would be at his house but he had every intention of finding out. "I'll be there within five minutes."

She hung up the phone at her end and Jordan accelerated underneath the Interstate sign that told him he had a mile and a half until his exit.

Chapter Fifteen

ഇ

Roxanne paced up and down the stone path that wound its way toward the very large estate in front of her. She stared at the varying shapes of rock that made up the path, and the perfectly manicured grass on either side. Hedges trimmed to perfection lined the brick wall that closed in the courtyard and prevented her from reaching the front door of the home. She had tried pushing the button on the intercom system built into the wall next to the black-iron gate that closed her out, but no one had answered.

Roxanne knew a small amount of history on Jordan Hall. She knew his father had worked hard to make a name for himself in the city, and had died of a heart attack while Jordan was in college. She didn't know a thing about Jordan's mother, other than the fact that Jordan had never mentioned her. Roxanne did know that everything she saw around her, Jordan had worked hard to obtain. The man hadn't been left a fortune by his father—Jordan had worked hard to get where he was, and this fine home showed how successful he had become.

Whoever was stealing from Hall Enterprises could ruin Jordan if they weren't stopped. Roxanne knew that to be the unspoken truth of the matter, and that with every day, Jordan faced the possibility of scandal that could mar his reputation beyond repair. They had clues though, and after an afternoon of aggravation over the thought that she was a prime suspect, Roxanne had decided that the best thing to do was to confront Jordan and share with him what she knew. Regardless of how he treated her personally, they had a business alliance, and as an employee of Hall Enterprises, Roxanne would show her loyalty.

She turned as headlights turned onto the quiet street. As the car turned into the driveway and Roxanne heard the sound of the garage door open, her heart began pounding and her palms grew damp.

"You can handle this man," she whispered to herself, and held her head high as she walked toward the car that parked in the dark garage.

Roxanne walked into the garage without hesitating and stood with her arms crossed as the garage door slid down, preventing her departure. Her eyes adjusted to the darkness, and she watched as Jordan opened his car door and stood with briefcase in hand, to stare down at her. He still wore the clothes he'd had on in Nebraska and Roxanne wondered if he'd dressed that way all day at the office. Knowing how often he worked late, she didn't find it surprising that he would be just now coming home, especially considering the serious issues that needed to be resolved.

Jordan closed his car door, but didn't move from where he stood in front of her. Roxanne clenched her hands to her waist, keeping her arms crossed, as if that small barrier would prevent her from feeling the sensations that rippled through her at Jordan's nearness. His broad chest was a mere foot in front of her, and she could smell his cologne, as well as the manly scent that seemed to intoxicate her whenever she was this close to him. Everything she had come here to talk to him about, the crisis that lay pending if they didn't resolve it soon, all of the matters at hand seemed to dissipate in a fog of uncontrollable desire that racked her senses.

Roxanne raised her head to look into his eyes, and his dark gaze met hers in a silent greeting. She knew he felt the same desire for her that she felt for him. And what terrified her was the knowledge that he knew how he could control her. Focusing on her breathing, she worked to regain control of her senses, and pulled her gaze from his as she turned her focus on the door leading to the kitchen.

"If you have a minute I'd like to speak with you," she said, turning to show him that she wasn't impressed by how sexy he looked at the moment.

The expression that crossed his face told her that she had failed. "We'll have more than a minute of time," he told her, and turned to lead the way into his house.

Roxanne didn't follow Jordan as he led her into the main portion of his home, and then began ascending a very wide staircase. She assumed he would change and then join her. Jordan didn't say a word when she chose not to follow him, and she chanced a glance as he disappeared at the top of the stairs. He had left her to browse through his home so Roxanne decided to do just that.

She stood in the living room, which appeared to be about the size of her house. Elegant furniture that could have been right out of a showroom, and without a trace of dust on it, had been arranged throughout the room. Roxanne felt like she walked through a model mansion, as if this one was just a sample of how a person could live if they made the big time. She left the living room, deciding it said nothing about Jordan, and sauntered down a hallway toward the next room. All walls in this room had heavy wooden shelves lining them, and every shelf was full of thick hardback books. The smell of the heavy bound books filled her nostrils as she faced one of the shelves and surveyed its contents.

She ran her finger idly over the leather bound backs of a row of books, and recognized names of classic literature, as well as poetry, and texts on government and law, finance and advertising. The books appeared to be a general assortment that could appeal to anyone, but she wondered if Jordan had read any of them or if they simply had been shelved for appearance.

She left the books, and ran her fingers over the ivory keys of a beautiful grand piano, and then studied the exquisite carvings in the wood surrounding a large fireplace, before settling her gaze on large glass doors that led to a patio along the back side of the house. Roxanne walked to the doors, feeling the thickness of the carpet through her sandals, and then flicked the lock so she could open them. A beep told her that an alarm system had acknowledged the doors being opened, and

Roxanne wondered if that beep would bring Jordan running. It dawned on her that the idea appealed to her, and she stepped out onto the long wooden deck that could easily hold a party of fifty people or more.

She left the glass doors open and crossed over the wooden floor toward the latticed fence that bordered the deck, and gazed at the extensive flower garden that spread for some distance before a thick row of trees began, which possibly bordered the property.

A fresh, wood scent filled her nostrils as she crossed the deck. The smell of the garden perfumed the air, a mixture of aromas from the roses that bordered the deck, to a variety of flowers she couldn't identify in the dark.

She could smell pine through the slight breeze, and recognized the shape of the trees at the edge of the large yard. The night air was cool against her skin and she wrapped her arms around herself as she leaned against the railing and stared across the picture-perfect landscape.

Footsteps creaked on the deck behind her and Roxanne turned to see Jordan, matching her attire in blue jeans. A black T-shirt hugged his torso, and he'd tucked the shirt into his jeans, allowing her to see ripples of muscles and a flat, well-toned stomach that she already knew was covered with downy black hair. The floodlights attached to the side of the house shadowed his expression and made his black hair shine like raw silk.

"You're drooling," Jordan drawled as he walked over to where she stood. The smell of soap clung to him as he came to stand next to her.

"I am not!" Roxanne turned to stare across the yard again, feeling as if she'd just been caught with her hand in the cookie jar. "We need to talk," she said, and they needed to keep the conversation on a professional level. "My hands are tied in trying to assist in finding this thief and I don't like it."

Jordan rested his hip against the railing so that he faced her, and Roxanne did her best not to look in his direction. She saw his hand rise toward her face, and quickly walked away from him along the edge of the railing.

Already just being in his presence had her aching to be with him. But that wouldn't solve any of their problems. Not to mention she'd already broken it off with him. Although apparently he seemed to think them a couple now — as memories of him telling the detective they were in a relationship echoed through her.

Damn it. She needed to keep her thoughts focused.

"I've never been accused of committing any crime before," she continued. "And if it weren't for that investigator of yours implying my guilt, I could possibly have found more information out about our thief."

"What information do you think you could gather?" Jordan asked.

He needed to keep his distance, but he ached to fuck her until she screamed, and then discuss these matters. It had been one hell of a long day already, and more than anything he'd like a few hours alone with Roxanne, upstairs, in his bed. Watching her now, dressed so casually in her faded jeans and T-shirt, she still stirred him to life more than any woman ever had before.

The floodlight on the porch captured auburn highlights in her hair, which fell past her shoulders. Her T-shirt hugged her torso, showing off her narrow waist the way she had it tucked into her jeans. And that ass, her sweet ass, curved so perfectly. Her jeans hugged her just right, accentuating the way her thighs met her rear end. He focused on that spot just at the end of her ass that he would love to run his tongue along, make her entire body quiver.

Roxanne turned to face him but hadn't realized he'd moved closer to her. Her nose just about brushed his chest and she stepped backward, almost tripping over a deck chair she hadn't noticed.

"I wanted to talk to the librarian," she said, as she sidestepped the chair. "Aaron told me that she mentioned he'd been the only man in there that day."

Jordan reached for her arm as she stumbled around the chair, and his long fingers scraped against her skin. Just touching her hardened every inch of him.

She slipped away from the touch, and again walked along the railing. He felt the odd sensation that a game of cat and mouse was underway.

"And when did you talk to Aaron?" Jordan followed her along the side of the deck, knowing now what she'd done all day.

'Today. He invited me to lunch to explain everything that happened to him." Roxanne decided moving around the deck did nothing to keep him from her side. She planted her feet, staring out into his backyard. "And if your investigator had been a bit more thorough, you would have known your thief was a woman and Aaron never would have gone to jail."

"Are you here to offer a confession?" Jordan watched the fire burn in her gaze when she turned on him, raising her hand quickly to slap at him when he reached for her.

"No, I'm not here to offer a confession," she hissed, turning to march back through the house toward her car. "But if that's what you think, there's no reason to continue this conversation."

The light attached to the side of the house cast dark shadows, making it impossible for her to see his expression.

She stopped when she reached the patio doors leading back into his home. Turning, she studied him. "I came here to exchange information. Hall Enterprises won't survive this if we don't do something soon. Money is disappearing, and you've just lost a damn good accountant. And it sounds like you might do better without me, too."

"You aren't going anywhere." Jordan spoke the words under his breath so that Roxanne almost didn't hear him.

He hadn't followed her this time. He still leaned against the railing that bordered the deck, and she could see his face clearly at this angle. For a second she thought she saw something gentle flicker in those black eyes. *He needs me*, she thought to herself. *Jordan Hall risks losing everything, and if he loses the people around him capable of helping him, he might not stand a chance.*

Why couldn't he acknowledge that fact himself? He had intelligence. Roxanne would stick to him like glue if he would let her know how much he needed her.

"I drove to Nebraska to help and couldn't move for fear of being arrested," she shouted out at him.

"That wouldn't have happened," Jordan said.

Roxanne blinked. His words confused her for a moment and she stared at him. "You think that I'm guilty of stealing money from you," she said under her breath.

"Did I say that?" Jordan straightened and walked toward her.

Roxanne forgot to move from his path as a dull throb began in the soft folds of skin between her legs. She craned her neck to watch him as he approached.

"Your detective implied it," she said, feeling suddenly confused by his question. "And so did Ralph Layette."

"I believe I heard something to that effect." Jordan stopped as he reached her, and still she seemed unable to move. It was as if he had placed a spell over her, forbidding her feet to take flight.

"I'm not your thief." Roxanne didn't know what else to say to him, shy of rehashing her every move over the past couple weeks in order to *prove* her innocence.

"I know you aren't," Jordan said, and brushed his knuckles over her cheekbone and then down toward her neck.

He slid his fingers toward the back of her neck, and then with the side of his hand, pressed against her chin so that she raised her face. His black eyes radiated like onyx, and she felt his breath mix with hers, before his lips pressed against her forehead. He began a path around the edge of her face with his soft, dry lips, and the dull throb between her legs exploded, her cream soaking her pussy. Suddenly it was as if the deck turned sideways, her world toppling over while he made her come with a simple kiss.

Roxanne took a step backward, and then paced across the deck into a darker corner. She stared at the shadowed landscape without focusing on any of it.

"Why did you let your investigator imply that I was guilty?" she asked, needing fresh air. Her entire body burned with need. Her legs were like wet noodles and she held on to the deck, inhaling the fresh scent of the flowers in the yard.

"Because he thought you were guilty."

She was going to explode, right here and now, just lose it and scream and yell until Jordan knew beyond any doubt that she was not his criminal.

He put his hand over hers, sensing her outrage. But she deserved the truth.

"Take a walk with me." And he needed assurance that she was really his.

He wouldn't make it without her. His business wouldn't make it, and he sure as hell didn't want to go another day wondering if she would remain by his side or not.

Jordan's request obviously baffled her, since it had nothing to do with her question, and she turned to stare at him. He extended a hand, and she dropped her gaze to it, then looked up toward his face again.

"The path through the gardens is beautiful," he told her, enjoying how her eyes sparkled with curiosity, the animosity still there, however. "Even at night, I think you'll enjoy it."

Roxanne looked out across the yard and then back at him. "I'm not going for a walk in the dark," she told him. "I want to understand why you let me believe you thought I would steal from you. I've been loyal to you for two years."

Jordan turned from her and walked over to the glass doors leading into the library. He disappeared into the warm flood of light from the room for a moment, and then Roxanne turned as suddenly the yard surrounding the large patio deck flooded with light. He reappeared in the next instant and she turned her attention to him as he walked up to her. Jordan slipped his hand around hers and led her toward the gate in the patio as if she were a child.

"Why did you come here this evening?" he asked as he opened the gate, and stepped down onto the cobblestone path that disappeared ahead of them into a line of well-trimmed hedges.

"I thought if we shared the information we had that we might be able to catch this thief together." Her hand absorbed the warmth of his.

Light streamed across the path from lights that appeared to be fixed in the larger trees. The surreal sensation it created gave the impression she'd just entered some sort of fantasy world. What a wonderful place to simply forget all of her problems. She wondered if Jordan used this place for just that.

"Excellent idea." Jordan slowed as the path split into two different directions, and then led them toward the right, deeper into the maze of flowers, trees and hedges. "And one you should have acted upon a lot sooner."

His heart leapt at the knowledge that she came to him to establish a truce. He hadn't been at all sure what brought her to his home, but knowing that she wanted to work with him, trust in his judgment, share everything she knew and then catch their thief together, brought peace to him. Suddenly he was a lot more relaxed than he'd been all day. She hadn't committed her heart to him but this was a start.

Roxanne cleared her throat. "All we have to do is put aside this physical attraction we have for each other and work together as two professionals again."

Jordan chuckled but didn't say anything. She didn't try to pull her hand free from his grasp and he had no intention of letting her go. She talked a pretty talk, but he doubted she wanted just a professional relationship with him. And he knew he would never be able to *just* work with her.

Nope. Roxanne was the woman for him. There was no doubt in his mind. The way she had come over to his house, so concerned for the well-being of Hall Enterprises, had lifted his heart, brought his mood up from pure grouchiness to seeing some hope. No one had ever cared about his business as much as he did. Hall Enterprises was his baby, and she loved it as much as he did.

But even more than that, he was falling in love with her. Her energy, her determination, her intelligence, and yes, that gorgeous body of hers. All of it turned him on and he had no intention of letting go.

"That isn't how it's going to be," he said after a minute, and let go of her hand as they reached the gazebo in the middle of his garden.

She said nothing, but walked toward the structure, stuffing her hands in her pants pockets.

"And I know you will submit to me if I wish it," Jordan said from behind her.

Roxanne turned around and gawked at him. "You pompous ass," she hissed. "I am not your slut, or your play toy. You'll just have to make do with one of your other women for that indulgence."

Jordan didn't comment, but Roxanne wasn't sure she liked the look that came over his face. Even in the scattered light, she could see his features darken.

"I do not wish to make do with another woman." Jordan stood facing her, and the predatory way he captured her with his gaze sent her insides to boiling point.

She turned from him, needing space, and feeling they were straying into dangerous territory. "

"None of this matters," she said with a wave of her hand in the air. "I came here to talk about business, not your desire to possess me."

Her heart about exploded within her when Jordan pressed along her backside, and leaned his head to whisper into her ear.

"You came here because you thought I believed you were guilty." His breath scorched her ear and the side of her face, sending a tingling sensation rippling through her. His hands gripped her hips, holding her against him.

"Your detective almost came out and accused me of stealing from you. And you did nothing to stop him," she argued. "The only reason I came here was because we have a thief to catch."

"That we do." Jordan didn't move, but continued to talk with his face right next to hers. "And you believe we'll think better if we're together."

"Well, yes," she agreed, but then hesitated at his wording. "No," she corrected herself. "I mean we need to work as a business team."

"But there is more than business between us."

Roxanne stepped away from the trance he seemed to be putting her into...again. She walked around the gazebo, glancing at the different paths, not sure where any of them went.

"I don't want there to be more between us," she said, unable to look at him.

"Yes, you do."

Roxanne didn't need to turn to know that Jordan followed her. He didn't rush to her, or hurry to grab her as if she would run, but moved with a slow pace, one of confidence, which matched the tone he used in countering her comment.

"You're wrong." Roxanne chose a path that she thought would lead toward the house, and began walking along it with sureness in her step.

Jordan followed, she knew that, but she didn't dare look over her shoulder to see how close. "Where are you going?"

"I'm not going to discuss business with you until you agree that is all that we share," she said over her shoulder.

"And what if I prove you wrong?"

His question challenged her, but the answer she was about to toss at him left her when the path stopped and she faced what appeared to be a forest. Random lights still spread over the denser foliage, but she hesitated in entering.

"The only way back to the house is if you pass me," Jordan challenged her. "But the path in front of you will wind back to the house too, if you dare trust yourself alone in the forest with me."

Roxanne turned, and attempted marching right past Jordan, but his arm, held out like a steel beam, blocked her path.

He gripped her forearm and then slid her sideways so that she stood directly in front of him. Before she could protest, he wrapped his arms around her, kissing her with so much intensity her knees buckled.

She gripped his shirt, holding on for dear life, while his tongue caressed hers, doing a dance of passion that made her head spin. The pounding of her heart throbbed into her pussy, creating a primal beat that wouldn't be denied.

Damn him for having control over her body like this.

Tugging her shirt free of her jeans, he traced his fingers over her skin until he cupped her breast. Molten hot liquid streamed through her, soaking her, preparing her for anything he might do. Everything inside her screamed to submit to him.

All the reasons why she needed to fight him dissipated, leaving her a puddle of craving need, unable to do anything but cling to him.

Jordan forced her mouth open further as he deepened the kiss. The night air teased her feverish skin as Jordan slipped her T-shirt up to expose her.

His fingers clamped down on her nipple and squeezed, and she about fell to her knees. Her nipples had always been a weakness with her. She could swear there was a nerve connected to them that ran straight to the hardened, throbbing knot just beneath the soft folds of skin between her legs. That focal point of her sex swelled with every pinch and twist that he applied to her nipple.

"Jordan, please," she murmured.

"Please what?" he growled, and then before she realized what he had done, he'd pulled her T-shirt over her head, leaving her half-naked in front of him.

Roxanne realized with a wash of clarity that he had half stripped her in the middle of his yard. "Give me back my shirt."

And although they were surrounded by foliage, she had no clue how close they were to his property line, or who could be out there.

"I think it would be a better idea for you to give me your jeans." Jordan let his gaze swoop down her, and Roxanne took a step backward.

"This isn't going to happen, Jordan," she informed him.

"Yes it is."

"You have no clue how to be faithful," she told him, placing the truth in front of him.

"That's your story," he said without hesitation, and she stared at him.

"I caught you, remember?" Roxanne couldn't believe he would try to deny the day she discovered another woman's perfume on him. He couldn't edge out of this one that easily.

She reached for her T-shirt, but he pulled it away from her, and then with an agility that made her curse, he wrapped his other arm around her waist. Roxanne twisted in his grip, but he held firm until her back pressed against his steely chest.

She breathed heavily, wishing for strength to overpower him, but knowing it would never exist. "Let me go," she whispered.

"You want this too." Jordan slipped his hand to the button on her jeans, and in the next second had it unbuttoned, and the zipper down.

"You are not going to strip me out here in front of God and everyone," she hissed, and fought with all her might to be free of him.

Jordan let her go, but then tugged on her jeans with both hands as she took a step away from him, and the denim material slid to her knees.

Roxanne tripped over the bulge of material trapping her legs, and stumbled forward, catching herself before she fell on her nose, and then found herself on all fours, naked with Jordan hovering over her.

He squatted behind her, and she felt him tug as she crawled forward. Before he could stop her, she had jumped to her feet, but without her jeans.

"I don't know about God," he told her, "but I'm almost certain you and I are the only ones out here."

"I'm naked," she gasped, not believing how easily the man had rid her of her clothes.

"And beautiful," Jordan added, unable to stop from grinning while he stared down at her. "I like you this way."

"You arrogant buffoon," she hissed, and his grin broadened.

"Oh!" She clenched her fists in aggravation, and then determined not to give in to him that easily, turned and bolted into the forest.

Chapter Sixteen

ဆာ

Shadows stretched in distorted patterns through the trees. Without a moon, the night air appeared as black as the sky. The flood beams he had installed throughout the yard intentionally were sparse throughout this wooded area. He had wanted the dense trees to offer the sensation of hiking through the woods.

He stepped onto the packed-down dirt path. He wasn't too worried if his noise alerted Roxanne to his whereabouts. She had disappeared, and was out of his sight within seconds, but that would make hunting her down all the more pleasurable. She didn't possess his tracking skills or his knowledge of the forest. It would take no more than minutes to find her. The only thing hindering him was moving with his cock hard as a rock. If he didn't sink deep inside her soon he would explode. It didn't take him long to find her. Roxanne had her back pressed against a tree, a wild look in her eyes, and her brown hair tousled down to her shoulders. All he could do was stand there for a minute as his eyes focused on the rise and fall of her breasts. The night air puckered her nipples and the distraction was pure torture. No longer concerned about being quiet, he moved in on her.

Roxanne jumped as her gaze shot to him. The white of her eyes stood out around her dark orbs. Instinctively, she took several steps away from the tree.

"It's spooky in here," she whispered at him.

"Then don't run from me," Jordan suggested, not seeing any reason to whisper.

Somehow she'd managed to keep her sandals on. But, that was all she wore—and her body looked better than any woman's body had a right to look. His cock throbbed so hard he wasn't sure he would be able to chase her if she started to run.

Obviously, she noted his predicament. Her smile was pure evil. "You're the one who told me I could go past you or into the forest." With that she turned and darted through the trees, quickly engulfed by the darkness.

Jordan cursed loudly and accepted the pain as he took off in a full sprint after her. There wasn't much of a competition at this point. He was head and shoulders taller than she was and there was no way she could outrun him. In the next minute, he reached out and grabbed the back of her head, grasping her tangled brown locks between his fingers. Roxanne stumbled and he almost fell on top of her when she went down.

Holding her tightly, he managed to keep her from hitting the hard ground. Chasing her naked through the night was one hell of a turn-on, but he didn't wish her bruised or scraped.

"You sound out of breath, Jordan. Are you out of shape?" Her purr sounded mocking as she fell to her hands and knees.

"I have a feeling you won't be saying that here in a bit," he growled into her hair as he lifted her off the ground.

The challenge in that purring laughter of hers about made him come right there on the spot. She seemed to realize his condition because suddenly she wasn't struggling to get away anymore. Instead, her naked ass twitched against his cock and a growl escaped him before he could stop it.

"Let me down," she whispered.

"Will you promise not to run?" He wasn't out of shape at all. But she was right. In his present condition, he could hurt himself if he didn't allow his cock freedom.

It crossed his mind to strip out of his own clothes and then the two of them could prance naked through the woods. Hell...once they caught this thief, the two of them were going to enjoy some much-needed time off. Maybe they would stay naked the entire time.

"I promise. I won't run." Some of her anger seemed to have dissipated.

Jordan released her and she took a couple of clumsy steps in front of him before gaining her footing.

"Don't ever run from me, Roxanne." He stroked her hair out of her face. The way she looked up at him, seeming to understand the meaning of his words, released emotions that he wasn't sure he'd ever experienced before. "I need you."

"Yes. You do need me," she whispered, and right now she couldn't stand it any longer. She needed him too.

Ignoring the little voice inside her to defy him, to walk away and not give in to her desires until she had a strong commitment, she ran her hand over his perfectly sculpted chest to the top of his pants.

All he could do was stand there when she knelt before him. Hands half the size of his overwhelmed him with their skill. Night air tickled the hair on his legs as his pants fell to his ankles. Heavenly heat engulfed him when her mouth closed around him. Whoever taught her to use that tongue of hers deserved a medal. She nipped and sucked until he could feel the blood pounding through his veins. Those torturing hands left his balls and grabbed his rear end, fingernails digging into him as she held on and let him ram his cock into her mouth again and again.

"Stand up." Jordan's voice was no more than a guttural whisper.

Roxanne obeyed silently, her lips swollen and parted as she looked up at him with lust-filled eyes. He grabbed her ass and lifted her up into the air before sliding her down on to his engorged shaft, impaling her with one thrust. She howled and threw her head back, moving her hands to his shoulders to hold on for dear life as he drove into her. Muscular legs wrapped around him and she arched to allow him full penetration.

Jordan pounded Roxanne's velvety folds without mercy. When her muscles constricted around his cock and her body tightened, he knew she was ready to explode. Pulling out of her quickly, he half-dropped, half-threw her away from him.

The protesting scream that escaped her lips brought a smile to his face.

"On all fours." There was no way Jordan could form a full sentence.

Roxanne didn't object. Anything. She would do anything to have him back inside her. Quickly, Roxanne scurried to her hands and knees, ignoring the uneven ground pressing into her skin.

Dropping to his knees, Jordan put a hand on her stomach to lift her to him, then probed the puckered hole that taunted him, rubbing himself up and down her, from one hole to the other, until she was as soaked at both ends, and he thought he would explode once again with need.

"Oh yes," Roxanne moaned, realizing what he intended to do.

Her body quivered with excitement. She felt like a wild woman, on her hands and knees being fucked by her man in the great outdoors. Arching her back, she was so exposed, so vulnerable, and a rush of intense pleasure over the knowledge took her off-guard. She would figure it out later, but right now, submitting to Jordan like this felt real damned good.

He eased his cock into her asshole and closed his eyes in an effort not to explode as tight heat almost suffocated him.

"Oh God, Roxanne," he breathed, as he started moving slowly. At that moment, he would have given the woman anything she asked for. The moon and the stars would be hers if she had requested it. Never before had he fit inside a woman so perfectly.

"Ummm." She attempted to speak as she adjusted her legs, raising herself, allowing him to go deeper.

Jordan moved slowly in and out of her ass, aware that he'd finally gained her full submission. And the knowledge burned at him, rushed through him with so much intensity he would lose it without fully being able to enjoy her, or give her the pleasure she deserved.

Her body relaxed underneath him, as she arched and allowed him to ease in and out of her. He knew he wasn't hurting her, although more than likely he'd have to carry her back home when they were done.

"Jordan," she cried, turning her head so he could see her moisten her lips, her cheeks flushed with such a crimson hue that he could see her pleasure even in the dim light.

He couldn't help himself. Moving faster, gripping her ass while he began pounding her, he closed his eyes, the pleasure she offered him better than he'd ever dreamed possible.

"Fucking shit...I'm going to come." He couldn't focus on a blessed thing other than the tightness of her ass.

Sweat trickled down his temples and his back as he slid in and out of her heat with all the ferocity he could manage. The ringing in his ears didn't distract him from the pounding of his blood through every inch of his body. No longer capable of holding back, he exploded deep inside her, as her muscles clenched and released against him. Roxanne trembled, unable to stop the tidal wave of her climax surging and exploding inside her. She screamed, sure of the fact that she would pass out from the intensity of her orgasm.

The two of them collapsed on the bed of twigs and dried leaves underneath them, and greedily breathed in the cool night air.

"I can't believe I let you do that," Roxanne said after a moment.

His cock slid out of her, and he pulled her to him, resting on his back while he cuddled her into his arms.

Jordan stared up at the trees above him, appearing like black contorted lines against the almost black sky above them. He turned to look at Roxanne, then shifted to his side and studied her expression. Her eyes were closed, and she lay naked on the ground, her hair tossed around her head. She breathed heavily, and her ripe breasts moved up and down as her dark nipples remained puckered and eager.

"Are you hurt?" He knew he had gotten carried away but she seemed to want everything he had given her.

She turned her head in his direction and opened one eye. "Only my pride," she said.

He loved that saucy look she gave him, and his insides stirred as he let his gaze travel down her body.

"You respond well to me," he told her. "That is nothing to be ashamed of."

"This isn't about physical attraction," she murmured, moistening her lips. "I need to trust you, know that I'm the only woman you're sleeping with."

"You are the only woman I'm sleeping with." He ran his fingers through her hair, enjoying its silky feeling.

No other woman even came close to grabbing his attention. And until Roxanne, the last thought on his mind had been entering a relationship.

Roxanne nodded and nibbled her lower lip. He stood and pulled his jeans up, then buttoned them. "Your jeans are back at the entrance to the forest." He held out his hand to help her stand. "Can you walk?"

"Yeah," she said, not looking at him. "I'm fine."

But she wasn't fine. He wasn't sure exactly what demons plagued her, but she remained quiet and walked alongside him on the path back to the entrance of the forest.

Any other time, Jordan would have thought such a stroll along this path that he never had time to enjoy, would have been a wonderful treat, especially with Roxanne. But so much weighed over the two of them at the moment that it was hard to take time to focus on their surroundings as they walked.

When they reached the point where the dirt path turned to cobblestone, Jordan went over to where he had tossed her jeans, and straightened them before handing them to her. "I think showers are in order," he decided. "And then you and I can sit down and brainstorm over this matter at work. Have you eaten?"

"I'm not all that hungry right now," she said, looking distracted. "But I think I will accept your offer of a shower."

She did look up at him then, and he could see the turmoil clouding her lovely eyes. "And I would like to shower alone," she added.

Jordan smiled, having assumed they would shower alone already. "That will be fine," he told her.

Jordan wasn't surprised to see missed calls on his cell phone when they returned to the house. He set Roxanne up in his bathroom, making sure she had clean towels and everything she needed. Then he had left her and returned downstairs to his den, to once again focus on the matters of his business. He checked the numbers to see who had called him, and decided to contact Dixon first, to see if he had gathered any new information.

A printout rested in the tray of his fax machine, and Jordan stood and walked to the machine, which sat on his side table. It took just a minute to recognize the information that had been faxed to him.

"Damn it," he swore, and fought the urge to crinkle the sheet into a ball and toss it across the room.

The phone on the desk rang, and Jordan yanked the receiver off the cradle. "Yes," he demanded.

"Where have you been?" Dixon asked.

"Busy," Jordan told him.

"Well, so has our thief," Dixon said. "Did you get my fax?"

"I just picked it up." Jordan focused on the fax that he still held in his hand and felt his mood grow sour.

"She nabbed another ten thousand right here in town," Dixon said. "I've sent the police over to Roxanne's house, and I'm not too surprised that she isn't at home."

"You sent the police to her house?" Jordan slammed his hand, holding the fax, onto his desk. "I will not have you harassing her," he yelled into the phone.

"I realize you have feelings for her, Jordan, but this is your life you're talking about. Many more thefts like this and she will put you under."

"Roxanne is not our thief," Jordan hissed. "I have told you that before. And if you can't get that into your head then I will find another investigator who will focus on solving these crimes."

Dixon didn't say anything for a minute, and Jordan walked around his desk and sat in his chair. He looked up at that moment, and realized that Roxanne stood in the doorway of his study.

She appeared dwarfed wearing his large white bathrobe, which she must have pulled off the hook in his bathroom. Her feet were bare, and her hair hung damp around her face, which glowed from her hot shower. Roxanne watched him with her dark eyes, and her lips drawn in a tight line. By her expression, Jordan guessed she had stood there long enough to hear his comments on the phone.

Jordan gestured for her to enter, and she took cautious steps toward his desk, bringing with her the clean scent of soap.

"Jordan, your father—" Dixon began, but Jordan interrupted him.

"This has nothing to do with my father," he barked, and glanced up when Roxanne frowned at him.

Roxanne wanted to run from his office, grab her clothes and get the hell out of there. Overhearing him defend her felt damn good, but his associates thought her a criminal. She needed to be out there finding the real thief. More than anything she wanted to show all of them that not only were they wrong, but that she could find out who was stealing from Jordan before the others could. Blame it on her pride, but she wanted respect, and didn't mind working to earn it. Not to mention she would love to rub all of those assholes' noses in the fact that she could pull off the job when they couldn't.

But another part of her couldn't leave Jordan's side. She glanced down at the fax that rested on his desk, recognizing the withdrawal statement and their client's name.

"Not again," she whispered, and collapsed into the chair facing Jordan while he listened to whoever spoke to him at the other end.

"Jordan, you've worked hard to establish your firm," Dixon was saying.

Again Jordan cut him off. "Do we know where the thief was when this unauthorized transaction took place?" Jordan watched Roxanne who held the fax in her hand.

"The police are working on it," Dixon said.

"How long ago did this happen?" Jordan asked.

"A little over an hour ago," Roxanne told him while studying the printout, and Dixon offered the same information over the phone.

"Do they know where the thief did this?" she asked, and Jordan shook his head.

Roxanne turned with the fax still in her hand, and walked out of Jordan's study. Jordan stood, wanting to know where she headed.

"I'm still down here at your office," Dixon told him. "Why don't you drive back down here? I'm sure the police have some questions for you."

"The police can come here." Jordan wanted to brainstorm with Roxanne and doubted he would be able to do so if he brought her with him to the office. "I'm staying in for the night."

"Very well," Dixon said, and didn't sound pleased with Jordan's comment but that was just too damned bad. "I'll be in touch."

Jordan hung up the phone and then walked into the main part of his home, looking for Roxanne. "Where are you?" he called out, but she didn't answer.

A beep sounded, and Jordan realized his front door had just opened. He walked to the main entryway as Roxanne reentered his home. "Where did you go?" he asked, noting she had just left his house wearing his long white bathrobe, and deciding at the same time that he liked the way she looked in it.

Roxanne held up her briefcase, and his robe slid open around her, revealing a fair amount of cleavage.

"Aaron found out that the thief had used that library because he had a friend who is a hacker," she told him as she re-secured the bathrobe and walked past him back toward his study. "I have Aaron's number in here. I'm not sure if he'll agree to help or not."

"You're going to call him?" Jordan had a feeling the young accountant would be more than willing to help, especially since Jordan had offered him a small fortune to leave the firm quietly, and had pretty much secured a position for the young man with a well-established brokerage firm.

Roxanne didn't answer, but set her briefcase down on the opposite side of Jordan's desk and popped it open. She pulled out her cell phone, and one of the company's laptops, and created a space for herself on the corner of his desk. Jordan pushed a chair up behind her, and she glanced at him for a moment before accepting it, and sitting.

"My clothes are too dirty to put back on," she murmured, and arranged his bathrobe around her.

"I like you in that," Jordan said, and sat on the edge of his desk so that he could look down at her.

She didn't comment nor did she look up, but flipped on the laptop, and then a minute later had Aaron Tipley on the phone.

Jordan sat and listened to her talk to the young man, noting how friendly and professional she could sound all at the same time. She had a gift for working with people, and a sound mind for business. All of that wrapped up in such a gorgeous body. Jordan never would have believed such a woman could exist.

"Of course, this would have to be kept quiet," Roxanne said, and Jordan quit focusing on her attributes, to listen to what she said on the phone. "But Hall Enterprises will pay for his services. We would like to meet with him as soon as can be arranged."

Roxanne nodded, smiled, and then laughed at something Aaron must have said to her. Jordan couldn't see how anyone who paid any attention to this woman would think her guilty of any crime. She had as much of a vested interest in Hall Enterprises as he did. He had no problem paying for the services of a hacker, but the fact that she would authorize something like this, without so much as a glance in his direction, showed him that she viewed the company as much a part of her life as he did.

"Yes, give him this number, and have him call me as soon as possible." Roxanne continued to smile. "Thank you, Aaron," she said, and then jotted something down on a notepad she had pulled from the inner pocket of her briefcase.

Jordan's phone rang, and he stood to move around his desk to answer it. He didn't recognize the number on his caller ID, but answered it, thinking it might be the police or someone else pertaining to the latest theft.

"Jordan, darling, it's Elaine Rothchild." The woman sang into his ear. "I just had to call you since I realized I caught you on the run the other day."

Jordan leaned back in his chair, wishing now he hadn't answered the call. "Hello, Elaine," he said, frowning while he picked up a pen and began tapping it against his desk. "I'm in the middle of something right now. This isn't a good time."

"Well, we had to stop in town to see my niece," Elaine continued, obviously ignoring the fact that he didn't want to talk to her. "I didn't tell Matthew about our conversation the other day. He would have been so upset with me if he thought I'd upset you somehow. I thought while we were in town I would make another attempt to get you to talk with my husband. You've got the most successful firm in the Midwest, and Matthew would be such an asset to you."

Jordan had conveniently put everything about the presumptuous woman out of his head the minute he had left her, but he nodded anyway. "Right now isn't a good time," he said.

"Then I'll call you tomorrow morning. We can make plans then," she said quickly before he could tell her he wasn't interested.

Damn pushy bitch.

"Well, I hope I haven't distracted your thoughts too much," she said with a laugh that told Jordan that she was very pleased with herself. "But I told my Matthew that I was willing to do anything to help him land a position with Hall Enterprises."

"I'm sure you would," Jordan said and doubted he would have time in the morning to give her husband any consideration. "I've got some matters to tie up this evening. I'll call you."

"You won't regret it," Elaine said, and he about cringed when she blew a kiss through the phone.

Jordan managed to get the woman off the phone in the next minute, and let out a sigh as he hung up the phone. At the least he could find solace in knowing Hall Enterprises still held its outstanding reputation.

Jordan looked up as Roxanne stood at the other side of his desk. "So this hacker is going to call you?" he asked, and then noticed the look of outrage on her face.

"How dare you," she hissed, and then turned and stormed out of his office.

Chapter Seventeen

ଔ

Roxanne raced up the flight of stairs as fast as she could without tripping over the long bathrobe. She fought the sensation to break out into tears as she hurried down his hallway, through his oversized bedroom, and into the master bathroom where she had left her clothes. Dirty or not, she would put them back on and get the hell out of there.

Emotions too strong and overwhelming flooded through her, making her want to puke. She fought to remain levelheaded as she slipped the heavy robe off her shoulders, and turned to put it on the hook where she had found it. She had a job to do, and she had every intention of doing it, but she would be damned if she would sit in Jordan's home, practically naked, and do his dirty work while he flirted with other women on the phone.

She picked up her wrinkled T-shirt, which smelled of grass and dirt, and gave it a hard shake.

"What are you doing?" Jordan stopped in the doorway to the bathroom, and crossed his arms over his chest.

A lump grew in her throat, and she turned her back to him while she slid the smelly shirt over her head.

"I'm going home, Jordan, or to the office—anywhere but here." Roxanne reached for her jeans, and felt Jordan's hands grip her bare hips. "No," she said, and grabbed her jeans as she struggled to make Jordan release her.

The lump in her throat grew a bit when he did release her, and then stood watching her while she dressed. "I thought you said those were dirty." He watched her slide into the jeans.

"Well I can't go home naked," she spat at him, and then walked around him, through his bedroom, and then down the hallway toward the staircase.

Roxanne heard her cell phone ringing as she reached the bottom of the stairs, and hurried back to Jordan's study to answer it.

Jordan was on her heels knowing there was no way in hell she would storm out of there on him. She had just jumped to some very wrong conclusions. He wouldn't go for her throwing a jealous fit every time a woman called him. But for now, he would sit on her if he had to and make her hear what that phone call had entailed.

"Hello," she said, trying to push thoughts of their recent sex out of her head.

"Is this Roxanne Isley?" a man spoke at the other end.

"Yes, who is this?"

"My name is Mark Dunne. Aaron Tipley asked me to call you. He said you might be interested in some computer assistance."

Roxanne reached for the chair she had been in minutes before and pulled her pad from Jordan's desk.

"Yes, when is the soonest you can meet?" she asked. "We have an emergency."

"That's what Aaron told me. And he said something about payment?" The young man sounded eager to help, and be paid for his assistance.

Roxanne negotiated with him until they agreed on the terms for his service. "Is there any way you could meet with me this evening?"

Excitement almost covered up the pain that had lodged in her heart when Mark said that he would meet her at her house in an hour. That would give her time to get home and put some clean clothes on.

"I'm going with you." Jordan didn't like the upset look she gave him. "You didn't hear what you thought you heard just now on the phone."

Roxanne straightened, her expression going blank, although she couldn't hide the emotion that swirled in her eyes. "Apparently I don't have a right to say whether you talk to other women or not."

Jordan took her arm once she'd lifted her briefcase. "Know this now, Roxanne. There are no other women, nor will there be."

She nodded, not sure what to believe, and headed toward her car.

* * * * *

Mark Dunne proved to be invaluable, and Roxanne really felt they might be able to narrow in on their thief soon with his help.

"The most obvious pattern here is that your thief uses library computers every time they access your accounts." Mark offered the list of locations to Jordan.

"I'd like to hire you to assist me until this matter is settled," Jordan spoke while writing out a check several hours later. He handed the check to Mark. "I also need your word not to discuss any of this with anyone."

Mark simply stared at the check in his hand. "Holy shit. For this amount of money, I'll do whatever you want."

Jordan nodded, knowing he'd just bought the young man and not regretting it for a minute.

"First thing in the morning, I'll work up a new program that should make it impossible for anyone to access your clients' information. There will be all new passwords," Mark said, and then looked up sheepishly. "Of course, I won't put it into motion until you approve."

Jordan shook the man's hand and then walked him to Roxanne's door. She shook his hand as well and then stood behind him after Mark left.

"You're going home too, Jordan," she said, making her tone firm. She was beyond exhausted and not in the mood to fight with him.

Relief and disappointment swarmed through her at the same time when he didn't argue. She could ponder why he didn't insist that they sleep together, or worry that he'd left to go spend time with someone else. But she was too tired. Once he was gone, she simply turned off the lights in her house and then went to bed.

Chapter Eighteen

ဢ

The next day proved quiet at work even though she'd been out the day before. Little was going on, like the calm before the storm. But it gave her time to focus on her usual tasks, making sure all files were in order.

Standing and stretching, she left Jordan's office and walked down the hall to the small kitchen where a variety of snacks were kept. She'd overdosed on coffee lately and craved something a bit more nourishing. Grabbing a bottled water out of the small refrigerator, she noticed a basket of fresh fruit on the counter and helped herself to an apple.

"I must admit that this kitchen is a lot cleaner now," Dorothy said to her, as she closed the small refrigerator.

Roxanne looked around, not remembering it ever being dirty.

"Yes, it does look nice in here," she said, and smiled at the receptionist.

Dorothy still had her mouthpiece that she used to answer the phones attached to her head, and the cord dangled in front of her chest.

"My sister will be impressed that Sonya manages to do a decent job cleaning." Dorothy chuckled and turned her back to Roxanne as she began slicing an apple on the counter.

Roxanne remembered authorizing one of Dorothy's relatives to do the cleaning. She unscrewed her water bottle and took a long sip. "Your niece, was it?"

Dorothy looked over her shoulder and smiled. "Yes, Sonya. It's a good summer job for her cleaning this place." Dorothy chuckled. "Keeps her out of trouble."

"I'd forgotten that we agreed to let her clean the office." Roxanne took a minute to survey the kitchen and decided that it did look clean. "Well you can let her know that she is doing a good job."

"I'll do that." Dorothy patted Roxanne's arm as she passed her with her plate of sliced apples.

Roxanne walked back to Jordan's office, noting Ralph Layette's closed office door and feeling a bit betrayed and left out. Joe Dixon and Jordan were in the office with Ralph and that they had been in a closed-door meeting most of the afternoon. She hadn't been asked to join them and she didn't know what they were discussing. It irked her to be left out of matters and the urge to push open the door without knocking and demand to know what was going on made her pause before she convinced herself it wouldn't be a good move.

Jordan told her he needed her to remain at work while he was in the meeting. "Hold down the fort for me," he had said, and she'd hated the way he had smiled at her. He really looked like he cared about her. She could see how preoccupied he was with solving these crimes. And rightly so. They were driving her nuts with each passing day. It was just real lousy timing that she'd happened to enter into a full-blown affair with her boss at the same time all of this scandal had occurred.

They never had an opportunity to discuss the phone call he had received from Elaine, whoever she was, while Roxanne had been at his house. Not that Roxanne was sure she wanted to know anything about Elaine. The mere idea of the woman's existence had Roxanne steaming with jealousy. She recognized the ugly emotion, and hated that she experienced it.

Roxanne put her water on her desk and then turned to acknowledge Pedro when he appeared in the doorway.

"Got a minute, boss?"

"Since when am I your boss?" Roxanne laughed, and slumped into her chair, wishing it was five so she could go home and take a nap.

Pedro Romero looked over his shoulder, as if to ensure that they were alone, and then grinned as he said, "You know as well as I do that Mr. Hall couldn't run this place without you."

Roxanne rolled her eyes, and Pedro winked at her. "What do you need, Pedro?"

"You've got a Sonya Wisdom, who has been on payroll for six weeks now."

"Yes. I was just talking to Dorothy about her. Is there a problem?"

"I'm only mentioning it because she hasn't cashed any of her checks yet." Pedro held out a balance sheet, which showed the hours Sonya had worked, and her rate of pay being eight dollars an hour.

Roxanne noted Sonya worked two hours a night, and often the hours were logged around the midnight hour.

"Why don't you check with Dorothy, and we'll make sure Sonya gets her checks cashed."

"Good enough," Pedro said, and left Roxanne alone with her bottle of water, and the slow-moving clock on the wall.

She wondered why Sonya would work such late hours, doing a job that couldn't be that enjoyable, and then not bother to cash her paychecks.

* * * * *

Roxanne woke later that evening with Matisse sleeping on her back, her face pressed into the cushion of her couch, and her cell phone ringing on her coffee table. Matisse protested when she pushed herself up to a sitting position, and reached for her phone.

"Hello," Roxanne said, and stood to stretch before padding toward the bathroom.

"Roxanne, this is Mark Dunne," the man on the other end said. "I've compiled some stats for you, do you have a minute?"

"What do you mean by stats?" After the bathroom, Roxanne headed toward her bedroom, and flipped on her light, then walked over to close her blinds. She couldn't believe it was after nine. She had fallen asleep shortly after getting home from work, and if anyone had called before now, this was the first time she had heard the phone ring.

"I've gathered all the information I could find on our thief, and looked for all the similarities. We already knew that she always used a library, so I thought I would see if I could find any other patterns."

"Good idea." She sat down on her bed and began stroking Matisse, who climbed onto her lap and began purring. "Did you find any other patterns?"

"Well, we know she started accessing the accounts a little less than two months ago," Mark began, "and she uses libraries. It also appears that she has only accessed accounts that you have had with your clients for only a few months."

"That isn't true," Roxanne said, waking up as she listened. "One of our largest clients has had several of his accounts accessed, and money taken."

"You would be referring to Roger Uphouse," Mark said, and Roxanne listened as she heard papers being shuffled. "I said she has accessed new accounts, not new clients."

"Interesting." Roxanne wondered what that might possibly mean. "You find anything else?"

"Nothing that seems to stand out," Mark told her. "She has been to ten libraries that we know of, has done the dirty deed at only libraries, and she never uses the same library twice."

"I'm sure Jordan has his investigator contacting each library," Roxanne said, thinking out loud.

"You would think so," Mark said.

"Have you talked to him about all of this?" Roxanne thought again about the new accounts, and wondered what connection might be there.

"Yes. He told me he was in a meeting, and to call and give you the information," Mark told her.

Roxanne wondered what meeting he might be in this late at night. Possibly he still brainstormed with Layette and Dixon. But what if he was with Elaine? Her stomach twisted into an unpleasant knot, and she tried to keep her thoughts on the conversation. Never had she realized that she could get so damned jealous.

"Well, I don't have a clue what any of it means at this point," she confessed.

Mark promised to keep in touch and then said goodbye. Roxanne thought about their conversation a minute longer, and then her thoughts strayed back to Jordan. If he was still in his closed-door meeting with Layette and Dixon, then they must be making some headway. Roxanne didn't like feeling left out when she felt she had as much vested in Hall Enterprises as Layette, and as for Dixon, well, she wouldn't allow ill thoughts to kindle.

On an impulse, Roxanne decided she would join them.

Hurrying back into the bathroom, she stripped. "I know Jordan won't turn me away," she told Matisse, who brushed her back against the doorway. She hopped into the shower before she lost her nerve to head to the office.

And if he wasn't at the office, then maybe a drive past his house, just to ensure there weren't any other cars parked there. She had no idea what she would do if there were.

You'd walk into his house and punch any bimbo who might be with him right in the nose.

* * * * *

Roxanne used her master key to unlock the building, and then headed across the lobby to the elevators. Since the central alarm system was off, someone still worked somewhere on one of the floors. She rode the elevator up the many floors of the office building and then stepped out when the doors slid open and walked over to the glass doors that had the words "Hall Enterprises" painted on them. The doors were locked, but that didn't surprise her, any more than the light trickling down the hallway from Jordan's office. It would make sense that the men would have moved to the larger office at the end of the workday.

The office had a clean smell as she let the glass doors swing shut behind her. She glanced toward the secretarial pool, and noticed the bottom drawer open to the first filing cabinet in the row against the wall. She took a step toward it, and then recognized cleaning supplies filling the drawer.

"That's right," she mumbled to herself, remembering that Dorothy's niece cleaned the place in the evening. Roxanne left the drawer open, and wandered down the hall toward Jordan's office. None of the other offices had their lights on, and Roxanne wondered where the cleaning girl was at the moment. It dawned on her too that she didn't hear any voices. What were Jordan and the rest of them doing?

"Hello." Roxanne didn't know what else to say, as she walked into Jordan's office and found a teenage girl sitting at her desk, using her computer.

"Oh shit!" The teenage girl jumped up and away from Roxanne's computer all in one motion. "You scared the crap out of me."

"I'm sorry," Roxanne said, recovering after a moment from her own surprise to find a stranger at her desk, instead of the three men she expected to find in there. "What are you doing?"

The girl moved toward the computer with lightning speed, and moved the mouse frantically, as she clicked a few times.

"Nothing." The girl wore a halter top with baggy workout pants that rested on protruding hipbones. Her flat tummy was tan, and a single hoop earring hung from her belly button. The girl had brown hair that stuck out underneath a bandana she had tied over her head in the contemporary fashion Roxanne had seen other teenagers wear. Her nails were short, and painted a florescent green, and she wore a shade of green eyeliner that Roxanne thought she would have looked better without. One ear had too many stud earrings lining it for Roxanne to count, and she couldn't see the other ear to tell if it was equally pierced.

"Mr. Hall told me I could do this," the girl muttered, and moved past Roxanne after turning off the computer.

"Oh," Roxanne said, and turned to follow the teenager. "Did you see Mr. Hall tonight?"

The teenager had already reached the doors leading to the elevators, and pulled one of them open. "No, not tonight," she said over her shoulder and then she was gone.

Roxanne stared down the empty hallway for a minute, trying to gather her thoughts after being startled by the teenager. She walked toward the doors to lock them, since the girl hadn't bothered to do so, and then noticed the still open bottom drawer, and walked over to close it.

Roxanne pushed the drawer closed with her foot, and then turned to stare at the row of empty cubicles that made up the secretarial pool. She had been in this office many times at night, and almost as many times had stared in this direction in the dark. Something didn't seem right to her at the moment though, and she couldn't place what it was. She moved slowly down the row of desks, each separated by the cream-colored partitions offering a small amount of privacy for each employee. Nothing seemed amiss, and Roxanne chastised herself for allowing the tightening of her tummy from nerves, as she searched for something that seemed out of place.

"You're being silly," she scolded, and turned toward the hallway, and then walked with a sure foot to Jordan's office. "Now, Mr. Hall," she said to the empty room, "where is this meeting you claim to be in?"

Roxanne stood over her desk, staring at the familiar items on it, and allowing her thoughts to return to the time in Jordan's study at his home. She remembered the conversation Jordan had with that woman, Elaine, while she had sat there listening. Jordan had shown no remorse at all about flirting with some other lady right after the two of them had been so intimate with each other.

Roxanne cringed as humiliation swept through her once again. She had enjoyed the wild sex they had shared in the forest, enjoyed it very much. She liked being the prey, hunted down and then surrendering. It had been a very erotic experience, but then Jordan had made her feel cheap. He hadn't cherished her as she wanted him to, but had moved on and within less than an hour flirted with another lady on the phone.

"You have got to quit thinking about it," she scolded herself, and took a quick look around the office, before turning off the light, and walking toward the main doors.

Roxanne glanced at all the cubicles as she reached for the panel along the wall to set the alarm, and then stopped.

"What is wrong with this picture?" she mumbled, and stared at the quiet, dark work area for a moment. "My God! That's it."

Roxanne walked over to the main server, which sat behind Dorothy's desk, and noticed it was off, as it should be. Usually when she and Jordan worked nights, the light from the server glowed behind Dorothy's desk, but tonight that area remained dark. More than likely, when Jordan and the others left, Jordan had shut it off. But if he had given Dorothy's niece permission to use the computer, wouldn't he have left it on for her?

Roxanne turned, and then noticed what she hadn't noticed before. Linda Rickmeier's computer was still on. The glow from the lights on the tower spread enough light to catch Roxanne's attention. And normally that computer would be off as soon as business hours were over.

Turning to the processor's desk, she tapped the keyboard to bring the monitor out of sleep mode.

The area filled with more light as the screen came to life, and Roxanne realized that this amount of light had been in the secretarial pool just a few minutes before, when she had tried to determine why things looked different to her tonight. The monitor must have just entered sleep mode, which meant it had been used recently. A list of recently processed loans appeared on the screen.

"Linda should know better than to leave her computer on like this." Roxanne leaned over the keyboard, and began to shut down the computer. Then she froze. "Mark said all the accounts accessed were new accounts."

Roxanne straightened, and stared at the list of accounts on the screen. She glanced at Linda's desk, wondering if she could determine the last thing she had worked on before leaving that day.

"She asked me a question toward the end of the day." She chewed at her lip until she remembered the question about determining income on a self-employed client.

Roxanne looked at the baskets at the edge of Linda's desk, and found the one where Linda placed completed work. The file on top belonged to the client Linda had asked the question about. Roxanne opened the file and stared at its contents, and then glanced at the screen. The file that was open on the screen was a different account than the account in the file folder.

Roxanne glanced through the rest of the files in the basket. None of them matched the file that was open on the computer.

"Why would Linda be in this file on the computer?" Roxanne continued to stare at the screen, and then the contents in the file, but could make no sense of it.

She closed the file and placed it back in the basket where it would be collected and filed the next day, and then reached for the mouse to shut down the computer. Tomorrow she would have to remind Linda that she needed to close down her computer every night. The woman worked hard, and had learned a lot in the short amount of time that she had been with the company, so Roxanne wouldn't make a big issue out of it.

But it was important to remember to do even the small things, like turning off the computer.

"The last thing we need is an open invitation to allow our thief access to the rest of our accounts," Roxanne grumbled, but then her hand froze on the mouse.

Then it hit her. Suddenly everything made sense. Her fingers shook when she pulled her cell phone out.

"Please answer." Roxanne listened as the phone rang for the second time, and then smiled when a man's voice answered. "Mark, this is Roxanne. I'm sorry to bother you so late in the evening, but would you be able to meet me at Hall Enterprises right now?"

Chapter Nineteen

෨

Roxanne stood in Jordan's office staring down at her desk. Jordan stood on the other side and watched Mark Dunne as he sat at Roxanne's computer.

"Are you sure no one has been at this computer since your cleaning lady was here?" Mark frowned at the screen in front of him.

"Sonya Wisdom was the last person to sit here." Roxanne had confirmed the young lady's name when she got to work that morning. Mark Dunne had told her he couldn't make it out the night before, but had agreed to meet her at the office first thing the next morning. "I left everything the way I found it last night, just as you asked."

"Good." Mark continued to punch keys on her keyboard. "And what about the computer out front? Can you make sure no one touches it?"

"Already done." Jordan had a cross expression on his face and Roxanne could only guess that the thought of a teenager besting him for so much money didn't sit well.

"I don't want anyone in the office aware of what we have learned," Roxanne said, and Jordan met her gaze.

"Well, we haven't learned anything yet," Mark told her.

Roxanne nodded and sighed. "You're right. Part of me wishes it wasn't Sonya because she is just a kid, and I can't imagine what she would want with that kind of money."

"You'd be surprised," Mark muttered, but didn't elaborate.

Mark Dunne seemed an odd friend for Aaron Tipley to have. Roxanne had thought that of the man the first time she met him. Where Aaron was a clean-cut young man, just out of the service, with a wife and a lucrative career, Mark Dunne seemed to be just the opposite. To the best of Roxanne's knowledge, the man didn't work. His brown hair fell past his shoulders and was tied into a neat ponytail. Mark wore blue jeans that had seen better days, and a well-worn T-shirt. He had thick glasses, and to all appearances looked very much the computer geek. Roxanne didn't take to labeling people, but this man could be on a television show as a hacker, he fit the stereotype so well.

"What have you told the ladies out front?" Jordan asked her.

"Nothing, really." Roxanne shrugged. "I told Linda that her computer wasn't acting right, and until further notice she needed to stay off it. The women think that Mark is here to service the computers."

Mark chuckled at that, but didn't look up from what he was doing. Roxanne edged behind him so that she could watch, curious to see how he would be able to determine what Sonya had done on it last night.

The room fell into silence for a minute until Mark leaned back in his chair and sighed.

"What?" Jordan and Roxanne asked him at the same time.

"This." Mark looked up at the two of them and waved his hand. "The two of you are breathing down my neck and it's making it hard for me to concentrate."

"Oh." Again they both mumbled at the same time, and Jordan moved toward his desk while Roxanne took a step backward and wondered what she could do to make herself busy.

"Is there anything the two of you can do and I'll contact you as soon as I'm through going over these two computers?" Mark looked first at Jordan and then at Roxanne.

"We'll give you some peace," Jordan told him, and gathered his briefcase, then turned to Roxanne. "Gather your things and you can run errands with me."

Roxanne wanted to protest, feeling she should keep herself busy in the office in case Mark needed her. "Maybe I should stay," she began.

"Don't worry," Mark looked up at her and smiled, showing two front teeth, which were slightly crooked. "I will be sure to call you if I find anything, or as soon as I'm done. Sound good?"

Roxanne nodded and then gathered her things. "Shall we?" Jordan held his hand out toward her in a gallant manner.

Roxanne narrowed her brow at the gesture, took her briefcase in hand, and headed toward the office door. "I have my cell phone on me," she told Mark over her shoulder.

"I'll talk to you soon," Mark said.

Jordan placed his hand on Roxanne's back as they entered the hallway, and Roxanne realized he had never touched her intimately like this during business hours. She wanted to step out of his reach, but at the same time liked him next to her.

Joe Dixon stepped out of Layette's office and faced the two of them. "What's going on in there?" His question was directed at Jordan.

"He needs some time to do his work," Jordan offered. "We're going to run some errands."

Dixon nodded and then turned his gaze to Roxanne. "Young lady, I believe I owe you an apology."

Roxanne didn't know what to say. "Yes, Mr. Dixon?" she asked, curious as to what the man had to say.

"I misjudged you, young lady, and I see that now," Joe Dixon told her.

Roxanne didn't realize that she held her breath, and exhaled at the man's words.

"Yes, Mr. Dixon, you did misjudge me," Roxanne said quietly. "I've never committed a crime in my life and I would never steal from anyone."

Joe Dixon smiled, and Roxanne couldn't believe how it changed his appearance. "I hadn't met Jordan before this investigation, but I knew his father well. I didn't want to see history repeating itself."

Roxanne didn't know what Joe Dixon referred to, and so had no response. She glanced up at Jordan and saw how masked his expression was. She couldn't tell if he was pleased with Joe's words or possibly embarrassed. But Roxanne couldn't imagine Jordan being embarrassed over anything.

"Well, I wish you two the best of luck." Again Joe nodded and smiled at Roxanne.

"We'll find the thief." And she meant it. She knew neither of them would rest until this matter was settled.

Jordan's hand nudged her, guiding her toward the main doors of Hall Enterprises.

"Will you two be back soon?" Dorothy asked, as they entered the secretarial pool.

Roxanne turned her attention to their receptionist, and noticed the older woman's warm smile as she focused on Jordan's hand resting on Roxanne's back. Roxanne stepped out of Jordan's protective hold and approached Dorothy's desk.

"Mr. Dunne needs some time to work on the computers," Roxanne told her. "Make sure he isn't bothered, and if he needs to work out here, please give him plenty of room and let him do what he needs to do."

"Of course, dear," Dorothy said, still smiling.

"If there are any client calls, forward them to my cell phone. I'm in the way in there." Roxanne returned the smile, hoping the ladies wouldn't break into a whirlwind of gossip over her and Jordan as soon as they left the building.

"Yes, call if you need us," Jordan said over her shoulder, and Roxanne watched Linda look up from her filing at the two of them.

"Shall we?" This time Jordan put his hand on Roxanne's shoulder, and urged her toward the doors.

Roxanne swore she could hear one of them make a comment about her and Jordan being a cute couple as the glass doors swung shut behind them.

They'd reached the elevator when his cell phone rang.

"Hall here."

A female's voice sounded through the phone, although Roxanne couldn't tell what she said.

"I'm not sure yet what my schedule looks like today. Lunch?" Jordan's expression wasn't readable, and he didn't look at her but focused on the ground.

They stepped into the elevator and Roxanne reminded herself that he'd told her there were no other women. The woman's voice continued through the phone. It was hard not to edge closer to him so that she could hear.

The doors opened and Roxanne bolted free of her confinement with Jordan. She didn't like the surge of emotions that rampaged through her like a prairie fire, burning her insides with intense curiosity as to whom he'd been talking to. She needed a distraction and moved toward the main doors of the building as she tried to clear her brain of Jordan Hall.

She needed to focus on what Mark Dunne was doing upstairs with her computer. He had the ability to determine what Sonya had done on her computer as well as Linda's. And Roxanne hoped they would hear from him soon.

Roxanne hated the turmoil going on inside her over Jordan. The two of them needed to discuss what type of relationship they had. Obviously they had a great sexual relationship but Roxanne didn't want just that. And hadn't Jordan just made a show in the office that made it appear they were a couple?

"Have you given any thought to contacting the libraries we know our thief has visited and seeing if they've seen a young lady matching Sonya's description?" Jordan asked her as he held the door and Roxanne stepped out into the morning sun.

"While I was in Nebraska, I made a friend out of the waitress," she told him.

Jordan kept his hand on her back and she knew if he were only to remove it then she would be able to rid her mind completely of all sexual thoughts of him and focus completely on their conversation. At the same time, the possessive way he guided her made her feel important.

"The waitress that I had send breakfast to you?" Jordan looked down at her surprised. "You didn't tell me this."

"There are many things I don't tell you," she said, wanting to add that when he started telling her everything, then maybe she would return the favor. "But she gave me her phone number. I could call her and see if she would question the librarian."

"You two got chummy enough that she gave you your phone number?" There was humor in Jordan's face, and she squinted up at him.

"She sat with me while I ate, and we talked some," Roxanne said, then looked away as they approached her car.

"And you told her why we were there?"

They stopped at her car, and Roxanne again squinted against the morning light, to see his expression.

"Yes," Roxanne said, and then smiled as she remembered. "She thought we were FBI."

Jordan grinned at her comment and appeared to be focused on something over her shoulder. She guessed his mind churned on several different thoughts at once, and she watched him until he looked down at her.

"Give her a call," he said. "Let me know what she says."

Jordan leaned forward and kissed her then, right in the middle of the parking lot. His cell phone rang again and vibrated between them at the same time. Jordan straightened to answer it and Roxanne found she couldn't move. She stood in front of him, her face close enough to his chest that she could feel his body heat, smell his masculine scent, and it intoxicated her.

She listened to him discuss several possibilities concerning investments and then agree to prepare a proposal for whoever it was he spoke with.

Roxanne left him standing there and got into her car, pulling out her cell phone so that she could place her own call. Unfortunately, all she reached was Emily's voice mail. Leaving a message for the waitress, she looked up to see Jordan standing outside her car door, watching her.

"It's calls like that one that reassure me the reputation of Hall Enterprises is still on solid ground," Jordan told her as he clipped his phone to his belt. He smiled down at her, and she could tell that something he'd just discussed really pleased him. "Paul Bradford, a brand-new client I just picked up from out in New England, has informed me that he wishes to put the rest of his accounts with us."

Roxanne recognized the name as the one Linda had asked for help with the other day, but she hadn't taken time to browse the contents of the file.

"Now that is good news," Roxanne said, returning his smile, and then taking a moment to admire how the morning sun made his hair look like black silk, shiny and smooth. There were rare moments when she saw Jordan look this pleased, and she wanted to cherish the moment. "I left voice mail for Emily to call me back," she added.

Her cell phone rang, and Roxanne grabbed it, noticing the Nebraska area code.

"Hello," she said.

"Hi, Roxanne, this is Emily, I just got your message off my machine." Emily sounded just as she did in person, upbeat and happy.

"Do you have time to stop in to your library?" Roxanne asked. "I need to know if the librarian remembers seeing a teenage girl at the computer the day my friend was arrested."

Roxanne gave Emily a detailed description of Sonya, and Emily sounded thrilled to help. Roxanne hung up the phone, knowing Jordan had listened, and glanced at the long legs that blocked her exit. Her phone rang again and this time Roxanne didn't recognize the number. She pushed her talk button and answered.

"Hello," she said, and then paused when she didn't get an immediate response.

"Roxanne?" The voice didn't sound familiar, and Roxanne frowned at the connection. Whoever it was, their voice seemed to vibrate.

"This is Roxanne. We have a bad connection. Who is this please?"

"Back off, Roxanne. That is an order." The line went silent, and Roxanne sat there, staring at her steering wheel, repeating the vibrating words in her head.

"Back off from what?" Roxanne muttered, but then realized the party at the other end had disconnected.

She lowered the phone and stared at the blank screen that told her she had a strong signal. A second passed, and barely that before fear gripped her, making it hard to breathe.

"Jordan," she whispered, and realized then that he had squatted next to her and slipped the phone from her hand.

"Who was that?" he asked, and began pushing numbers on her phone. "You're white as a ghost. What did they say?"

"They said to back off, and that it was an order." Roxanne took a deep breath, and heard the vibrating voice in her head. "I think I've just been threatened."

Chapter Twenty

❦

Roxanne sat in one of the chairs that normally faced Jordan's desk, and listened to the police officers talk to Jordan and Mark Dunne. Jordan had pulled the chair around to the side of his desk, and planted Roxanne there the second they returned to his office. He had called the police, while a baffled Mark Dunne had listened as Roxanne explained what had happened.

Two officers arrived—Officer Rick Houser, and Officer Janet Holten—and Mark explained to them how Roxanne's computer had been used to transfer money out of one of the accounts with Hall Enterprises, and into a private savings account with a small bank in Olathe, Kansas. The officers took notes, and listened as Roxanne tried to explain how the caller had sounded.

"I can't think of another way to describe it other than the voice seemed to vibrate." Roxanne watched Officer Holten, who sat in the chair across from Roxanne, as the woman used very thin pliers on the inside of Roxanne's cell phone. "I'm not even sure if the person who called me was a man or a woman," she added.

Joe Dixon leaned against Jordan's desk with his arms crossed, turning his head to focus on whoever spoke at the moment. Ralph Layette leaned against the wall, also listening.

"That should do it," Officer Holten told her, and handed Roxanne her phone. "Any call that comes through that phone will be recorded."

"Thank you." Roxanne didn't know what else to say. The last thing she wanted was every one of her phone calls listened to, but she knew this had to be done.

"Just make sure if you want to have a private conversation that you do it on another phone," the officer said, and she smiled at Roxanne. "It's no fun having your privacy invaded."

"I just want this person stopped." Roxanne watched the officer as she put away the small tools she had used to install the device into Roxanne's phone. "If that means having my phone tapped, then so be it."

"The caller used a pay phone to contact you." The other police officer, Officer Houser, who stood talking with Jordan, turned his attention to Roxanne, apparently having overheard what she had just said. "Unfortunately that means we'll have to wait for them to place another call to you, and hope we can trace it."

Roxanne didn't want to hear that vibrating voice again, and cringed at the thought. The more she played the few words her caller had said to her over in her head, the more it gave her the creeps.

"I'm assuming they wanted me to back off from investigating these crimes," she said, thinking out loud.

Roxanne could see the outrage that Jordan tried to suppress and she had to admit to feeling more than frustrated over the thought that a teenager could be responsible for threatening Hall Enterprises.

"We can question Miss Sonya Wisdom," Officer Houser mused, "but I'm not sure this is grounds for an arrest." He studied the printout Mark Dunne had offered him. "Do we have proof it was this teenager who did this?"

"You have her passwords there. She logged on to the Internet through an ISP that she probably has at her house." Mark nodded to the papers the officer held in front of him. "But I think if you can lift prints you might have the proof to back all that up."

"It won't take much to verify what ISP she uses at home." The officer studied the papers again, and the room grew quiet as everyone watched him. "Who all has touched the computer since the girl was on it?"

Mark Dunne lifted latex gloves he had recently stripped from his hands. "I used gloves," he said, and smiled.

"I'm pretty sure no one else has used the computer," Roxanne offered.

"We'll send someone over to dust for prints." Officer Houser glanced at his partner.

Roxanne watched the group slowly leave the office, and stood to follow them out toward the lobby. She could only imagine how hard it would be to get everyone to remain focused on work after this little escapade ended. The ladies in the secretarial pool would be full of questions, and all the accountants stood in the doorways to their offices as the officers left the building. A quick glance told her that no clients were in the office at the moment, and for that much, Roxanne gave silent thanks.

"What is all the fuss about?" Dorothy had stepped around her desk, her earpiece still attached to her head, and sidled next to Roxanne as Jordan escorted the officers out of the office.

Roxanne watched him through the glass doors as the small group stood in front of the elevators. Dorothy deserved an answer of sorts, and Roxanne thought of a way to summarize everything for the receptionist.

"The police are helping the investigator that Jordan hired," Roxanne told her, and then watched Dorothy nod solemnly.

"They're figuring out who is screwing with the accounts?" Dorothy asked, and looked like a worried mother as she focused her attention on Jordan and the others through the glass doors.

"Yes, I think we've narrowed it down." Roxanne watched Dorothy and concluded in a second that the woman had no clue her niece was a prime suspect.

Dorothy looked worried over the drama in the office and sounded curious as to what had occurred. But she didn't appear to be prying for information, and her expression revealed no fear that someone she cared about could be arrested.

Roxanne spent the rest of the day working from her old cubicle in the secretarial pool. She seldom had time to sit, as she helped answer the phone, and hovered from desk to desk, answering questions, mostly work-related, but everyone was curious about the police, and Roxanne did her best to answer their questions.

Around five, her cell phone rang, and Roxanne felt her tummy spasm when she picked it up to look at the caller ID box. She relaxed when she noticed the Nebraska area code, but decided to take the call privately, and instinctively walked down the hallway to Jordan's office.

He looked up questioningly from behind his desk as she entered, but when he noticed her cell phone in her hand he scooted around his desk and reached for it.

"Who is it?" he demanded, when she put it to her ear instead of handing it to him.

"Hello?" Roxanne placed a hand on Jordan's chest, and his arm went around her shoulder as he pulled her into him and leaned his head by hers so that he could hear the caller.

"Hi sweetie," a cheerful voice sang out. "This is Emily. I got up town to talk to Betty."

"Who is Betty?" Jordan whispered.

Roxanne glanced up at him, and felt his power saturate through her. Jordan's protective instincts were on full alert, and Roxanne felt she could take on an army wrapped in his arms.

"Betty is the librarian?" Roxanne asked Emily.

"Oh, yes." Emily giggled. "Sorry. I forget everyone doesn't know everyone sometimes."

Jordan straightened, and ran his hand over Roxanne's hair. She felt her body respond to his caresses, and worked to focus on Emily when she wanted to cuddle into Jordan, and feel that virile body against her.

"What did she say about the description you gave her?" Roxanne asked.

"Betty is pretty sure there was a teenager in here who matched that description," Emily began. "And we don't have a lot of teenagers around these parts who are decked out and all." Emily laughed. "They'd stand out like a sore thumb up here."

"Emily, you've been a wonderful help," Roxanne told the waitress.

"Well, you got to tell me what this all means," Emily said. "I don't get much excitement around here. Don't just leave me hanging like this."

Roxanne smiled. "I'm not sure what it means yet. But I promise that when I know for sure, I will call and tell you."

Emily consented, and the two women said goodbye to each other.

"It sounds like Sonya made a trip to Nebraska." Roxanne placed her cell phone on her desk and faced Jordan.

"Well, your phone is tapped so the call was recorded." Jordan turned from her and moved to his desk, then punched a button on his phone. "Dorothy, see if you can reach Officer Houser for me."

Roxanne's cell phone rang again, and Roxanne turned with a start to stare at it. Jordan reached it before she did, and picked it up to stare at the little caller ID box. "Do you know that number?"

Roxanne sighed, and put her hand over her heart, feeling it pound under her dress. "It's Joanie," she said, and reached for the phone.

"Hi, lady," Roxanne said, as she answered the phone.

"Hi, yourself," Joanie said. "How's your day going?"

"Don't ask." Roxanne laughed, trying for a light tone.

"Well that doesn't sound good," Joanie said. "I called to see what you're doing tonight. There's only a week until my wedding, you know. And I wondered if you wanted to help me go through everything tonight, and make sure I haven't forgotten anything." Joanie sounded nervous.

"Of course I can do that." Roxanne hadn't looked forward to going home alone anyway.

She looked at Jordan, and he raised a questioning eyebrow at her. His phone buzzed, and Roxanne heard Dorothy tell Jordan that she had one of the officers on the line.

"Great." Joanie sighed. "Can you come over after work?"

Roxanne agreed to be there and then hung up her phone. She faced Jordan and listened while he talked to the officer on the other line, and then waited after he hung up the phone for him to fill her in.

"The police department is contacting the Auburn library," Jordan told her. "If they can fax a picture of Sonya to the librarian, and get confirmation, then they will pull the girl in for questioning this evening."

Roxanne blew out a puff of air, and stared into those raven black eyes that studied her. Jordan still remained such a mystery to her, and she accepted the fact that that bothered her. She wanted to know his thoughts and his feelings, but worried the man didn't have it in him to open up to her and share enough of himself for them to truly have a relationship. At least the type of relationship Roxanne wanted.

"What did your girlfriend want?" Jordan asked.

"Her wedding is a week away, and I'm going to go over there and help her make sure everything is in order." Roxanne felt better letting Jordan know her plans, and realized she liked him knowing what she was doing. She felt protected somehow, and cared for, and it was a good feeling. If only she could get the man to commit to her.

"And how do you plan on getting there?" Jordan took his attention from her, and began organizing the items on his desk, then reached for his briefcase.

Roxanne realized it was five, and he was gathering his things to leave. She wondered what he planned on doing, and felt a loss that he didn't see the need to share his itinerary with her.

"I'm going to drive over there as soon as I leave here," Roxanne told him. "I guess I'll stop by the house first and change clothes."

Jordan snapped his briefcase shut and stood up. "You're not going anywhere by yourself."

Roxanne opened her mouth to respond, but Linda appeared in the doorway behind them and spoke, and Roxanne turned to face her.

"I'm sorry to interrupt," Linda began, and Roxanne turned to see the processor smiling at the two of them. "I wanted you to know that the Bradford file is done, and I left it on my desk for you to go over, like you asked," Linda said to Roxanne.

"Thanks, Linda. I'm sure you did everything just fine." Roxanne walked toward Linda, realizing her purse was out at her old cubicle in the secretarial pool. She turned to grab her cell phone, but Jordan picked it up for her.

"We have no way of knowing how serious this prankster is who called you," Jordan said to her, after Linda had left the doorway. Jordan held the phone up in front of Roxanne. "Having your line tapped isn't enough insurance to protect you."

Roxanne stared up into Jordan's dark eyes and watched his gaze lower to her mouth.

"I'll be careful," she whispered, feeling his predatory instincts engulf her and wanting desperately to submit to him.

"You'll be with me," he growled, and met her gaze.

Roxanne reached for her cell phone, which Jordan released to her, but then put his fingers under her chin and tipped her face to his.

"Don't fight me on this," he told her, in a softer, less gruff tone. "Someone has threatened you."

Jordan consented to driving Roxanne to Joanie's apartment, although Roxanne could tell he didn't like the idea of leaving her there.

"She's nervous about her wedding, and I'm her best friend," Roxanne had told him.

He left her at the edge of the parking lot closest to Joanie's door, and Roxanne noticed he didn't drive off until Joanie had answered the door.

The two women chatted about the wedding, as they organized everything to be hauled to the chapel the following weekend. Roxanne could see how nervous Joanie was, but at the same time her best friend glowed with excitement. Every time David appeared to help with something, or just to see how they fared, Joanie wrapped her arms around him and showered him with kisses. David had a hard time keeping his hands off his soon-to-be wife too, and Roxanne enjoyed seeing real love on display.

The three of them ended up on the patio, enjoying the night air, after Joanie announced that she thought everything on her list had been checked off.

Roxanne told her friends about her day, and the prank call she'd received.

"I'm going to have to agree with your boss on this one," David said, after listening. "You shouldn't be alone."

Joanie nodded her agreement. "You're welcome to stay here if you want."

"Something tells me that Jordan wouldn't be thrilled by that idea." David patted Joanie's hand, and she squeezed his fingers. "You've got to realize, darling, he doesn't know us yet."

"I don't answer to him," Roxanne protested, but knew in her mind that she would let Jordan know if she did plan on staying with her friends.

"Is he planning on picking you up and taking you to your car?" David asked.

"I don't know." Roxanne had forgotten that her car wasn't here. "We didn't discuss it."

"I have no problem taking you to it," David said. "And you're welcome to stay here. But you might want to call Jordan and discuss it with him."

As Roxanne reached for her phone, David and Joanie's doorbell rang, and the three of them turned to look through the sliding glass doors into the apartment.

"I'll get the door." David went inside, and Roxanne helped Joanie gather their glasses so they could return inside also.

Roxanne entered the apartment and then stopped in surprise when Jordan stood inside the front door, shaking hands with David. David turned when the women entered.

"And I would like you to meet my fiancée, Joanie," David said, and held his hand out as Joanie walked forward. "This is Jordan Hall."

"I think we've met in passing at the office once or twice," he said, shaking Joanie's hand but then turning his attention to Roxanne.

"Is the wedding all organized?" he asked, walking over to her and pulling her into his arms.

Roxanne nodded, distracted by the strong scent of man that overwhelmed her as she stood in his arms. Everything around her seemed to fade, and she grew very aware of the powerful arms that held her so gently. She reached up and ran her hands over his biceps, wondering if they would ever have the happiness that Joanie and David had found.

"I think these two could organize weddings for a living," David joked, and Joanie smacked his chest with her hand.

David grabbed Joanie, and wrapped his arms around her stomach, pressing her back up against his chest. He rested his chin on her head, and his expression grew serious. "Roxanne told us about her disturbing phone call earlier today. I don't blame you a bit for not letting her out of your sight for long."

"Have there been any new developments?" Roxanne asked, adjusting herself in his arms so that she could look up at him.

"I just got a call from the police," Jordan told all of them, and Roxanne looked up to see him focusing his attention on her. "They're getting ready to make an arrest."

"They're arresting Sonya," Roxanne said, more than asked.

It was such a shame to see a young lady throw her life away like that. The criminal charges that would be pressed against her would be steep.

Jordan nodded. "Apparently they sent Sonya's picture to several libraries today. Two librarians will testify that they have seen her. Fingerprints match up on your computer with the prints lifted at one of the libraries, and they've already seized one bank account where money had been transferred."

Roxanne lowered her gaze, and then looked over to Joanie. "This will devastate Dorothy, Sonya's aunt. I'm sure she had no idea her niece was doing more than cleaning the office."

"She was cleaning us out," Jordan mumbled.

"I can't imagine why she did it." Roxanne continued to focus on her best friend. "I'm pretty sure she comes from a good family."

Jordan stroked Roxanne's back, and she tingled in reaction to his touch.

"Why don't we all go back out to the patio?" Joanie suggested, and pulled away from David as she headed for the kitchen. "What can I get you to drink, Jordan?"

"You're kind to offer," Jordan said, and Roxanne watched Joanie grin like a schoolgirl. "I stopped by to see if Roxanne was ready to go. If she is needed down at the police station, I want to be with her."

"We completely understand." David nodded.

Roxanne gathered her things, and hugged her friends goodbye. Jordan assured Joanie that the four of them would get together soon, and then escorted Roxanne to his car.

"Will you take me to my car?" Roxanne asked, as she walked through the parking lot with Jordan.

"There's no harm in leaving it there for the night."

Roxanne realized Jordan intended for them to spend the night together. Need for him sizzled through her and she imagined Jordan planning an erotic adventure for the two of them.

"I don't want any of your employees noticing it parked there if they arrive before I do in the morning." Roxanne forced herself to focus, and not dwell on the wicked sensations Jordan sent through her when he ran his hand down the back of her head to her rear end. "It won't look good if my co-workers believe I'm sleeping with the boss."

"You are sleeping with the boss," Jordan teased, and gave her rear a playful slap.

"You know what I mean." Roxanne rubbed her rear where he'd just spanked her, and smiled when she looked up to see passion fill his gaze as he watched the act.

They reached the Porsche, and Jordan unlocked the passenger door and then opened it for her.

"Please take me to my car," she asked again, as she slid into the passenger seat.

Jordan watched her skirt slide up her thigh when she slid into his car. She'd worn thigh-highs instead of her usual pantyhose. His insides hardened, blood suddenly pumping through him faster than it had a moment ago. He wondered if she had on panties, or if that pussy of hers was completely exposed.

"It will cost you," Jordan told her, and then shut her door, and strode around to the other side.

Roxanne saw how his mood seemed to have lifted, and understood the release of tension he must be experiencing with the knowledge that the thievery would stop. Tonight would be a good night to discuss the standing of their relationship, Roxanne decided, and felt a knot of anticipation and anxiety form in her tummy.

Chapter Twenty-One

ಬಾ

The parking lot next to the tall office building appeared quiet and abandoned when Jordan pulled the Porsche alongside Roxanne's Probe. Roxanne got out of his car before he could make it around to help her, and fished for her keys in her purse. Jordan moved around the Porsche, and took her purse from her hands, placing it on the roof of her car behind her.

Roxanne looked up at him, and felt her insides dance to life at the predatory look on his face. Why was it such a turn-on to be stalked like prey?

"I am going to spend the entire night making love to you, lady," Jordan said. "I don't plan on stopping until you accept that fact that you are mine."

He stood inches from her, forcing her to look up so she could see his face. He didn't touch her, but the nearness of his body, as he stood inches from her, engulfed her with an ache that begged for attention. A pulsing need between her legs, as pressure and moistness made the smooth folds of skin ache for his touch, forced her to adjust how she stood. She shifted from one foot to the other, wanting nothing more at the moment than to rub her fingers around her clitoris, and spread the thick juices from her need over her shaven skin.

Roxanne licked her lips, and Jordan moved in on the action, capturing her lower lip with his teeth and scraping her tender skin before moving his mouth over hers. Roxanne stretched into him, pressing her body against his, and ran her hands up his muscular arms, then held on to his shoulders. She wanted to make love to him, and hoped that he would want her to, after she said what needed to be said.

Jordan pulled his mouth from hers, and Roxanne gazed into those midnight eyes that matched the color of the sky behind him. His black hair hung around his face as he looked down at her, and she reached up to run a finger over a silky strand.

"There's more to a relationship than me belonging to you," she whispered, her heart aching with each beat. "There are other women in your life and every time I bring it up, you offer no explanation, as if I'm simply supposed to accept that."

"There are no other women in my life, Roxanne. Just you. And that's how it's going to be."

He scanned her face, seeing her worry, and searched for words that would calm her. This was such new territory. Never had he wanted something so bad that he couldn't buy, or gain, simply by taking it. Roxanne wanted more from him than he'd ever given another person before. He wouldn't live without her, but wasn't sure he had what she needed in return.

"What about Elaine? And the phone call yesterday," she asked, inevitable pain wrapping around her heart.

"Elaine Rothchild is the wife of an accountant who needs work. She's propositioned me, but Roxanne, you have nothing to worry about. She called me again yesterday, begging for work for her husband and making it clear she would do anything to help him get a job." He didn't like telling her this.

More than anything he wanted to protect her from the ugly side of his job. But she wouldn't have it that way. And somehow he would learn to give her what she wanted. Roxanne was worth it. He sighed, enjoying how her bare thighs felt against his hands. His blood boiled with need but he fought to keep his head clear to answer her questions until she was satisfied. "They are a couple who partake in a different type of sexual lifestyle. She wanted to fuck me while her husband watched."

"Would you do that?" she asked.

"No," he told her, the smoothness of her skin against his palms driving him crazy. "Not with them. Hall Enterprises has a strong reputation. We've managed to keep scandal away from our business and I won't chance doing anything to tarnish it."

Jordan didn't take his gaze from hers as his hands moved to her hips, and then slowly raised her dress.

Roxanne looked around the dark parking lot, and then back up to his aroused gaze. "Jordan, we're in a parking lot."

Roxanne felt the second her dress raised to her hips, and the fresh air teased the moist skin between her legs. Her eyes widened as one of Jordan's hands moved over her rear end, and his other hand slid between her legs and fingers spread her and exposed her swollen knob of desire, which now pulsed with an erratic beat spawned from desire and nervous excitement.

"You're not wearing any underwear," Jordan growled in a husky whisper into her ear, sending instant chills through her entire body.

Roxanne had so many sensations running through her that all she could manage was a small smile in response. He had exposed her in a public place, albeit quiet and unoccupied, her heart pounded with that knowledge. It also pounded as her breathing quickened, and her mind grew more focused on what his hands were doing to her.

But something else clicked inside her while a sensual fog threatened to take over her thoughts. "Our business?" she asked, his words suddenly hitting her.

Jordan watched her, it hitting him at that moment that he'd referred to Hall Enterprises as theirs. He smiled, liking the idea.

"I can't live without you, Roxanne," he whispered, crushing his groin against her exposed pussy. "We're the perfect team, whether it's work or pleasure."

He watched the wall of resistance she'd placed around her emotions lifting as happiness lit up her dark eyes and flushed over her expression.

"Will you submit to me here?" Jordan's tone had a husky edge to it. He needed her so desperately he wasn't sure he could move until he'd had her. And taking her publicly like this had that edge of danger to it that sent a rush of adrenaline through him, making him feel more alive while blood pumped into his cock.

"No," she said instantly, and then her legs quivered when he pressed a finger against the bulging throb between her legs. "Jordan," she cried, and hung on to him as he pressed harder.

"Are you going to fight me?" he whispered, and she stared up into those demanding eyes.

Roxanne couldn't answer though. Jordan spread his fingers across her rear and pressed her into him while his other hand stroked her wetness, and played a wicked dance around her hardened clit.

"Unzip my pants, Roxanne," Jordan told her.

Roxanne stared at him, and felt her mouth go dry. Her hands slid from his shoulders to his elbows, but then stopped. Jordan found the rock-hard nub surrounded by her juices, and patted it with one finger.

"Do it now," he ordered with a gruff whisper.

Roxanne inhaled a shattered breath, and let her hands slide to his pants. She shook with nervous energy, the thought of him fucking her so publicly, where they risked the chance of getting caught, scaring and exciting her all at once. Her fingers stumbled over his belt and zipper, while her heart raced with so much energy that she was lightheaded.

Jordan's arousal leapt into her hands once she had his zipper down, and she licked her dry lips as her fingers circled the steely shaft.

Jordan moved his hand that spread over her exposed rear end, and ran his fingers toward her inner thigh, then pulled and lifted her leg.

"What if we get caught?" She shot a nervous look around the parking lot.

She wanted him so bad. And fucking him there had a naughty thrill to it that made her so wet she couldn't stand it.

"I'll protect you. Take this adventure with me," he whispered, and lifted her leg to his waist, then angled his hips so that she could feel his cock press into her moistness.

"I will have you anywhere," he told her. "Move your hands."

Roxanne let go of the velvet skin that covered steel, and put her hands around his biceps. Nervous energy ran through her and combated with raw desire, causing her heart to race, and blood to pump through her at an exciting pace. Someone could pull into the quiet parking lot at any moment. They could get caught doing it in between their parked cars like two high-school kids, and the thought scared and excited her all at the same time.

Jordan pressed against her, and then shifted her body toward him. At the same time he thrust, and Roxanne felt his engorged erection slide through her feverish entrance and fill her, as he stretched and penetrated her, matching her need with his.

Jordan retreated slowly.

Roxanne felt the pressure he left behind, and her lower muscles gripped at him, unable to prevent his slow escape. She dug her fingers into his arms, her mouth open, not wishing to breathe.

"Jordan," she begged, no longer caring that they stood in a dark parking lot, next to the office building where they worked, in the heart of Kansas City, with life buzzing around them on the street, and for blocks after that.

Jordan bent his legs slightly, and began a lazy cruise within her again, sliding his massive shaft deeper inside her, pressing against the pressure he had left behind moments before. She felt her muscles cling to him, as once again he filled and stretched her.

"Who do you belong to?" he asked.

Roxanne couldn't look away from those black orbs that stalked her. She licked her lips and tried to tell him that she didn't belong to anyone. If he wanted to own her, make her into his sexual toy, then he had the wrong woman. But as Jordan filled her again, and then stopped before he had completely penetrated her, and let his erection rest within her soaked, aching muscles, she couldn't make herself form the words.

"Tell me," Jordan whispered, and stood holding her, buried deep within her, and not moving.

"I…" she tried to say it but then stopped. She wanted to tell him that she belonged to herself.

Jordan once again began to slide away from the one spot that would bring her release. She gripped at his arms with her fingers, digging deep into the material of his shirt, and tried everything her inner muscles were capable of to prevent his regression.

"No," she wailed, as he made a torturous journey back toward the entrance of her sex, leaving her in a fog of frustrated passion as the pressure built further inside her.

"You know the answer, Roxanne," he told her. "I want to hear you admit it. Tell me who you belong to."

"Tell me who you belong to," she cried, and wanting more than anything to belong to him, to be his forever.

Jordan slammed into her with such force that Roxanne felt she had been punched when stars exploded in front of her. She threw her head back, gasping for air, as her muscles grabbed onto his cock, and exploded with so much force that Roxanne felt her legs go weak. He maneuvered his hands quickly to help her remain balanced on her one foot, and at the same time slid completely out of her. Roxanne had barely felt her orgasm begin when she found herself empty, and her leg sliding down the side of him, until both her feet were on the ground.

"Get in your car, and drive to my house." Jordan straightened, and adjusted himself, then zipped his pants, taking away from her what she needed most at the moment. "I'll be right behind you."

Roxanne wanted to cry, and scream at the same time. She wanted to lunge at Jordan and demand that he finish what he started. He adjusted his pants and then turned toward his car.

The asshole! He got her all hot and bothered, and then left her in a state where she could hardly focus, let alone move. And now he expected her to drive. She couldn't believe his nerve. She yanked her car door open. Roxanne threw her purse to the passenger seat, and slid behind the wheel of her car, staring ahead for a moment before she reached for her key. She had felt his arousal, knew he was hard with need for her. How could he walk away from her when he wanted her as badly as she wanted him?

Roxanne grabbed her keys and started her car. She lurched the car forward, grinding her gears, and left the parking lot while cursing his name.

"You are a fool!" Roxanne let out an exasperated breath, and forced herself to relax as she moved through traffic. "He tried to fuck you in a parking lot, for crying out loud. Now listen to you. You're throwing a tantrum because he stopped."

Roxanne scolded herself out loud, and then took slow calming breaths as she reached to turn on the stereo. A hard object pressed into the side of her neck, and Roxanne had to hit the brake to prevent hitting the car in front of her when a man's voice spoke from behind her.

"The man was a fool not to fuck you blind."

"What the fuck?" Roxanne cried out, fear gripping her so hard that she could barely see the road in front of her.

"Pick up your phone and call him. Tell him to go on to his house and that you'll be there in a minute," the man behind her said with a sinister growl.

"I can't." Roxanne couldn't think. Her heart pounded so hard she knew she would puke.

"You will," he told her, pressing the hard object into her neck so hard that it hurt. "Get your phone now and tell him."

She couldn't think. Tears blurred her vision and she couldn't tell if there were cars in front of her or not. Try as she would, she couldn't see anyone in her backseat through her rearview mirror. Whoever pressed the cold, metal object into her neck was crouched down low enough that he couldn't be seen.

Chapter Twenty-Two

❧

Jordan couldn't get comfortable as he focused on traffic and Roxanne's car in front of him. His engorged arousal made it very difficult to sit or do anything else for that matter.

Every inch of his physical desires screamed, *"Stupid, stupid!"* for leaving that hot, moist sweetness he could still feel surrounding his dick.

Roxanne had been as aroused by his spontaneous, public attention as he had been, if not more so. He could have pounded her into pure ecstasy, and probably indulged in a few other sexual pleasures too. He doubted she would have stopped him at any point. Roxanne was a sexual dream come true, with her eagerness to experience everything he administered to her. She had been dripping with cum when he first touched her, and the fact that she had worn thigh-highs, and not those pantyhose she usually wore, had made access so much easier.

Jordan groaned, and then hit his brakes when Roxanne slowed suddenly due to traffic. She didn't increase her speed, and he matched her pace, remaining behind her.

"It was necessary," he told himself, as he fought not to regret ending their lovemaking before it had even started.

The pulsing throb that pounded through his arousal disagreed with him but Jordan worked to focus on traffic and not think about Roxanne's hot body. He had made a decision, and in order to see it through he needed to stick to his game plan.

Jordan had fought the reality that he felt anything more for Roxanne other than as a consenting adult who shared his desire for wild sex. Other women had fulfilled that need for him in the past, but Roxanne had more to offer, and she wanted more from him.

He had realized she wanted a serious relationship from him and at first had shrugged it off as a female thing she would overcome. But what had nagged at him was that he wanted more from Roxanne as well. He wouldn't deny any longer that he loved her—needed her—and would meet any terms to have her.

When she wasn't with him he couldn't keep his mind off of her, and he had to know what she was doing, and who she was with, or he couldn't concentrate on his own work. She had become a part of him, and if they were going to enter into a relationship, then he needed to hear her commit to him.

It was what she wanted, or he wouldn't make her accept complete submission. She had told him in so many words, and had shown him through her jealousy when she thought he had been with other women. She had shown him that she wanted to be the focus of his attention, and that she wanted him to tell her that she would be the only woman in his life.

But then she'd demanded his submission too. It shouldn't have surprised him. In fact, when she asked him who he belonged to, it had finally clicked what had made him fall in love with her. Her strength, her determination, her mind that never let go, never gave up. In a state of complete surrender to him, she had still managed to demand that he admit he belonged to her.

There was nothing passive about Roxanne. She was a fiery woman full of energy and spark. They would walk side by side through life, dealing with all matters together. That thought made him even harder than her sweet pussy had.

His phone rang and he glanced down to see Roxanne's number.

"Jordan. I'm going to run by my house to get some clothes first and then I'll be over." Her voice sounded shaky and he watched her in front of him while he listened on the phone.

"Sounds good but if you aren't at my place in thirty minutes I'll chase you down." Thoughts of chasing her through the woods behind his house, and how hot it had made her, rushed through him. He shifted to ease the pain in his throbbing cock, still wet from her juices.

"No. You told me that you love me. And you know that I love you. Now go home and I'll be there shortly." She hung up on him and then darted into the next lane, dodging cars until suddenly she was two lanes over and hitting the next exit.

Jordan stared at his cell phone for a minute while watching the traffic around him. He'd never told Roxanne that he loved her. And she'd never voiced it to him. His insides hardened, worry attacking him hard enough to steal his breath. Something wasn't right with this picture.

He punched the button on his phone to call her back.

"Hello." She'd answered on the first ring but said nothing. "Hello?" he said again.

There were muffled sounds, car noise. But she didn't answer him.

Jordan cut into the other lane, dodging cars and racing toward the next exit. He kept his cell pressed to his ear, struggling to interpret the sounds he heard.

"Is that a gun?" Roxanne's voice sounded far away, like she had the cell phone put down somewhere.

Damn it to fucking hell! She was in trouble!

Why the hell hadn't he stayed on her ass? She'd pulled off on the previous exit and could be anywhere right now. Turning onto the first side street that would trace him back in the direction he had to be, a hardness spread through him, causing him to grip his steering wheel until his knuckles hurt. If anyone laid a hand on her, he would kill them.

* * * * *

"My car is almost out of gas." Roxanne rubbed her fist over her eye to clear her vision, and keep the car on the road.

Her captor said nothing. In fact, other than to tell her when to turn, he hadn't said a word to her since making his presence known. Roxanne had managed to keep the car on the road, although she'd been tempted more than once to intentionally drive into a ditch, or try to flip the car — anything! She would do anything to get that gun to quit pressing into the side of her neck. She hadn't seen the weapon, but it had been pressed there long enough for her to feel its hard surface, a small circular object, hollow in the middle, that remained in a solitary position below her right ear.

"I'm serious," Roxanne tried again. She didn't know why she wanted the man behind her to speak, he hadn't had anything nice to say to her so far, but it bugged her that he sat behind her with that gun, just out of range of her rearview mirror, and remained silent. "We've got less than a quarter tank of gas and we aren't headed anywhere near a gas station. Where does county road 1500 take us?"

She glanced down at her cell phone, resting next to her on the seat. In the darkness she couldn't tell if Jordan was still on the line, or not. The police had put a listening device in it, and she prayed with all of her might that they were being recorded, and that Jordan had heard what road she was on.

The man behind her in the seat leaned forward for the first time. The gun left the side of her neck, although she could still feel the indention from where it had been pressing for the past ten minutes.

"Slow down. There's a gravel road up here to your left. Turn there." The man behind her nudged her with the gun when he spoke, and Roxanne jumped in spite of herself.

"I don't see a road," she said, and her voice cracked from fear.

Roxanne took a deep breath and focused on the surroundings, hoping for a mile marker or something to give a clue as to where they were. In the darkness, all she could see were the thick meadows that spread to either side of the road, broken occasionally by a group of trees.

"Turn left," the man instructed.

A gravel road appeared in her headlights, and Roxanne turned onto it, wondering how anyone would ever know where she was. She took a minute to glance up and down the county road she had been on and saw no cars in either direction. Dust from the gravel flew up on either side of her car, and Roxanne slowly headed toward a destination, having no clue what to expect, and not knowing how she would ever get out of there.

The bumps on the road scraped the gun up and down her neck, but Roxanne didn't dare try to put her hand on the spot that grew more and more agitated the further they drove. She almost felt relief when a doublewide trailer appeared ahead, and wondered if that was their destination.

"Turn here." The man nudged her with the gun, and Roxanne obeyed, turning onto a paved driveway.

As they approached the house, Roxanne did her best to take in her surroundings, although she didn't know what to look for in the dark that might enable her escape. A doublewide trailer that appeared to have been on the property for some time sat at the edge of a circular drive. It had been well-kept, and in the dark Roxanne could see trimmed bushes and flower gardens bordering the house.

"Park here." The man pulled the gun away from Roxanne's neck, and she instinctively put her fingers on the spot where it had been, still feeling the pressure of the hard metal against her skin.

As she put the car into park, her captor pushed the passenger seat next to her forward, opened the passenger door, and slid out of the car. Roxanne got her first confirmation that a gun had indeed been pressed to her neck. She now stared at it as a small man, wearing black jeans and a pullover collared shirt that hung untucked past the waistline of his jeans, walked around the front of her car and then opened her car door for her. Her mouth went dry and she felt her stomach heave.

This was it. She grabbed her phone, glancing at it quickly, but too scared to make a show of trying to see if she was still connected to Jordan, and stepped out of her car on shaky legs. Roxanne stared the man in the face as he nudged her with the gun, and tried her best to reason with him. She had to do something to save her life.

"Why are you doing this?" she asked, adjusting her phone so it clipped to her skirt. Her fingers were so damp she swore she wouldn't be able to complete the simple act. If he took her phone from her, it would be her last hope for rescue. "We're in the country, out in the middle of nowhere. Why did you bring me here?"

"We need insurance. And you're it." He didn't elaborate.

The man took her arm and guided her toward the front door, and Roxanne did her best to walk alongside him without tripping. A small porch light hung next to the front door, but otherwise it was dark and Roxanne couldn't see much past the small circle of light that cast over the front yard.

"I haven't done anything, and I don't know why you're bringing me here." Now she was babbling but Roxanne didn't know what else to say and her mind seemed unable to find a good argument that might convince this man to let her back into the safety of her car.

Someone opened the front door, although Roxanne didn't see anyone at first. She felt her stomach heave, and thought for sure she would throw up all over the two wooden steps she stumbled up as her assailant gave her a not-so-nice shove toward the entrance of her prison.

One of Roxanne's heels caught in a gap between boards on the step and she stumbled, reaching forward to grab the doorknob and balance herself. A hand gripped her wrist, steadying her, and at the same time guiding her inside.

"Very nice work," a man's voice said.

Roxanne felt herself guided by the wrist now into a modest-looking living room. At first glance she felt she had been brought to the wrong place, and a sense of giddiness flowed through her. She wanted to smile at the relaxed atmosphere the warm colors of the living room offered, and knew she must be bordering on hysteria.

The door closed behind her and Roxanne turned at the sound, realizing in the same instant that her kidnapper had not followed her inside. She turned again and stared into the face of a man she had never seen before.

"Why am I here?" she asked, taking in the contents of the room she was in.

Dark tan furniture, end tables and a coffee table were arranged in a simple manner. The place looked clean, and a lamp had been turned on that rested on the far end table. Long cream-colored drapes covered the windows, and they were all closed, giving the room an intimate, quiet feeling. None of this comforted Roxanne, however. She had been kidnapped, and the place could have been a mansion, but it still remained her prison.

"You fucked up when you showed up at your office the other night," the man answered, and Roxanne shot her attention back to the man. "Now we have to clean up the mess you've made."

The man wasn't tall. He wore baggy jeans, and a simple black T-shirt with no wording on it. If asked to describe the man she would have given such a generic explanation it would have been little to go by.

She couldn't help but wonder if his appearance had been carefully planned. Nothing about him stood out—no tattoos, scars, or anything that would help in identifying him.

The man turned and, still holding her wrist, walked through an arched doorway into a kitchen and dining area. The carpet on the floor changed to vinyl, and Roxanne's shoes clicked as she followed him.

"Sit there," he instructed as he released her wrist, and pointed to one of the chairs at the dining room table.

Roxanne sat and watched the man pad over to the refrigerator and pull out a bottle of wine. She noticed he had no shoes on, and wore gray socks that moved silently over the floor. He grabbed two wineglasses and returned to the table.

"Miss Roxanne Isley, may I call you Roxanne?" The man sat in the chair next to her, and turned it so they faced each other.

Roxanne didn't answer but watched him as he popped the cork and poured wine into each glass. He handed one of the glasses, half full of the golden liquid, to her, and she knew if she drank much more than a sip she quite easily could puke. Just the smell of the wine turned her stomach. Her fingers shook as she accepted the glass, and she placed it on the table in front of her quickly, without tasting it.

"I imagine it would be terrifying to be stolen from your car at night," the man said, as he watched her actions. "Especially when you thought you would be in the arms of your lover shortly."

This comment seemed to amuse the man, since Roxanne noticed a slight turn of the edge of his mouth into something that might resemble a smile. She didn't see a need to comment since she doubted anything she had to say on the matter would affect this man's opinion to release her. God. Please let the police show up soon.

"But it is important that I bring you here because now I need your help." The man took a long sip of his wine, watching her over the edge of his glass.

"You need my help?" Roxanne wanted to say it would be a cold day in hell before she helped the man do a thing. "You have a strange way of asking for it," she said instead.

"I am not asking for your help." There was a hard edge in the man's tone. "You will help me."

Roxanne straightened at the coldness in the man's words. "You have snooped around a bit too much, and years of hard work will not be ruined because you wish to impress your boss." He didn't sound bitter with his comment, instead Roxanne detected determination. The man had an agenda, and she didn't see any harm in being curious about what he was doing.

"What work do you do?" she asked.

This time the man smiled at her question, and she saw a change in his expression, as a person did when they were preparing to talk about their favorite subject.

"Consider me a Robin Hood of sorts," he said, and his smile faded.

Roxanne watched him, thinking that he must not smile much because there were no lines of any kind around his mouth. She would have a tough guess at his age.

"Are you saying you steal from the rich and give to the poor?" The longer they sat there and talked, possibly her rescuers would arrive, and nothing more would happen to her. That is, if rescuers were on their way.

"Well, not exactly." The man had returned to his blank expression and watched her with green eyes as he explained. "Maybe I should say that I manage a Robin Hood-type society. I've never stolen a thing in my life."

He made this last comment as if it was something he was proud to say. And Roxanne instantly knew it was a lie.

When he stood, Roxanne edged closer to the table in her chair. She watched him walk into the kitchen, and she quickly looked around the room, as if her path to escape would be obvious in her brief moment of not being watched. A napkin holder sat in the middle of the table, half full with paper napkins. Otherwise there was nothing else on the table.

An overhead light hung from a chain, and when she glanced up at it, she could see a small spiral of dead bugs resting in the porcelain light fixture.

There were two windows in the room, both with cream-colored drapes, which were pulled closed. Through the doorway she could see the front door and part of the living room, but nothing stood out to her as a quick means of escape, other than bolting for the front door.

"The people who work for me understand that everyone benefits in what we do. I'm a very fair man." He returned to her side, but instead of sitting, he stood next to her for a minute. "The rewards I offer are beyond your wildest imagination, Roxanne."

She would have had to turn and look up to see him, and Roxanne decided to continue facing the table. He made her nervous hovering next to her though, and Roxanne wished he would sit down.

"What do you want more than anything in the whole world?" he asked her.

"I want to go home," she said without hesitating.

The man placed the wine bottle on the table in front of Roxanne, and then stepped behind her. Roxanne tensed, not sure what he was up to. When his fingers clamped down on her shoulders, she jumped.

He leaned forward so that his mouth was by her ear. "I'm not playing games, my dear," he whispered. "Now don't whine to me like a baby. I don't like it."

Something in his tone made Roxanne feel she was in true danger. She had been scared ever since she realized she'd been kidnapped, but terror trickled through her bloodstream now, and she turned her head so she could see him.

"I know you aren't playing games," she said, and her voice trembled.

"Good. Very good." He began kneading her shoulders, pressing his thumbs against the base of her neck, and making her muscles tighten further in fear. "Now what do you want more than anything in the whole world?" he asked again.

Roxanne feared this was a trick question, and searched her mind for the right answer, but came up blank. "I don't know," she said, blinking tears from her eyes.

"Everyone has dreams, Roxanne," he told her, and the soft caress of his voice made her skin crawl. "You want something and I can give it to you. Anything your heart desires will be yours."

His fingers left her shoulders, and his hands slid down her front. Roxanne held her breath and squeezed her eyes closed, allowing hot tears to run down her cheeks when his hands clamped down on her breasts.

"Don't you want beautiful clothes? Closets full? Jewelry? The ability to wake up and decide you are going to go visit another country that day?" His hot breath burned her neck as he spoke, and irritated the spot where the gun had prodded her.

Please be listening to all of this, Jordan. Please be on your way here to rescue me.

The man squeezed her breasts, rubbing his fingers forward until his thumb and forefinger pinched her nipples. He repeated the motion several times, and Roxanne remained frozen, unable to prevent the tears.

There has got to be a way out of here, she thought, trying to keep her mind off what the man was doing. If there wasn't someone on their way to rescue her, she had to figure out how to escape by herself. The thought of being raped terrified her. What would she do if this man forced himself on her? She had no idea what to say to him though in order to stop his actions, and panicked that anything she might say could escalate them.

"Imagine a life where you didn't have to work, Roxanne." His breath now burned her ear, and she fought the urge to bat at his face with her hand. "Imagine not having to pay attention to a time clock, or follow orders. A life like that is what we all dream about, and now you can have it."

She squeezed her eyes closed tighter, telling herself to not listen to the man ramble, but to focus on how she could get out of there.

"You will have your own home and beautiful clothes, closets full of them," he continued. "The world will be your playground, and all of your friends, millionaires.

"I will show you how to live a life like this," he told her, "and you will be amazed how simple it is.

"You already possess more knowledge than most I have trained." He pulled away from her for a moment and unzipped her dress. She felt the zipper slide down her spine, and his knuckles braised her skin. Her stomach burned, and she fought not to gulp into an hysteria of tears.

Please don't hurt me. Tears streamed down her face and she couldn't focus but didn't dare move to wipe them away.

"I will take you downstairs soon, and I will show you what you will need to do." He moved the material of her dress off her shoulders, and she heard him suck in air as his hands moved over her lace bra. "I will expect you to learn quickly, Roxanne," he said, and slid his hands inside her bra.

She couldn't allow this. She let out a small whimper when he squeezed her nipples, and then her breasts. Her breath came out in staggered gasps, and she fought to focus on something else.

The police. They are tracing this call and they will find me. God. Please don't let him notice that my phone is on.

"Until I am comfortable that you know our system well, and that I have your undying loyalty, you will remain here with me." In a quick movement, he stretched his hands and forced the straps of her bra off her shoulders. "We are a very tight family here, and you will be welcomed. And I am a very generous leader," he said, and ran his palms over her now exposed nipples.

"Once you understand everything, you will experience a freedom like you never thought existed. Nothing will be out of your reach, and everything life has to offer you will be at your fingertips.

"We are going to go downstairs now," he told her, moving from behind her. "You will not ask any questions, nor will any explanations be offered you at this time. I will show you where to stand and you will remain there, not moving but simply observing and learning what you can at this time."

He didn't ask her if she understood, which she didn't. But Roxanne had no problem with not asking questions. He pulled her to her feet, and her dress pooled at her waist. She made an effort to slide the material back up to her shoulders, but the man grabbed her wrist and prevented her. Apparently she would be made to stand where he put her, exposed to whoever might be downstairs. Roxanne prayed her cell phone, with its open line, had alerted the police to her predicament, because at this point, she had no idea what else to do in order to get out of there.

Chapter Twenty-Three

ഇ

Not often had anyone been able to infuriate Jordan to the point where he wondered if he thought clearly. He credited himself as a levelheaded man, even in situations where someone tried to get the upper hand with him. And seldom had anyone succeeded. Nor would they tonight, and he glared at the large trailer, concealed in the meadow.

His phone rang, and Jordan pounced on it. "Yeah," he said, without preamble.

"Mr. Hall, this is Officer Houser." There was static on the line, and Jordan pressed the phone to his ear as he glanced out his car windows and surveyed the dark meadow spreading across both sides of the narrow county road.

"Where the hell are you?" Jordan wanted the police here now, so they could get Roxanne out of that house. "I called you all a good fifteen minutes ago, and I'm about to go in after her alone if you don't get here quick."

"We're on our way." The officer verified directions, and Jordan repeated what he had told the dispatcher. "I'd say we are just about to you," the officer added.

Jordan looked in his rearview mirror, and noticed headlights turning off the county road.

"If that is you, I'd cut the lights so we don't alarm anyone inside." Jordan hoped it was the police since he wasn't armed, and didn't want to explain to anyone why he sat out there alone in his Porsche.

The lights in the car behind him went off, and Jordan exhaled, which made him realize how tense he was. He didn't like not being able to handle a situation, and had considered more than once trying to play superhero and go in and rescue

Roxanne on his own. The simple truth was he doubted he would be able to do it. And that pissed him off. They could be torturing her inside that house, and he sat out there feeling helpless.

The patrol car pulled up behind Jordan's Porsche, and an officer got out on either side of the vehicle. Jordan opened his own car door and turned to face Officer Houser, who had been to his office just that morning.

"Her phone is still on. Have you heard everything?"

"They're monitoring it at headquarters. And we have backup on its way." The officer studied the house, while the other officer, the woman who had been with Officer Houser, stood behind the two men, talking quietly into her radio.

"We don't have time to wait. We need to get her out of there now." He would go in there himself, if these cops didn't act pretty damn quickly.

"They're here." She pointed up the road. "Got two officers in a car at the county turnoff, and three walking across the meadow now."

Jordan was impressed at the amount of backup they had. He nodded his approval. "I want to get her out of there as quickly as we can. Are you ready?"

Officer Houser held a hand out, as if to block Jordan's path. Jordan stiffened at the gesture.

"Hold on, Mr. Hall. Let's let our men who are trained in this area do their job."

"I'm not standing here while she is in there having God knows what done to her." He turned and began walking toward the driveway of the house, and Officer Houser was next to him in an instant.

Officer Houser walked quickly and grabbed Jordan's arm. "I can't let you interfere right now, Mr. Hall. We don't know what risks are involved."

"Miss Isley is at risk," Jordan hissed at the man. "You better tell your men to act quickly before I go in there and do something that may cause you to arrest me."

Jordan yanked his hand free from the officer, and once again turned toward the house. He had almost reached where Roxanne's car had stopped earlier. Officer Houser grabbed Jordan again, and Jordan exerted serious effort not to turn and belt the man. The officer must have seen the anger peaking within him because he let go of him when Jordan turned to face him.

"Our men are entering the house now. But we need to get out of sight, and let them do their job."

Roxanne stood along the wall, watching the two men and woman who sat at computers and worked while the Robin Hood man stood over them talking to them in a tone she couldn't hear. It took everything she had to stand there in complete humiliation, with her dress pulled down to her waist, and her breasts exposed. The man had removed her bra before they descended the stairs, and then had guided her to the place where she stood now.

"For now you will stand here, watch and learn," he had told her, as he stood close to her and fondled her breasts. "I will not allow anyone to touch you, so you don't have to worry about that. But your appearance pleases me, and I will enjoy looking over here from time to time and seeing you on display for me."

Roxanne had wanted to spit in his face, but she kept her expression blank. He stood very close, with his face inches from hers, and his hot breath made her skin crawl.

"I want you to know," he added, and she watched as his eyes stared at her unblinking, a mixture of green and blue that appeared very clear and determined, "if you do anything that doesn't please me, then I might decide to let the others touch you too."

Roxanne felt her body quiver, and she fought not to shake uncontrollably in front of the monster who now offered her a small smile. "You will be a good girl though. I believe you only want me to touch you."

She didn't move a muscle when he leaned forward and smothered her neck with his hot breath as he kissed her collarbone.

When he backed away from her, she could see the three people at the computer had turned and watched the show. The man clapped his hands and told them to get back to work, as he adjusted his pants and moved to stand behind them. They did as he said, but each of them glanced over their shoulder at her from time to time.

Tears fell down Roxanne's cheeks as she glanced around the finished basement. From what she could hear of the conversation, this man, who the others referred to as Robin, was stealing from accounts all over the world. His setup looked so simple, she realized, as she took in the modestly furnished basement. But then again, all he needed were the computers and the knowledge to move around on them and hack into people's accounts.

She noticed sliding glass doors on the other side of the basement stairs, and realized the doublewide not only stood on a foundation with this basement, but also must have been built on a hill. Someone had gone to some effort to make the place appear a lot simpler from the road than it actually was.

She stared at the glass doors, and at the blackness beyond them. No outside light shone, and she had no idea what was out there. But at the moment, those doors, or the stairs, were her only means of escape. And neither looked too promising.

She jerked her head toward Robin when he walked back toward her.

"You appear to be daydreaming, my dear," he said in a calm voice that chilled her. "How will you learn if you don't pay attention?"

He raised his hand as if he would strike her, and Roxanne took a step backward in spite of his previous instruction not to move.

"No, don't," she whimpered, and turned her head from him, squeezing her eyes closed as she waited for the strike. She felt her muscles shake, and although she tried to stop them, she feared her legs would give out, and prepared to fall.

What sounded like an explosion blasted through the air, and Roxanne screamed, not sure at first what had happened. She covered her head with her arms, and collapsed to the floor, squatting as she began to cry harder. Her knees burned as they scraped the carpet, and her hands and elbows followed, as her dress twisted around her waist. It dawned on her that others were screaming too, and she looked around her through her tears. Robin had turned from her, and she scooted on all fours away from him.

More people had entered the room, and appeared to be wrestling with the men and woman who had been at the computers. That was when she noticed the KCPD letters on one of the men's jacket, and she cried fresh tears of joy. She slipped her arms through the sleeve holes of her dress, and tried to slide it up her body. The material twisted around her, and she looked down, trying to cover herself, and stay clear of the growing commotion in the room.

She had to get out of there, and she wasn't going to run before she had her clothes back on. She heaved a staggered breath as her dress finally straightened, and then fought to stand on trembling legs.

The officers all had guns poised on the small group who had been in the basement, and everyone seemed to be talking at once. More people entered, and she realized then that someone had broken through the glass doors, and fragments of glass lay scattered across the floor. An officer approached her, and spoke to her, but Roxanne could hardly make out what he said. He had a jacket extended and wrapped it over her shoulders, then began guiding her through the confusion toward the darkness that lay past the basement doors where the police had entered.

The night air hit her like a damp washcloth against her tear-soaked cheeks. The officer held onto her as she struggled to walk over the rough terrain behind the house and around the side of it, where lights seemed to shine from everywhere. She realized that several cars had their headlights beamed at different angles, and a tall, dark figure walked with long strides toward them, silhouetted by the lights. She pulled from the officer when she realized the figure was Jordan.

"Dear God, my love! Oh, thank God you're okay!" he exclaimed, and opened his arms so that she could fall into him.

"Jordan, I'm so glad you're here," she cried, and let him hold her, never wanting him to let her go. "I was so scared."

"I know you were, sweetheart. We got you out of there as soon as we could."

She didn't pay much attention to the commotion after that. Jordan led her to his car, and held her hand as they drove to the station.

"Did that bastard hurt you?" he asked when they got out of the car, and he ran his hands over her, as if confirming for himself that she was okay.

"No. He threatened to, but I'm not hurt." She smiled up at him, and then collapsed into his chest, still feeling shaky, and wanting nothing more than to be wrapped in his protective embrace.

Jordan held her for a moment, resting his chin on top of her head, and she pressed her cheek against his chest, feeling his heartbeat and the warmth of his body permeate through her. Jordan's hand brushed up and down her back in a gentle stroke while his other arm gripped her shoulders, holding her next to him. She let out an audible sigh, and felt her muscles relax further under his touch.

"I realized something while waiting to get you out of that house," Jordan said.

"What's that?" Roxanne asked, not moving from her very comfortable spot.

Jordan didn't answer right away, and Roxanne finally let curiosity get the better of her, and leaned her head back to look up at his face. "What did you realize?" she asked again.

Jordan put a few inches between them, which was too much space for Roxanne. He cupped her face with his hands, and she met his gaze.

"You used our love as a sign to me that you were in trouble." He stroked her cheek, loving the way she nibbled at her lower lip when he reminded her of the words she'd chosen to use to alert him that something was wrong. "And it's something I should have told you sooner. But I've never said this much in my life so it's going to take some getting used to. Roxanne, I love you."

Jordan's words hit her so hard, her heart exploded into a rapid pitter-patter while energy surged through her, and the desire to jump into his lap, wrap her arms around him, and hold on to him forever, enveloped her.

"I love you, too," Roxanne whispered, unable to stop the grin that spread across her face.

Jordan lowered his head to kiss her, and she went up on tiptoes to meet him halfway, her mouth as eager as his. In spite of the exhaustion she had felt moments before, and the aching muscles worn out from being clenched in fear, Roxanne grabbed his shoulders and pressed him to her.

She collapsed against him, feeling his strength, his heat, the comforting power that flooded through her.

She was thoroughly out of breath when their kiss finally ended, and their faces parted enough so they could stare into each other's eyes, and she could see a calm settle over his face that she hadn't seen before. He smiled down at her with the peace of a child coming home, she thought, and knew no one had ever graced her with such love before.

"Could I ask one favor?" she said, and he nodded before he said anything.

"You may have anything you want," he told her.

Roxanne ran her hands down those powerful arms. "Could we not do it in parking lots anymore?"

Jordan glanced around them and his smile faded. "Oh baby, I'm sorry." And his expression grew so serious that she suppressed a giggle. "No more parking lots," he assured her, and then held her close as they turned and walked toward the large judicial center.

Chapter Twenty-Four

ဆ

Roxanne opened her eyes when she heard the door open.

"If you don't get out of there soon, you'll still be covered in bubbles when your friends arrive." Jordan stood in the doorway of his bathroom, and Roxanne smiled lazily at him.

"I don't think they'd mind," she teased him, and then giggled when Jordan straightened, and gave her a stern look.

His expression softened immediately, and a wicked glint appeared in his eyes as he approached the tub. Roxanne shifted in the warm water, and ran her hands over the surface to bring the mounds of bubbles around her.

"Maybe I should present you that way then," he growled in a tone she recognized as one meant to torment her.

Jordan reached into the water and lifted her up from underneath her arms as water and bubbles slid down her body. She reached for him, laughing and trying to get him wet, but he held her at arm's length and surveyed her nakedness with blackened orbs that seared her skin with need as they gazed over her.

The week after Joanie and David's wedding, Jordan and Roxanne had taken some time off and gone to stay in his cabin buried in the Rockies. It was time both of them needed, after having worked many long hours at the office, and then dealing with the ordeal of so many accounts coming up short.

The doorbell chimed downstairs, and Roxanne wiggled in Jordan's grasp.

"Are you two decent?" Millie hollered up the stairs.

Jordan placed Roxanne on the floor next to the tub, and looked toward the open bathroom door. "Well, one of our guests has arrived," he said, and then turned back and reached for her nipple.

She slapped his hand away laughing. "Better go be a gracious host," she said, between giggles when Jordan grabbed her and yanked her toward him. She had learned that he didn't like to be denied access to touching her whenever he pleased, and enjoyed his aggression whenever she decided to push his hands away from her.

Jordan pulled her in for a quick kiss, and then spanked her bare rear end, which made a loud slapping sound against her wet skin. Roxanne felt the heat instantly on her rear, and a swelling ache develop at the same time that she knew she wouldn't get satisfied for at least the next few hours.

By the time Roxanne had dressed, she could hear laughing and chattering on the deck out back. She hurried down the stairs and ran a hand through her still damp hair as she hurried out to the large deck that had been well-lit for the planned gathering that evening. Jordan had waited for the office environment to return to its normal busy atmosphere before deciding to have a gathering for all of his employees, and a few of their friends, over at his house. Roxanne had loved the idea, since she hadn't had time to see Joanie since her return from the honeymoon, and Roxanne wanted her friends to meet Jordan in a more relaxed atmosphere than their first brief meeting. She had hardly had time to even talk to Joanie on the phone, and laughed out loud when her friend spotted her the second Roxanne walked out on the deck.

"There you are," Joanie said, handing David her drink, and then hurrying over to wrap her arms around Roxanne.

The two of them laughed and talked at the same time, immediately trying to share everything that had happened to them since they had last seen each other. Roxanne heard Jordan's baritone chuckle, and turned in that direction.

"Would you look at those two," Roxanne said to Joanie, as the two of them turned their attention to Jordan and David, who leaned against the railing on the other side of the deck. "I take it

Jordan took care of seeing that reintroductions were made. Those two are talking like old friends."

"Yes, he's made us feel right at home." Joanie nudged Roxanne with her elbow, and Roxanne turned to see her friend's mischievous smile. "And I am looking at those two. They are definitely the finest-looking men I've ever seen."

"I'd have to say you're right," Roxanne said, and then turned her attention to the men who now were both looking their way. Roxanne put her hand on Joanie's shoulder, and whispered, "They're watching us."

"Yeah, and they're trying to figure out what we're saying about them," Joanie whispered back, and the two of them broke into giggles.

"Of course they're assuming we're talking about them," Roxanne laughed, and turned to see that both men now had inquisitive expressions on their face.

"We are talking about them." Joanie looked so beautiful with her streaming long blonde hair, and her laugh was contagious.

Roxanne noticed several men from the office turned their attention to her, and Roxanne wrapped her arm around Joanie's and headed toward Jordan and David.

Every employee from the office managed to show up for the gathering, even Dorothy, who had seemed so subdued after finding out her niece had become involved with the Robin Hood thief. She had insisted that she should resign when she learned that her niece had used cleaning the office as a prime opportunity to access Hall Enterprises files after Robin had taught her what to do. Roxanne wouldn't hear of it, and insisted that Dorothy stay on at the office, reassuring the older lady that no one had ever suspected her of having any involvement with the deeds of her niece. Roxanne watched as Dorothy stood over chatting with Millie, and helping her as the housekeeper prepared two rows of picnic tables in the yard where they would all soon enjoy the barbeque, which could be smelled cooking on several grills.

"I can't remember when Jordan has thrown a party like this."

Roxanne turned to see Ralph Layette standing next to her, holding a bottle of beer that he had hardly touched, and fingering a cigar in the other hand.

"I don't think he has as long as I've known him," Roxanne said, cautious that the man who had thought her guilty for so long now appeared genial.

"I owe you an apology, young lady," Ralph stammered, and Roxanne stared at the older man, noticing that his boxer-like face truly did look a bit humble. "I made an error in judgment, and wish to clear the air with you."

"It's okay, Ralph. Please consider the matter closed." Roxanne smiled, and decided not to admit that she was thrilled to see the burly man ask for her forgiveness.

Ralph nodded, and took her words at face value. He chewed on his cigar for a moment, and glanced around at the group of people, enjoying each other's company on the large deck.

"I'm not sure what Jordan has shared with you about his past," he continued after a minute, and Roxanne gave him her attention.

Jordan had told her little about his younger years, and Roxanne couldn't help feeling curious about what Ralph meant by the comment. The older man studied her with a serious expression.

"I'm not surprised that he hasn't told you much." Ralph apparently guessed at the truth, and Roxanne's curiosity was piqued. "I knew Jordan's father, as you may know, and just didn't want to see the same thing happen to Jordan that happened to his father." Ralph turned and gave Roxanne a sheepish smile. "I see now that I was wrong, and am very glad to admit it."

The man nodded to her, and then walked away from her, leaving her standing at the edge of the crowd, wondering what had happened in Jordan's past. She looked over at Jordan, and noticed he had donned an apron, and held a large platter as he pulled steaks from the grill. Roxanne would have to wait until later to find out answers to her questions, and hurried over to help him prepare to feed their guests.

"Roxanne, we have another guest who has just arrived." Millie caught Roxanne's attention, as Roxanne helped carry a platter of steaks down to the rows of tables that already had large bowls of salads and potatoes, as well as platters of fruit on them.

Roxanne turned, and then grinned at the pretty young lady who stood next to Millie, looking a bit awkward as she glanced around at the large group of people.

"Emily, I'm so glad that you could make it." Roxanne placed the steaks on the table, and turned to greet her guest.

Although they'd met under odd circumstances, Roxanne had really enjoyed getting to know Emily. The two of them had several phone conversations since, and Roxanne had hoped she would show up for the party.

"Why would I pass up a chance to party like this?" Emily looked around at the beautiful yard and smiled, but Roxanne guessed her new friend felt uncomfortable at a gathering where she knew no one.

"I'm glad you made it. Did you bring your date?" Roxanne walked with Emily back toward the grill to grab the next platter, and help Millie who seemed to be in her glory as she scurried to prepare the tables for the feast.

"I didn't have anyone to bring," Emily confessed, and smiled sheepishly at Roxanne. "I just told you I had a boyfriend so you wouldn't realize how boring I was and that I had no life."

"Nothing about you seems boring to me." Roxanne gave Emily a quick hug, and then the two of them jumped in to help serve the guests.

Roxanne sat in between Joanie and Emily, with Jordan at the head of the long table, and David on the other side of him, facing his new wife. Roxanne enjoyed the quirky looks the two of them gave each other throughout the meal, and guessed that this was the first time in quite a while that they had gone so long without touching each other. True love glowed, Roxanne decided, and she wondered if she and Jordan had that same look about them that her friends did.

Toward the end of the meal, when conversation at the tables had grown to its loudest, and plates had been pushed away as everyone patted contented bellies, Jordan stood and announced that he had something to say.

"I want to thank all of you for making it out here this evening," he began, after everyone had quieted and turned to give him their attention. "And I would like to take this moment to make an announcement."

He grew quiet as he looked at his guests, and Roxanne wondered what he would say.

"She doesn't know it yet, but I would like to present a gift to the woman I love." Jordan produced a small box that sat on the table next to his plate, and Roxanne wondered when he had put it there.

She sat there stunned when he placed the small box in front of her. Gasps and whispers filled the air, and Roxanne knew everyone stared at her, but she couldn't take her eyes off the box in front of her.

"Open it." Jordan spoke so only she, and those right around her, could hear.

Roxanne felt Joanie squeeze her leg, and she couldn't help grinning as she fumbled with the paper that sealed the box, until she held a velvet ring box in her hand. She looked up at Jordan, not able to hide her surprise, and noticed the confidant, powerful man watching her with a very pleased smile on his face. She opened the box, and gasped along with Joanie and Emily as they all stared at the wonderful ring that sat inside.

Roxanne's fingers shook as she took the delicate gold band, with the very large diamond housed on it, out of the box.

"Roxanne. Marry me," he said in front of all of their guests.

Then he reached for her, and Roxanne stood next to him on legs that suddenly felt shaky. He took the ring from her, and then slid it on to her ring finger. "Will you marry me?" he whispered, suddenly looking terrified that she might say no.

"Hell yes, I'll marry you," she cried out, and the guests cheered and applauded their approval.

Roxanne sat on a stool in Jordan's kitchen later that evening, staring at her engagement ring, and replaying the events of the evening in her head. It was just like Jordan to be so confident in her decision that he would propose to her in front of all their guests. She loved him even more for that trait in him. He knew what she wanted, and he went out of his way to give it to her. They hadn't discussed marriage in detail prior to that night, but she knew that she wanted to be with Jordan for the rest of her life, and she relished the fact that he had sensed that in her.

She looked up when he entered the kitchen. He had removed his shirt and shoes, and padded over to her silently. "You like the ring?" he asked, smiling down at her.

"You know that I do," she said, and grinned when he smirked.

"I make it my first priority to always know what you want, and to give it to you before you can ask." He took her hand with the ring on it, and placed a kiss over the diamond. "And I took Joanie with me to pick it out," he confessed with a roguish grin.

Roxanne laughed, and decided not to ask when he had managed to sneak out with her girlfriend without her knowing about it. Jordan would give her a life of surprises and joy, and all she had to do was love and trust him. Her job was the simple one.

"I want to ask you something," she said, hoping she had chosen the right moment.

Jordan must have noticed the seriousness of her comment, because he pulled up the stool next to hers, and sat down next to her.

"Ralph Layette talked to me briefly this evening," she began. "He asked me to forgive him, but he made a comment I didn't understand. He said that he didn't want to see the same thing happen to you that happened to your father. What did he mean by that?"

Something guarded passed over Jordan's expression, and she watched him as he stared across the kitchen at the recently wiped down counters.

"My father started his business from scratch just as I did," Jordan began. "He made his fortune quickly, and moved up the ranks of society here in town."

Jordan took her two hands in his and squeezed them. "He fell in love with his secretary, and married her. Society didn't approve, saying she was a bimbo and gold digger, and it turned out that they were right."

"You aren't talking about your mother, are you?" Roxanne asked, trying to imagine a boy growing up thinking such things of his mother.

Jordan nodded. "When I was three, my mother cleaned my father out for everything she could get her hands on, and disappeared. Some say she fled to Europe, I'm not sure."

"You haven't talked to her since?" Roxanne couldn't believe a mother could leave her child like that.

"We were told she was killed in a yachting accident when I was about ten." Jordan offered the news as if it meant nothing to him, and Roxanne felt for the boy who had never been given the opportunity to have a mother to love. "He never admitted it, but I think Father always hoped she would come back to him. But after that, he seemed to give up on life. He died alone and bitter."

"How sad," Roxanne said, not knowing what else to say.

"Yes. And I vowed not to live my life as my father had."

Roxanne had noticed before that Jordan seemed bitter toward his father, and wondered what had caused that. She couldn't figure out how to ask the question though, so stood and wrapped her arms around him.

He nuzzled his face into her shirt, and then nipped at her nipple through the material. Roxanne ran her hands through his hair, and her breath caught at the wicked sensation his teeth caused when they brushed her skin through her shirt.

"Well I'm afraid you're stuck with me for life, mister," she whispered into his hair, and he lifted his head.

"I've never worried about your loyalty to me for a second," he told her, and she smiled at his cocky nature. "It's been me that I've worried about."

"I can't find a thing wrong with you," she said, and ran her hands over his shoulders and then down his arms, making a show of trying to find a blemish.

"My father never missed an opportunity to remind me that I was my mother's son." Jordan's comment stilled her hands and she stared at the stormy look in his eyes. "He despised her for leaving him, and embarrassing him in front of polite society. And of course there were the rumors that I wasn't really his son, but a bastard that she saddled him with when she left town."

"How awful," Roxanne cried out, wanting to do anything to douse the pain she heard in his words.

"Our blood types matched." Jordan shrugged. "I think it was just the gossip that annoyed him. Either way, we were never close."

"Well, I think you would make a good father." Roxanne watched the clouds leave his expression, and a smile crossed his face. She smiled too.

"I think I would too." She watched the wicked glint return in his smirk, and knew he had let the past return to that remote corner where he buried such demons. He had some painful memories that might take him many years to work through, but he had shared it with her, and that was enough for the moment.

"Maybe if we practice enough, someday we can experience parenthood." She teased him with her breasts as she rubbed then again up against his face.

Jordan gripped her rib cage with either hand, and stilled her motions, then clamped down on a nipple with his teeth. Roxanne felt the sting of her nipple being bitten soar through her clear to the depths of her womb, and groaned as she grabbed his hair.

Jordan lifted her and placed her on the island in the middle of the kitchen, then spread her legs as his hands worked their way up the inside of her miniskirt. He smiled down at her shaven, moist center that appeared as the material of her skirt scrunched around her waist.

"Do you see something you want?" she teased.

"Oh yes." Jordan slid a finger down her moist outer lips, and Roxanne tossed her head back and groaned. "But there is still a question you haven't answered."

Jordan slid a finger inside her, and then pulled it out and teased the smooth entrance.

Roxanne couldn't lift her head. "What's that?" she groaned.

"Who do you belong to?" he asked.

Roxanne smiled before slowly lifting her head to stare at him. He thrust two fingers inside her this time, and she felt them move back and forth once inside her. She bit her lip, loving the sensations that rippled through her. His dark eyes watched her like a predator who has captured his feast, and deciding where to indulge himself first.

"I belong to you, Jordan." She smiled as she watched satisfaction spread across his face. She slid forward, thrusting his fingers inside her further.

Roxanne grabbed his silky black hair on either side of his head, and pulled his face toward her pulsing heat. "And, my love, you belong to me."

She knew she couldn't force him to eat her if he decided not to, but he lowered his head willingly, and pressed his open mouth over her moist entrance. Roxanne sucked in air, and let her head fall back again, as she spread her legs as far apart as she could to allow him more room.

"What if one of our guests decides to come down for a midnight snack?" he asked, and rested his chin on her shaved mound.

Roxanne brought her head up and met his gaze as she smiled mischievously. She had almost forgotten that they had David and Joanie in the guest bedroom so that the four of them could wake in the morning and spend the day together. Emily had tried to leave and Roxanne had insisted she stay the night as well. The large house had plenty of unused bedrooms, and Millie had done a wonderful job of keeping all the rooms in tidy order.

"What will you offer them? Something out of the refrigerator? Or something here on the counter?" Roxanne asked, and ran her fingers through his raven black hair.

Jordan's laugh was filled with desire. "Maybe one day I'll consider sharing you with another, but first I want to get my fill of you."

He scooped her into his arms, and headed for the staircase.

"That is just fine with me," she said, and wrapped her arms around his shoulders as he carried her to their bedroom.

Why an electronic book?

We live in the Information Age—an exciting time in the history of human civilization, in which technology rules supreme and continues to progress in leaps and bounds every minute of every day. For a multitude of reasons, more and more avid literary fans are opting to purchase e-books instead of paper books. The question from those not yet initiated into the world of electronic reading is simply: *Why?*

1. *Price.* An electronic title at Ellora's Cave Publishing and Cerridwen Press runs anywhere from 40% to 75% less than the cover price of the exact same title in paperback format. Why? Basic mathematics and cost. It is less expensive to publish an e-book (no paper and printing, no warehousing and shipping) than it is to publish a paperback, so the savings are passed along to the consumer.

2. *Space.* Running out of room in your house for your books? That is one worry you will never have with electronic books. For a low one-time cost, you can purchase a handheld device specifically designed for e-reading. Many e-readers have large, convenient screens for viewing. Better yet, hundreds of titles can be stored within your new library—on a single microchip. There are a variety of e-readers from different manufacturers. You can also read e-books on your PC or laptop computer. (Please note that Ellora's

Cave does not endorse any specific brands. You can check our websites at www.ellorascave.com or www.cerridwenpress.com for information we make available to new consumers.)

3. *Mobility.* Because your new e-library consists of only a microchip within a small, easily transportable e-reader, your entire cache of books can be taken with you wherever you go.

4. ***Personal Viewing Preferences.*** Are the words you are currently reading too small? Too large? Too... ANNOYING? Paperback books cannot be modified according to personal preferences, but e-books can.

5. ***Instant Gratification.*** Is it the middle of the night and all the bookstores near you are closed? Are you tired of waiting days, sometimes weeks, for bookstores to ship the novels you bought? Ellora's Cave Publishing sells instantaneous downloads twenty-four hours a day, seven days a week, every day of the year. Our webstore is never closed. Our e-book delivery system is 100% automated, meaning your order is filled as soon as you pay for it.

Those are a few of the top reasons why electronic books are replacing paperbacks for many avid readers.

As always, Ellora's Cave and Cerridwen Press welcome your questions and comments. We invite you to email us at Comments@ellorascave.com or write to us directly at Ellora's Cave Publishing Inc., 1056 Home Avenue, Akron, OH 44310-3502.

THE
☥ ELLORA'S CAVE ☥
LIBRARY

Stay up to date with Ellora's Cave Titles in
Print with our Quarterly Catalog.

TO RECIEVE A CATALOG,
SEND AN EMAIL WITH YOUR NAME
AND MAILING ADDRESS TO:

CATALOG@ELLORASCAVE.COM

OR SEND A LETTER OR POSTCARD
WITH YOUR MAILING ADDRESS TO:

CATALOG REQUEST
c/o ELLORA'S CAVE PUBLISHING, INC.
1056 HOME AVENUE
AKRON, OHIO 44310-3502